"DISCARD"

ROGUES

STORIES OF
SWINDLERS, THIEVES,
AND CONFIDENCE MEN

ROGUES

STORIES OF SWINDLERS, THIEVES, AND CONFIDENCE MEN

Edited by Leo Hamalian

THOMAS Y. CROWELL   NEW YORK

Designed by Kohar Alexanian

Library of Congress Cataloging in Publication Data
Main entry under title:
Rogues : stories of swindlers, thieves, and
confidence men.

CONTENTS: Erskine, J. Francois Villon meets
a woman.—Morier, J. The adventures of Hajji Baba.
—Aleichem, S. Tit for tat. [etc]
    1. Rogues and vagabonds—Juvenile fiction.
    2. Short stories, American. 3. Short stories,
English. [1. Rogues and vagabonds—Fiction.
2. Short stories] I. Hamalian, Leo.
PZ5.R57 1979   [Fic]   78–19512
            ISBN 0–690–03913–1

First Edition

When a rogue kisses you, count your teeth.

ARMENIAN PROVERB

ACKNOWLEDGMENTS

The author and publisher gratefully acknowledge permission granted to use:

"François Villon Meets a Woman" by John Erskine. From *The Brief Hour of Francois Villon* by John Erskine copyright 1937 by John Erskine, Renewed 1965. Reprinted by permission of The Bobbs-Merrill Company, Inc.

"The Great Uranium Hoax" by Robert Traver. From *Smalltown D.A.*, E. P. Dutton, 1954. Reprinted by permission of Robert Traver.

"The Hustler" by Walter S. Tevis. Originally appeared in *Playboy* Magazine; Copyright © 1956 by *Playboy*. Reprinted by permission of Walter S. Tevis.

"The New Deal" by Charles Einstein. Originally appeared in *Playboy* Magazine; Copyright © 1963 by *Playboy*. Reprinted by permission of the author's agents Blassingame, McCauley & Wood.

"No Petty Thief" by Jesse Stuart. From *A Jesse Stuart Reader*, McGraw-Hill, Inc., 1963. Reprinted by permission of Jesse Stuart.

"The Spoils of Sacrilege" by David Fletcher. From *Raffles*, G.P. Putnam's Sons, 1977. Reprinted by permission of Anthony Sheil Associates, Ltd.

CONTENTS

INTRODUCTION

This collection of stories is about thieves, swindlers, frauds, confidence men, and other assorted hustlers who populate the pages of fiction. These stories are not concerned with the world of violent crime, but with the realm of roguery wherein we encounter those unscrupulous characters who live by their own wits and their own laws, whose signature is bold and sophisticated cunning rather than blood or bullets.

What do we mean by the term "roguery"? The expression is almost as old as the activity itself. One of the terms introduced into the English language around the sixteenth century to designate the business of beggars and vagabonds, it may have originated from the word "Roger," the name given to begging vagabonds who pretended to be students from Oxford or Cambridge. By the next century the word "rogue" had become an expression of endearment for a person of mischievous disposition. It was not until law and order began to replace lawlessness and disorder that the term gradually became synonymous with diverse forms of fraud.

Before these stories themselves are discussed, some distinctions must be made. Roguery is not to be confused with villainy. By the latter we mean something that is extreme in its evil and that is often expressed through ruthless cruelty or violence—rape, torture, assassination, homicide. Roguery is never violent and rarely vicious. Rogues in literature are regarded very often with tolerance, even with humor or compassion. Their acts of rascality are seen as a result of social environment rather than of warped character.

Just as the typical crime of the villain is violence, so the typical crime of the rogue is likely to be some form of theft or deception. What ordinary people must gain by sweat or muscle, the rogue seeks to win by his wits. All rogues have in common a distaste for honest labor, for any schedule that ties them to the clock, for any morality that enforces the golden rule. Without qualms of conscience, rogues may cheat at cards or dice, forge manuscripts or checks, scheme for fortunes or love, rustle someone else's livestock or lady, or prey on the citizenry as smugglers, counterfeiters, or fakers.

Why is the figure of the rogue so irresistible to the reader? Why is Robin Hood so appealing even to the most moral-minded? The answer probably lies in the nature of the relationship between the imagination and reality. In the hands of a craftsman, the characters who strut and fret their brief hour on the pages of the story hold up the mirror to our own identities. We are invited to see what is good and bad, what is virtue and what is vice, within ourselves. We are touched by our own reflection. Indeed, we may derive secret pleasure from the drama of the rogue who lives out our own deepest antisocial urges by defying received convention, authority, or morality. That the culprit is caught and punished for his temerity may also be part of the identification process. Punishment as well as crime is woven into our vision of an orderly universe. Though that vision is ambiguous, it should be clear that the theme of this collection is roguery observed, not roguery condoned.

I have arranged these stories to suggest the changing nature and scope of roguery in a world that has grown increasingly sophisticated over the past five centuries. As we range from the Parisian vagabond of the fifteenth century to the pool-hall hustler of the twentieth, the movement is from a relative innocence to the possibility of evil, from the congenial to the edge of violence.

Perhaps the most famous rogue in history is François Villon, a medieval poet of considerable talent. Though he deplored his dissipated life as a vagabond, he also derided the vanity of all life, whether or not like his own. Over the years, his popularity grew as a colorful outlaw who brought charm, dash, and a quixotic code of honor to the profession of roguery, and legendary episodes about him, like the one that John Erskine turns into a delightful romance, abound in literature. For many readers, Villon became the archetype of anti-Establishment dissent, the voice of the underworld poor who were deprived of power by official authority. The phenomenon of the rogue as radical is familiar in our own time, and represents the ultimate rehabilitation of this anti-hero.

James Morier's Hajji Baba represents the trickster of the seventeenth-century Moslem world. He sells adulterated tobacco—the worst to the wealthiest customers—and aspires to rise through the ranks of roguery with the advice of deceitful dervishes. It is an entertaining, lighthearted account written by an English diplomat who knew that costume could not disguise human habit. Though the anecdotes have the aura of fun and games, we are nonetheless reminded that in Moslem as well as in Christian society the religious fraud was a favorite butt of satire and that the confidence man without means was often an object of sympathy.

Tricksters were apparently not uncommon among the Jewry of the Old World, if we accept the word of Sholom Aleichem, the great Yiddish humorist, whose work inspired the musical *Fiddler on the Roof.* In "Tit for Tat," a tradesman outfoxed by his rabbi tells a story about a "rabbi who liked to play tricks" on his people, implying that within the man of religion there lies a potential rogue no different from the rascals of the profane world. Not to be outdone by an ordinary scoundrel, the rabbi responds with his own story about a conspiracy of citizens who are rogues at heart. Beneath the surface is the feeling that the rabbi in the *stetl*, the village, had to assume the role of Robin Hood in order to protect the poor against the wiles of tradesmen.

Jeff Peters in O. Henry's story may seem to be a version of Morier's Dervish Sefer transplanted to the New World, selling false cures and nostrums instead of beard combings. Wise in the tricks of the trade, Peters prevails by his native American wits when the mayor of the town—the symbol of law and order—tries to trap this genial fraud. We are not offended by the triumph of trickery so long as it is good-natured, Yankee ingenious, and geared for a laugh.

In David Fletcher's "The Spoils of Sacrilege," Raffles the cricketer and amateur cracksman is brought back to life in this adaptation based on the stories of E.

W. Hornung, who was the brother-in-law of the creator of Sherlock Holmes, Sir Arthur Conan Doyle, that implacable enemy of rogues and criminals. Even as Raffles lifts the precious necklace, his elegance of style, his graciousness of manner, his coolness in danger, quite overthrow all moral scruples, no less effectively than does the magic of François Villon.

Much of the renowned humor of P. G. Wodehouse stems from the idle gentleman of the English upper class "who generates as it were a store of loopiness which expends itself with frightful violence on his rare visits to the center of things." Of course, it is a special brand of violence: Uncle Fred walks the thin line between comedy and roguery, and as we follow his misfortunes, we watch the law of the land and even of gravity defied with such insistent chaos and absurd logic that everything—including manners and morality—explodes into farce.

The narrator of Jesse Stuart's tall story, "No Petty Thief," becomes a rogue in spite of himself; he has never stolen before in his life and his father raised him— "jerked him up by the hair of the head"—in decency and order. So powerful is the appeal of the machine that he embarks upon one of the most unusual acts of theft imaginable. When the trial jury refuses to believe that he could commit such an act, he himself provides the proof. He is what used to be known in Shakespeare's England as an "honest rogue." Nonetheless, he must be punished harshly by the hill dwellers of Kentucky, where life is held more cheaply than property.

"The Weather Prophet" by Dillon Anderson is about a pair of professional gamblers who run their streak of luck with the dice into an adventure that also pays off.

Like rogues of pedigree, they refuse to compromise their professional standards and demonstrate that there can be honor among their kind. In "The New Deal" by Charles Einstein, Rafferty the gambler tries his hand at blackjack in Las Vegas. To change his luck, he calls for a new deck of cards. The subsequent match reveals how effective an ingenious rogue can be even against the odds of Las Vegas gambling houses.

Robert Traver's "The Great Uranium Hoax" may remind some readers of Frank Stockton's classic "The Lady or the Tiger?" in its ambiguous ending. Is Robbins a fraud or is he a genius? He manipulates the stock market with brilliance and iron nerve and pits his mind against the most formidable power brokers on Wall Street. Robbins is such an outrageous rogue that we are tempted not only to forgive him but to envy him as well as he luxuriates in Parisian extravagance.

In Leslie Charteris' "The Wicked Cousin," two rogues match wits. A swindler who buys old letters that he thinks are valuable locks horns with Simon Templar, who makes it his business to visit justice on those rogues whom the law fails to apprehend. We are all a lot of scurvy rogues, the author implies, but some of us are better than others—a sentiment, we feel, Sholom Aleichem would endorse.

"The Hustler" by Walter Tevis pits a rogue against a villain. Sam Willis, a pool shark newly released from prison, decides to hustle the great Louisiana Fats on his own grounds. The rogue outwits and outplays the villain, but at the end is forced to pay the price for his temerity. With this story, we move out of the domain of roguery and toward the underworld of violent crime—an appropriate place to close this collection.

So in our imagination we have completed the journey to regions too risky to try in real life. We have lived out moments of adventure, and we have performed deeds of roguery. And what if these moments are nothing more than moonshine? The mystery is solved; the deed discovered; and the story brought to a peaceful conclusion. After trial and travail, the harmony of the universe is restored. Without arousing our own flow of adrenalin, we have escaped from mundane reality and then returned back to it. By magic we have had our cake and eaten it, too. What more can we ask of good fiction?

Leo Hamalian

JOHN ERSKINE

François Villon Meets a Woman

François Villon, poet in flight, turned on his side, woke in a state of panic, and tried to recall where he was.

The light was gray, an hour before dawn.

The stamp of a horse! Had they found him? He sat up on the haymow.

No, it was the farmer below, working at the cow. He could hear the swish of milk in the pail. Master Villon collapsed upon his stolen bed.

God, but he was hungry! Just listen to that milk! And in the farm kitchen, for honest care-free men, there would be eggs and bread, perhaps a slice of pig or chicken.

His thoughts went back to the wrongs he had suffered. Old stories, all of them. Except Marguerite, of course. Before Marguerite—Catherine. If ever he got his hands on Catherine again, he'd cut her throat. Or break her neck. Or strangle her slowly, till her beautiful eyes popped out. There's womankind for you—take your love while the pocket is full, leave you in your bad hour.

And Noah Jolis, who to please Catherine had beaten him—and Margot, his fat sister—and Robin Turgis, of the Pine Cone Tavern, who had Margot for wife and deserved no better!

These memories pained him most when the stomach
was empty, hunger and indignation being twins. With
that one windfall of food, five miles out of Paris, he had
recovered a modicum of Christian charity. Except for
Catherine. Heaven be his aid, he would hate her to the
end.

There was of course that affair at the College of
Navarre, the prick to his conscience which made flight
easier, the strongest excuse he had given the provost to
stretch his neck. Fortunately, the provost didn't yet con-
nect him with the crime. Meanwhile Master Villon reflected that justice is a slippery thing, hard to define and
rarely enforced. All theft is disorderly and should if possible be avoided. To rob a church is sin. And unprofitable.
From the college chapel his share had been one false
piece of silver and four genuine sous. The provost would
do his duty as to the four sous, but the worshiper who had
offered the bad piece would be free to go to church again.

Because he loved Catherine, he had told her the
truth. You can't cheat a girl you really love, and she had
been the first to make him wish he were a decent man.
But when she learned his danger she drove him into the
night, and when he came back desperate she had those
ruffians at the door, to beat him up. And Noah Jolis,
standing by, laughed. Noah might be sleeping with her
now.

The farmer below, having exhausted the cow, was
climbing the ladder for hay. Master Villon held his
breath, in prudence rather than in fear. The lout would do
no worse than swear at him.

The pitchfork touched his left leg and drew an in-
voluntary grunt. His hand went to his knife, by instinct,

but the peasant didn't wait. Master Villon heard a thump as the fellow slid down the ladder and hit the ground, then made for the farmhouse, where a dog barked, asking to be unchained.

Master Villon, having finished his sleep for the day, got over the farm wall and plied his legs, the scratched one and the sound, along the river road, toward the southeast.

His head was dizzy by the time he came to the château, two hours before noon. Villages on the way had been few and sleepy-looking, yet he had skirted them all. The château seemed austere, not the sort of place the provost's men would stop at. Master Villon found the gate and pulled the bell chain.

He could hear the tinkle inside, but no one answered. He pulled once more. The house was, as you might say, dead.

It wouldn't do to climb the front wall, not in the broad sun, but around at the back, where you might expect a garden, an old apple tree furnished a screen for his gymnastics, and once down among the rosebushes he aimed straight for the kitchen door.

Locked tight. All the doors. To his regret Master Villon was forced to enter by an unshuttered window.

At the foot of the stairs, in the main hall, he halloed, to establish an honorable relation with the inmates, but only the echo was roused. Having eased his conscience, he sought the kitchen from the inside; that door also was bolted. Had Master Villon been a man to despair, his weakened knees would have sunk under him altogether.

But while there was still a pencil of strength in his legs he mounted the stairs and inspected the richly garnished bedrooms where those could sleep whose fathers, he reflected, had done their stealing for them.

And in one room he paused, with extra bitterness: a woman's boudoir, laced and silken. A wardrobe for her gowns—a massive dresser full no doubt of whatever went next to her delicate skin—a canopied bed with a blue pillow. He could see the white thing resting there, head cushioned, eyelids closed. Catherine! Damn her!

From the window he learned why the house was silent. In yonder vineyard the servants, male and female, gathered grapes. Among them must be the cook.

So the woman who used this room was on a journey with her husband, and the servants expected no early return. Doubtless a handsome creature with a selfish heart, like Catherine's, and an itch to see the world, and her husband would rather be home but she needed watching. The devil help the man! Master Villon would walk on.

Before he walked, however, he pulled out the trays of the dresser, he being thorough in all his visits, and the contents were what he had supposed, dainty, intimate and troubling—fresh-laundered, scented, neatly folded.

On a pair of black stockings, in the middle of the top drawer, lay a shining gold piece.

What heaven sends, heaven sends! The muscles were working again in Master Villon's legs as he dusted down the road in search of meat and drink.

Midway through the afternoon he found what belonged to him, where the Seine forks with another river, and a tree-shaded town nested between shores. The inn was called "La Belle Image." There was a woman's face on the sign. Master Villon removed his hat, ran his hand over his bald head, stroked his long nose, and recognized the will of God.

When he opened the door the innkeeper, missing baggage and means of transportation, remained at ease in his chair, with his apron on.

"Food!" said Master Villon. "Beef, red wine, bread!" With that he stepped over the bench by the inn table and thrust his tired legs underneath.

"Money?" said the man in the chair.

Master Villon rang his gold piece on the board, at which music the host rose, as to Gabriel's horn.

"Put your bonnet on the nail yonder," said he, "while I fry an egg. There's a roast on the spit but it won't be cooked through till sundown."

"An egg," said Master Villon, ringing the nail with his hat, "will render appetite endurable without killing it. Let cheese and ale be included in this temporary sustenance."

In a moment his cheeks were full of bread and cheese, and without ale he would have choked, so ravenously he went at it, but before the egg was fried, a coach thundered up to the inn door, and Master Villon had been too close to his plate to note the direction it came from. Moreover, there was a convoy of three horsemen, well armed.

While the innkeeper was out in front, bowing to this unusual company, Master Villon got his hat from the peg, found a window in the taproom, and sought the picturesque bushes along the riverbank.

Once there, he repented of his haste. Though screened from possible pursuers, he couldn't inquire whether he really was pursued. His shelter had no lookout. Why hadn't he examined the coachload first? There, someone was hunting him now!

It was a girl of nineteen or twenty, swinging her sunhat by the ribbon, a reasonably tall young woman with engaging endowments of person and, it seemed, qualities of mind. To Master Villon, who had expected the provost, she was beauty itself. His own quick black eyes observed that hers were brown, wide-set with long lashes. When she saw him she betrayed neither astonishment nor fear nor boldness. She accepted him with the rest of the sunset-colored landscape. Her linen gown, plain but well-fitted, hid little of a bosom which Catherine would have envied—a gray dress, a broad white collar, a blue ribbon at her throat. Of what such a body might say to a man, her sincere eyes were not aware. By her hands, had he seen nothing else, he would have known a lady.

"I couldn't wait," she said.

Master Villon bowed cautiously.

"Father says the river is loveliest at this bend. After dinner it would be too dark."

Master Villon, who had given the river no study, turned to look at it.

"The dark green of the trees over there, the purple shadows, the dreamy slide of the water—it *is* the best hour, wouldn't you say?"

Master Villon returned her smile. "I have enjoyed none better."

"Do you come often?"

He shook his head. "Seldom."

"Then you don't live in Corbeil?"

Attending to the name of the town, he let slip the truth. "My home is in Paris."

"From choice?" she asked sympathetically, then corrected herself. "Of course I don't really know Paris."

"I can see that," said he.

She laughed. "Father will have a fit. You stay at the inn?"

They walked back side by side.

"How," she asked, "do you pass the time, when you are in Paris?"

He couldn't tell her he was a thief. Nor a Master of Arts—not in that dusty jacket, with the knife slung from his belt. "I lack a reputable profession," said he. "I am a bad poet."

She laughed again, to deride his modesty, but her father at the inn door was displeased. "You detain us all from dinner, Louise!"

A tall gentleman with white beard trimmed to a point, neat mustaches, keen eyes.

"I found a poet in the river," said she, unrebuked.

"My lady honored me," said Master Villon, bowing to the tall man. "François des Loges, at your service."

The keen eyes fastened on him. "Which Des Loges?"

"There is but one of me," said Master Villon, "born, such as I am, in Paris or nearby."

"Are you sure?"

"I am not," said Master Villon. "I take my mother's word for it."

The tall man held out his hand, not yet letting go with his eyes. "The Seigneur de Grigny, at *your* service."

Master Villon knew the Seigneur de Grigny did not like him, but he had faced adverse opinion before, and just then the innkeeper summoned them to dinner.

"The egg was wasted," he complained. "I thought you had left without paying."

"Your river view," said Master Villon, "is worth a dozen eggs."

"Not to mention," said the girl, "the pleasure of conversation with me. Will you sit at our end of the table, master poet?"

From then on the innkeeper thought well of him, whatever may have been in the seigneur's mind, and the girl with her cheerful questions gave him scarcely an interval for soup-swallowing.

"Do you write poems every day, or only while you are at home?"

Master Villon broke off a piece of bread. "As heaven decides, my lady."

"What are your poems about? Love?"

The seigneur looked up, to watch his reply.

"I deal with that theme, from time to time. Also with hate."

"Hate? That wouldn't be poetry!"

Her father interrupted. "Monsieur des Loges, have you ever eaten at the king's table?"

Master Villon shook his head, his mouth being full.

"You know my friend, D'Estouteville?"

Master Villon swallowed hard. "Who?"

"The Provost of Paris."

Knowing the provost entirely too well, Master Villon shied away. "The Duke of Orleans is a friend of mine, in a sense my protector."

"Ah!" said the girl. "There's a poet for you!"

The seigneur smiled, ever so slightly. "I *thought* we had met before."

Master Villon let the subject die, more willingly as the girl looked up, ready with another idea.

"The fine folk kill each other, don't they?"

"Where?"

"Paris. Father says so. And the poor starve. Don't they, Father?"

The seigneur was examining his knife, which edge to cut with.

"In all cities," said Master Villon, "there is mischief. The evil with the good. We have the river, this same river, and the islands, and the markets, and the churches, of course, and the inns, and the streets."

"Leave nothing out," said the seigneur. "Mention the jail."

"Father!" said the girl, brushing aside the discordant suggestion. "The streets," she went on, "are crooked and crowded."

"Men and women," said Master Villon. "Give me those, and I can live."

The seigneur's eyes almost lifted, then chose not to.

"The women," said the girl, pleased with her inexperience for knowing so much. "You don't need the men. Why did you come away?"

There was no impertinence in her questions, only a cordial turning over as of a book's pages, to get at the plot quickly.

"In summer," said he, "when the town is hot, I take to the road."

She laughed. "For peace?"

"Among other things."

"And even here a woman interrupts!"

"Louise," said the seigneur, "talk less and eat. We must be on our journey."

"Father, if Monsieur des Loges is homeward bound —you are, aren't you?"

He was, so long as the seigneur listened. To be headed openly for Paris might establish credit.

"Then he can ride with us, can't he? There's room in the coach."

"Unless I walk," said Master Villon hastily, "I miss the flavor of travel."

"You're not walking to Paris?" said the girl. "Not with your trunk on your back?"

"On these short rambles, my lady, I exchange the convenience of luggage for an easier touch of earth and weather."

"So far as our paths are the same," said the seigneur, with unforeseen complacence, "we shall be glad of your company, Monsieur des Loges."

Master Villon had met danger too often not to recognize the signs. The tall man must have something up his sleeve.

"At any other time, my lord—"

"Now!" said the girl. "We won't take no."

So the innkeeper, who had his ear out, came to the side of the seigneur's chair, and at his invitation recited from memory the cost of feeding one gentleman and one daughter, together with one coachman, one footman, and three outriders, who ate in the kitchen, together with five horses, who ate in the stall.

"Monsieur des Loges," said the seigneur, more affable than the innkeeper himself, "since you are for the moment my guest, will you give me the pleasure—"

"A thousand thanks," said Master Villon, starting to fish in his pocket, "but I happen to have—"

"There was also," said the innkeeper, "an egg, cooked though not consumed. Half a pound of cheese. A quart of ale."

"Naturally," said the seigneur, untying his purse. "Will you now fetch the coach?"

So the horses clattered up, the footman held the door, the girl stepped in, Master Villon with his gold piece unbroken took the seat on her left side, the seigneur the place of honor on the right. The innkeeper waved them off into the darkness, but no one noticed him.

They rode in silence, because the highway was rough, and for better reasons. Twice the girl spoke, but since it would have been equally appropriate for her father or the poet to reply, each left the privilege to the other.

"Suppose I hadn't cared to look at the river!"

Master Villon was estimating his chances of slipping away. Sooner or later the coach would stop. Should he thank them bravely, affect the lighthearted minstrel, and walk on humming a tune? Or should he dodge behind the coach and run?

"I feel as though we'd been absent a lifetime!"

He wouldn't run. He had no wish to slip away. Her knee was touching his, and if he could reform his impulses so as not to emphasize the pressure, she might continue to believe he was the upholstery.

To steady himself against the jolting of the coach, he put his hand down, where he expected to find the leather cushion between them, but her hand was resting there.

"Pardon!" He drew back from the warm softness, wondering at his flush of shame.

A moment later the seigneur roused himself, leaned forward to look out the window, recognized a gleam in the night.

"We are home," said he. "Monsieur des Loges, might we interrupt your walk a second time by providing you with a bed?"

Master Villon saw a trap. "My lord, your kindness is already beyond measure. With your permission—"

The girl put her hand on his, and held it there.

"My lord, with your permission I will accept an honor which I do not deserve."

Hardly were the words out of him when the coach wheeled through the gate of the château from which he had stolen the piece of gold.

There was such a twist of conscience around his heart that he turned faint, standing in the great hall at the foot of the stairs, with the servants of the house greeting the man and his daughter, and the outriders helping in with the bags.

"Home again, and how I've missed my room!" said the girl, running up to be sure it was still there. Master Villon felt the sweat spring on his brow.

"Monsieur des Loges," said her father, leading the way to a small office behind the stairs, "if you'll draw the other bench to my desk, we'll share a bottle before we sleep. I like to wash out the dust."

Master Villon wiped his forehead with his hat, and sat down.

"My dear wife," continued the seigneur as the butler

poured, "was a Des Loges. Louise des Loges. God rest her soul! I have been curious, ever since we met, as to the nearness of blood."

The butler having withdrawn, the white-bearded man raised a red glass, and Master Villon, for want of other ingenuity, returned the salute but did not drink.

"So far as the records are known," the seigneur went on, smacking his lips and stroking his mustache, "no Des Loges was ever a poet. A weakness for the arts was first detected in my side of the family."

Master Villon heard the girl coming from her room upstairs.

"Until this afternoon I had understood that no Des Loges was ever born in Paris, none at least of the authorized strain. . . . This wine is excellent—or would you prefer—"

Master Villon had counted her slow steps down the stairs, till she stood before them, calm but pale.

"Father, our house has been entered!"

The seigneur looked at her. "Nonsense! The servants were here. Nonsense!"

"My things have been moved around. The dresser has been searched. A gold piece is gone."

"Monsieur des Loges will form a sad opinion of us," said the tall man, rising with no great hurry. "Shall we examine the evidence, Monsieur des Loges?"

Though he pronounced the name somewhat too often, as it seemed to Master Villon, there was nothing for it but to follow them up the staircase and look again at what, to his regret, he had already seen.

"In the morning," said her father, finishing what you might call a surface survey, "I'll have it out with our people. You'd better not sleep here tonight, Louise."

"But of course I will! This is my room!"

"Then I'll show Monsieur des Loges to his bed across the hall," said her father, as docile as you could wish.

"Good night, poet," said she, quite herself again, holding out both hands for him to kiss. "I was silly to speak of this accident. Rest well!"

"There's a gown on the bed, Monsieur des Loges, and my other pair of slippers," said her father, closing the shutters against the night air. "Shall I send up some fruit, to nibble on?"

Master Villon cleared his throat. "I need nothing."

"Good dreams, then. I rise early but my daughter is usually late. Take your time."

Master Villon put off his shoes and stretched on the bed. The seigneur had removed the candle and the shutters were locked, unless a practiced ear could mistake. In the hall below waited, no doubt, the men who had ridden beside the coach.

Yet it wasn't danger that kept him awake, but the gold piece and the girl to whom it belonged. Her hand on his! If she alone still thought generously of him, what might she learn at dawn?

Strange that he should melt before a creature so childlike, he who had shunned innocence and paid tribute rather to what was scarred and scorched. At the goodness which knows little, he had laughed. But lying there on the bed he wished the gold piece were where it should have stayed. He wished he could return with her to the riverbank and admire the sunset. He wished he were— whatever she imagined him to be.

If her father intended to hold him till the Des Loges

records could be examined, the provost might happen along with his rope, and if the girl were looking on while they searched his pockets, she would recognize the money and know he deserved to swing.

If on the other hand he could put the money back, then even if he hanged—

Calculating the hours by the growing wear on his patience, Master Villon gave the household ample time to fall asleep. With his shoes in his hand he then drew open his door, inch by inch. Diagonally to the left, if he could remember the precise angle—

When his groping fingers told him her door was not entirely closed, he stepped back, as from peril. It couldn't be true! Of another woman, yes, but not of her! How many times had he thanked fortune for a ripe adventure dropped in his hands! But now he wasn't thankful. His heart ached with fear that she might be like all the rest.

Well, he would restore the gold piece and take his chance with the watchmen downstairs. In every house, no matter how timid, one window is overlooked. . . . The dresser would be to the right—the top drawer.

In the darkness he fancied he could trace the figure on the bed. He tried not to breathe. The top drawer came out, noiseless . . . he smoothed down the folded black stockings . . . he laid the coin gently, felt it sink upon the fabric.

To his horror the lovely form sat up in bed, struck a vigorous flint, lighted a candle.

"François Villon," said the seigneur, bringing his boots down on the floor and rising fully clad, "the compliment which you meditated, the tribute to my daughter and therefore indirectly to me, is not acceptable. On your rambles, as I observed, you wear no sword, but happily I possess two. Take your choice!"

Master Villon, very weary of life at that moment, raised a limp hand and grasped one of the hilts her father was holding toward him in the candle gloom.

"There is more space in the hall," said the man, kicking a chair out of the way, "but it will be a pleasure to kill you here."

"Father! No!"

They both turned and saw her at the door, candle in hand, clad somewhat hastily in a trailing night-robe.

"Go back to my room, daughter!"

"You mustn't kill him! He meant no harm!"

"The worst rascal in France," said her father. "At the inn table I knew him. He accepted my hospitality, then stole here to dishonor you. I was sure he would."

Master Villon dropped his sword on the girl's bed, with the hilt toward the seigneur. "I'm not in the mood," said he. "Run the blade through me, and be done with it!"

The seigneur reached for the bell cord. "You're no gentleman, François Villon. The two swords were for my daughter's sake, and because you happened to borrow my wife's name. Bring a rope," he went on as the outriders stuck their heads in. "We'll hang him from the window."

"Not from *my* window!" pleaded the girl. "Not from this house! I couldn't live here! I'd see his body swinging outside! I'd—"

"You have your mother's practical sense," said the seigneur. "Why soil a good home? François Villon, have the courtesy to be hanged elsewhere. I'll give you six hours' start. It is now past midnight. At seven or eight in the morning my dogs and my men will join you, under some convenient tree."

The outriders took him by the elbows and rushed him down the stairs.

"My hat," said Master Villon, "I left it in the office."

"His hat!" exclaimed the seigneur. "Give it to him. His hat!"

When they kicked him through the gate, she was standing by her father, motionless, with the night-robe around her.

Nine o'clock or thereabouts, next morning, she was walking in the rose garden when a bough cracked in the apple tree over the wall. The fruit that bounced at her feet was Master Villon.

She began to smile, then turned white. "Father is looking for you."

"I saw him ride off, my lady."

"I'm sorry you returned."

"My lady, do you regret our meeting in the first place?"

For a moment she stared at the ground.

"As Father said, you took his hospitality and then you—"

"He was playing a trick," said Master Villon with some heat. "He was catching a fly in honey. Hospitality should be too sacred for treacherous use!"

"You and Father may debate that, if you wish. *I* wasn't treacherous. I liked you. You knew I did. Yet you came looking for me where—where you thought I was."

Master Villon did not laugh at the sequence of her

ideas; his mind was on what he must now tell her, and how she would take it.

"You believe, with your father, that I entered your room to possess you? I had no such purpose! The next time I come there, yes, but not last night."

She put those honest brown eyes on him. "Why did you come?"

"To return your gold piece."

For once she flinched, under the full blow of that news.

"That's how it came back! Then you are a thief!"

"I was. Until I met you."

They stood silent, the longest of moments.

"Why did you return this morning? Just to make certain that I knew the worst?"

"No!" said he with sudden vigor. "To learn whether you too enjoy stamping on those who are found out!"

She may not have understood him. Or perhaps she did.

"The gold piece is not important. Not in the slightest!"

"To me," he said, "it is. Very!"

He bowed, hat on heart, as though closing the episode for the time being, and she watched while he climbed the wall, took hold of the apple bough for a safe purchase, and leapt to the turf outside.

JAMES MORIER

The Adventures of Hajji[1] Baba

I held a consultation with myself as to what I should do for my livelihood. Various walks in life were open to me. The begging line was an excellent one in Meshed, and, judging from my success as a water carrier, I should very soon have been at the head of the profession. I might also have become a *lûti,*[2] and kept a bear; but it required some apprenticeship to learn the tricks of the one, and to know how to tame the other: so I gave that up. Still I might have followed my own profession, and have taken a shop; but I could not bear the thoughts of settling, particularly in so remote a town as Meshed. At length I followed the bent of my inclination, and, as I was myself devotedly fond of smoking, I determined to become an itinerant seller of smoke. Accordingly, I bought pipes of various sizes, a wooden tray, containing the pipe heads, which was strapped round my waist, an iron pot for fire, which I carried in my hand, a

[1]A hajji is someone who has made a pilgrimage to a holy shrine. Meshed is the holy city of the Sufi sect of Moslems. The dervishes are Sufis. They originally had their mosque in Konya, Turkey.

[2]The *lûties* are privileged buffoons, usually keeping monkeys, bears, and other animals.

pair of iron pincers, a copper jug for water, that was suspended by a hook behind my back, and some long bags for my tobacco. All these commodities were fastened about my body, and when I was fully equipped, I looked like a porcupine with all its quills erect. My tobacco was of various sorts—Tabas, Shiraz, Susa, and Damascus. It is true that I was not very scrupulous about giving it pure; for with a very small quantity of the genuine leaf I managed to make a large store, with the assistance of different sorts of dungs. I had a great tact in discovering among my customers the real connoisseur, and to him I gave it almost genuine. My whole profits, in fact, depended upon my discrimination of characters. To those of the middling ranks, I gave it half mixed; to the lower sort, three-quarters; and to the lowest, almost without any tobacco at all. Whenever I thought I could perceive a wry face, I immediately exerted my ingenuity in favor of the excellence of my tobacco. I showed specimens of the good, descanted on its superior qualities, and gave the history of the very gardener who had reared it, and pledged myself to point out the very spot in his grounds where it grew.

I became celebrated in Meshed for the excellence of my pipes. My principal customer was a dervish, who was so great a connoisseur that I never dared to give him any but pure tobacco; and although I did not gain much by his custom, as he was not very exact in his payments, yet his conversation was so agreeable, and he recommended so many of his friends to me, that I cultivated his goodwill to the utmost of my power.

Dervish Sefer (for that was his name) was a man of a peculiar aspect. He had a large aquiline nose, piercing black eyes, a thick beard, and a great quantity of jet-black hair flowing over his shoulders. His conical cap was embroidered with sentences from the Koran and holy invocations: the skin of a red deer was fastened loosely upon his back, with the hairy side outwards: he bore in hand a long steel staff, which he generally carried on his shoulder, and in the other a calabash, suspended by three chains, which he extended whenever he deigned to ask the charity of passengers. In his girdle he wore large agate clasps, from which hung a quantity of heavy wooden beads; and, as he swung himself along through the streets and bazaars, there was so much of wildness and solicitude in all his words and actions, that he did not fail to inspire a certain awe in all beholders. This, I afterwards learned, was put on, in order to suit the character which he had adopted; for when he smoked my pipes, if no one chanced to be present, he was the most natural and unreserved of beings. Our acquaintance soon improved into intimacy, and at length he introduced me into a small circle of dervishes, men of his own turn and profession, with whom he lived almost exclusively, and I was invited to frequent their meetings. It is true that this did not suit my views in the smoking line, for they consumed more of my good tobacco than all the rest of my other customers put together; but their society was so agreeable that I could not resist the temptation.

Dervish Sefer, one evening when we had smoked more than usual, said to me, "Hajji Baba, you are too much of a man to be a seller of smoke all your life. Why do you not turn dervish, like us? We hold men's beards as cheap as dirt; and although our existence is precarious, yet it is one of great variety, as well as of great idleness.

We look upon mankind as fair game—we live upon their weakness and credulity; and, from what I have seen of you, I think you would do honor to our profession, and in time become as celebrated as even the famous Sheikh Saadi himself." This speech was applauded by the other two, who pressed my entering upon their profession. I was nothing loath, but I pleaded my ignorance of the necessary qualifications.

"How is it possible," said I, "that a being so ignorant and unexperienced as I am can at once attain the learning requisite for a dervish? I know how to read and write, true; I have gone through the Koran, and have my Hafiz and Saadi nearly by heart; besides which, I have read a great part of the Shah Nameh of Ferdûsi, but beyond that I am totally ignorant."

"Ah, my friend," said Dervish Sefer, "little do you know of dervishes, and still less of human kind. It is not great learning that is required to make a dervish: assurance is the first ingredient. With one-fiftieth part of the accomplishments that you have mentioned, and with only a common share of effrontery, I promise you that you may command not only the purses, but even the lives of your hearers. By impudence I have been a prophet, by impudence I have wrought miracles, by impudence I have restored the dying to health—by impudence, in short, I lead a life of great ease, and am feared and respected by those who, like you, do not know what dervishes are. If I chose to give myself the trouble, and incur the risks which Mahomed himself did, I might even now become as great a prophet as he. It would be as easy for me to cut the moon in two with my finger as it was for him, provided I once made my hearers have confidence in me; and impudence will do that, and more, if exerted in a proper manner."

When Dervish Sefer had done talking, his companions applauded what he had said; and they related so many curious anecdotes of the feats which they had performed, that I became very anxious to know more of these extraordinary men. They promised to relate the history of their lives at our next meeting, and, in the meanwhile, recommended me strongly to turn my thoughts to a line of life more dignified, and fuller of enjoyment, than that of a vagabond seller of adulterated smoke.

When we had again collected ourselves together, each with a pipe in his hand, seated with our backs against the wall, in a room, the window of which opened into a small square planted with flowers, Dervish Sefer, as the acknowledged chief of our society, began his story:

"I am the son of the Lûti Bashi, or head Merry-Andrew of the Prince of Shiraz, by a celebrated courtesan of the name of Taous, or the Peacock. With such parents, I leave you to imagine the education which I received. My principal associates, during my infancy, were the monkeys and bears that belonged to my father and his friends; and, perhaps, it is to the numerous tricks in which they were instructed, and to the facility with which they learnt them, that I am indebted for the talent of mimicry that has been so useful to me through life. At fifteen I was an accomplished _lûti_. I could eat fire, spout water, and perform all sorts of sleight of hand, and I should very probably have continued to prosper in this profession, had not the daughter of the prince's general of camel artillery become enamored of me, as I danced on the tightrope before the court on the festival of New Year's Day. A young camel driver under his orders had a sister who served in the harem of the general: he was my most intimate friend, and his sister told him of the effect my appearance had produced upon her mistress. I immediately went to a *mîrza,* or scribe, who lived in a small shed in a corner of the bazaar, and requested him to write a love letter for me, with as much red ink in it as possible, and crossed and recrossed with all the complication he could devise. Nothing could be better than this composition; for at the very outset it informed my mistress that I was dead, and that my death was owing to the fire of her eyes, which had made roast meat of my heart. Notwithstanding this assertion, I ventured at the end to say that as I had never yet seen her, I hoped that she would contrive to grant me an interview. In the joy of my heart for the possession of such a letter, in great confidence I told the scribe who my charmer was, which he had no sooner heard, than, hoping to receive a present for his trouble, he went forthwith and informed the general himself of the fact. That the son of the Lûti Bashi should dare to look up to the daughter of Zambûrekchi Bashi was a crime not to be forgiven; and because the latter had influence at court, he procured an order for my instant removal from Shiraz. My father did not wish to incur the prince's displeasure, and fearing, from my growing celebrity, that I should very soon rival him in his own profession, rather urged than delayed my departure. On the morning when I was about quitting Shiraz, and was bidding adieu to my friends the monkeys, bears, and other animals under his care, he said to me, 'Sefer, my son, I should be sorry to part with you; but with the education which you have received, and the peculiar advantages which you have had of living almost entirely in the society of me and my beasts, it is impossible that you will not succeed in life. I now endow you with what will ensure you a rapid fortune. I give you my chief ape, the most accomplished of his species. Make a friend of him for your own sake, and love him for mine; and I hope in time that you will reach the eminence which your father has attained.' Upon this he placed the animal upon my shoulder, and thus accompanied, I left the paternal roof.

"I took the road to Ispahan, in no very agreeable mood, for I scarcely knew whether to be happy or sorry for this change in my circumstances. A monkey and independence were certainly delightful things; but to leave my associates, and the places that were dear to me from infancy, and, above all, to abandon that fair unknown, whom my imagination had pictured to me as lovely as Shireen herself, were circumstances which appeared to me so distressing, that by the time I had reached the hut of the dervish, at the Teng Allah Akbar, my mind sank into a miserable fit of despondency. I seated myself on a stone, near the hut, and, with my monkey by my side, I gave vent to my grief in a flood of tears, exclaiming, *'Ah wahi! Ah wahi!'* in the most piteous accents imaginable.

"These brought the dervish out; and when he had heard my tale, invited me into the hut, where I found another dervish, of much more commanding aspect than the former. He was clad nearly in the same manner that I am now (indeed the cap I wear was his); but there was a wildness about his looks that was quite imposing.

"At the sight of me and my companion, he appeared struck by a sudden thought. He and the other dervish having talked together in private, he proposed that I should accompany him to Ispahan, promised that he would be kind to me, and, if I behaved well, would put me into the way of making my fortune. I readily agreed; and after the dervish of the hut had given us a pipe to smoke, we departed, walking at a good pace, without much being said between us during some time. Dervish Bideen,[3] for that was his name, at length began to question me very closely about my former life, and hearing in what my accomplishments consisted, seemed to be well pleased. He then descanted upon the advantages attending the life of a dervish, proved them to be superior to the low pursuits of a *lûti*, and at length persuaded me to embrace his profession. He said, that if I would look upon him as my master, he would teach me all he knew; and *that*, he assured me, was no small portion of knowledge, inasmuch as he was esteemed the most perfect dervish in Persia. He began to talk of magic and astrology, and gave me various receipts for making spells and charms, to serve on every occasion in life; by the sale of which alone I should be able to make my fortune. The tail of a hare, placed under the pillow of a child, he assured me, produces sleep; and its blood, given to a horse, makes him fleet and long-winded. The eye and the knucklebones of a wolf, attached to a boy's person, give him courage; and its fat, rubbed on a woman, will convert her husband's love into indifference: its gall, used in the same manner, produces fruitfulness. But the article which bore the greatest price in the seraglios was the *kûs keftar*, the dried skin of a female hyena; which, if worn about the

[3]The Persian for "give me."

person, conciliated the affection of all to the wearer. He discoursed long upon these and such like subjects, until he gradually excited so much interest in my heart, by thus placing my fortune apparently in full view, that at length he ventured to make a proposal, which he easily judged would be disagreeable.

" 'Sefer,' said he to me, 'you know not the treasure you possess in that ape—I do not mean as he stands now alive, but dead. If he were dead, I could extract such ingredients from him to make charms, which would sell for their weight in gold in the harem of the Shah. You must know that the liver of an ape, and only of that particular species which you possess, is sure to bring back the love of a desired object to the person who may possess it. Then the skin of its nose, if worn round the neck, is a decisive preventive against poison; and the ashes of the animal itself, after it has been burned over a slow fire, will, if taken internally, give all the qualities of the ape, cunning, adroitness, and the powers of imitation." He then proposed that we should kill the beast.

"I was certainly alarmed at the proposal. I had been brought up with my ape: we had hitherto gone through life together in prosperity as well as in adversity; and to lose him in this barbarous manner was more than I could bear. I was about to give a flat refusal to the dervish, when I observed that his countenance, which hitherto had been all smiles and good humor, had changed to downright furiousness; and fearing that he would take by force that which I could not protect, I, with all the reluctance imaginable, consented to the execution of his project. We then deviated from the road; and having got into a solitary glen, we gathered together some dry stubble and underwood, made a fire, striking a light with a flint and steel, which my companion carried about him. He took my poor ape into his hands, and, without farther ceremony, put it to death. He then dissected it; and having taken from it the liver, and the skin off its nose, burned it in the pile we had made; and when all was over, carefully collected the ashes, which having packed in a corner of his handkerchief, we proceeded on our journey.

"We reached Ispahan in due time, where I exchanged such parts of my dress as belonged to the *lûti* for the garb of a dervish, and then we proceeded to Tehran. Here my master's appearance produced great effect; for no sooner was it known that he had arrived than all sorts of people flocked to consult him. Mothers wanted protection for their children against the evil eye; wives a spell against the jealousy of their husbands; warriors talismans to secure them from harm in battle. But the ladies of the king's seraglio were his principal customers. Their most urgent demand was some powerful charm to ensure the attention of the king. The collection of materials for this purpose, which the Dervish Bideen had made, was very great. He had the hairs of a lynx, the backbone of an owl, and bear's grease in various preparations. To one of the ladies, who, owing to her advanced age, was more pressing than the others, he sold the liver of my monkey, assuring her, that as soon as she appeared wearing it about her person, his majesty would distinguish her from her rivals. To another, who complained that she was never in favor, and frustrated in all her schemes to attract notice, he administered a decoction of the monkey's ashes; and to a third, who wanted a charm to drive away wrinkles, he gave an ointment, which, if properly applied, and provided she did not laugh, or otherwise move the muscles of her face, would effectually keep them smooth.

"I was initiated into all these mysteries, and frequently was a party concerned in a fraud, whenever my master was put to the necessity of doing something supernatural to support his credit, if by chance his spells were palpably of no avail. But whatever profit arose either from these services, or from the spoils of my monkey, he alone was the gainer, for I never touched a *ghauz*[4] of it.

"I accompanied the Dervish Bideen into various countries, where we practised our art: sometimes we were adored as saints, and at others stoned for vagrants. Our journeys being performed on foot, I had good opportunities to see every place in detail. We traveled from Tehran to Constantinople, and from that capital to Grand Cairo, through Aleppo and Damascus. From Cairo we showed ourselves at Mecca and Medina; and taking ship at Jedda, landed at Surat, in the Guzerat, whence we walked to Lahore and Kashmir.

"At this last place, the dervish, according to custom, endeavored to deceive the natives: but they were too enlightened for us, and we were obliged to steal away in disgrace; and we at length fixed ourselves at Herat, where we were repaid for our former want of success by the credulity of the Afghans, who were good enough to admit all that we chose to tell them. But here, as the dervish was getting up a plan to appear as a prophet, and when our machinery for performing miracles was nearly completed, he, who had promised eter-

[4]A *ghauz* is a small copper coin.

nal youth to thousands, at length paid the debt of nature himself. He had shut himself up in a small hut,
situated at the top of a mountain near Herat, where we
made the good people believe he was living upon no
other food than that which the jinns and *peris* brought
to him; but unfortunately he actually died of a surfeit,
having eaten more of a roast lamb and sweetmeats than
his nature could support. For my own credit, I was
obliged to say, that the jinns, jealous of us mortals for
possessing the society of so wonderful a person, had so
inflated him with celestial food, that, leaving no room
for his soul, it had been completely blown out of his
body, and carried away into the fifth heaven by a strong
northeast wind, which was blowing at the time. This
wind, which lasts for 120 days during the summer
months, and without which the inhabitants would almost die with heat, I endeavored to make them believe
was a miracle performed by the dervish in their favor,
as a parting legacy to them and their descendants for
ever. The old men, indeed, who recollected the wind ever
since their youth, were incredulous; but their testimony
bore but little weight, compared to the influence which
we had acquired. He was buried with the greatest
honours; and the Prince of Herat himself, *Eshek Mirza,*[5]
lent his shoulder to bear his coffin to the grave. A mauso-
leum was erected over it by some of the most pious of the
Afghans, and it has ever since been a place of pilgrimage
from all the country round.

"I remained at Herat for some time after the death
of my companion, in order to enjoy the advantages which

[5]Roughly, "Mr. Jackass."

might accrue to me from being the friend and disciple of one of such high reputation, and I did not repent of my resolution. I disposed of my spells at great prices, and, moreover, made a considerable sum by selling the combings of my deceased friend's beard, and the cuttings of his nails, which I assured my purchasers had been carefully preserved during the time of his retirement in the mountains; although, in fact, they were chiefly collected from my own person. When I had sold of these relics enough to make several respectable beards, and a proportionate quantity of nails, I felt that if I persisted in the traffic, notwithstanding the inordinate credulity of the Afghans, I might be discovered for a cheat, therefore I took my departure, and, having traveled into various parts of Persia, I at length fixed myself among the Hezareh, a large tribe, living for the most part in tents, and which occupy the open country between Kabul and Kandahar. My success among them was something quite beyond my expectation, for I put into practice what the Dervish Bideen had planned at Herat, and actually appeared in the character of a prophet."

The Dervish Sefer then, laying his hand upon the shoulder of the dervish who sat next to him, said, "My friend, here, was my accomplice on that occasion, and he will remember how ingeniously we managed to make the Hezareh believe that we possessed a caldron which was always full of boiled rice—a miracle which even the most incredulous did not fail to believe, as long as they got their share of it. In short, I am the celebrated Hazret Ishan himself, he of whom you have lately heard so much in Khorassan; and although my sacred character was not proof against the attacks made upon it by the arms of the

Shah, yet, while it lasted, I collected enough from the zeal and credulity of my disciples to enable me to pass the remainder of my life in comfort. I have lived at Meshed for some time; and it is but a week ago that we contrived to perform the miracle of giving sight to a blind girl; so now we are held in the highest veneration."

Here the Dervish Sefer ended his history, and then called upon his next neighbour to give an account of himself.

This was the dervish who had been his accomplice among the Hezareh, and he began as follows:

"My father was a celebrated man of the law, of the city of Qom, enjoying the reputation of saying his prayers, making his ablutions, and keeping his fasts more regularly than any man in Persia; in short, he was the cream of Shias, and the model of Mussulmans. He had many sons, and we were brought up in the strictest practice of the external parts of our religion. The rigor and severity with which we were treated were combated on our part by cunning and dissimulation. These qualities gradually fixed themselves in our character; and without any consideration for our circumstances, we were early branded as a nest of hypocrites, and as the greatest cheats and liars of our birthplace. I, in particular, was so notorious that in my own defense I became a dervish, and I owe the reputation which I have acquired in that calling to the following fortunate circumstance:

"I had scarcely arrived at Tehran, and had taken up my quarters opposite to a druggist's shop, when I was called up in a great hurry by an old woman, who informed me that her master, the druggist, had just been taken exceedingly ill, after having eaten more than usual; that the medicine he had taken had not performed its office; and that his family wished to try what a talisman would do for him: she therefore invited me to write one suited to his case. As I had neither paper, pens, nor ink, I insisted upon going into his *anderûn*, or women's apartments, and writing it there, to which she consented. I was introduced into a small square yard, and then into a room, where I found the sick man extended on his bed on the ground, surrounded by as many women as the place could hold, who cried aloud, and exclaimed, *"Wahi, wahi,* in the name of God he dies, he dies!"* The implements of medicine were spread about, which showed that everything had been done either to kill or save him. A large basin, which had contained the prescription, sat on the shelf: the long glass tube, that instrument of torture, was in a corner; and among other furniture, the doctor himself was seen seated, unconcernedly enjoying his pipe, and who, having found that human means were inefficient, had had recourse to supernatural, and had prescribed, as a last resource, the talisman, which it was my fate to write. A new dervish excited new hopes, for I saw that I produced much stir as I entered the sickroom. I asked for paper with an air of authority, as if I felt great confidence in my own powers (although, in fact, I had never written a talisman before), and a large piece was produced, which seemed to have been the wrapper to some drug or other. Pen and ink were also given me; and then calling up all my gravity, I scrawled the paper over in a variety of odd characters, which here and there contained the names of Allah, Mohammed, Ali, Hassan, and Hossein, and all the Imâms, placing them in different anagrams, and substituting here and there figures instead of letters. I then handed it over with great ceremony to the doctor, who calling for water and a basin, washed the whole from off the paper into the basin, whilst the bystanders offered up prayers for the efficacy of the precious writing. The doctor then said, 'In the name of the Prophet, let the patient take this; and if fate hath decreed that he is to live, then the sacred names which he will now swallow will restore him: but if not, neither my skill, nor that of any other man, can ever be of the least avail.'

"The draught was administered, and every eye was immediately fixed upon the wretched man's face, as if a resuscitation was expected to ensue. He remained for some time without showing any symptom of life; when, to the astonishment of all, not excepting myself and the doctor, he groaned, opened his eyes, raised his head on his arm, then called for a basin, and at length vomited in a manner that would have done credit to the prescription of Abu Avicenna[6] himself. In short, he recovered.

"In my own mind, I immediately attributed the happy change to the drug which had once been wrapped in the paper, and which, with the nausea of the ink, had produced the effect just described: but I took care to let the bystanders know that the cure was entirely owing to the interference and to the handwriting of one of my sanctity; and that but for me he would have died.

"The doctor, on the other hand, took all the merit of the case to himself; for as soon as his patient had opened his eyes, he exclaimed, 'Did I not tell you so?' and in proportion as the draught operated, he went on exulting thus, 'There, there, see the efficacy of my prescription!

[6]A famed Arab physician of the Middle Ages.

Had it not been for me, you would have seen the druggist dead before you.'

"I, however, would not allow him to proceed, and said, 'If you are a doctor, why did you not cure your patient without calling for me? Keep to your blisters and to your bleedings, and do not interfere with that which does not belong to you.'

"He answered, 'Mr. Dervish, I make no doubt that you can write a very good talisman, and also can get a very good price for it: but every one knows who and what dervishes are; and if their talismans are ever of use, it is not their sanctity which makes them so.'

" 'Whose dog are you,' exclaimed I, in return, 'to talk to me after this manner? I, who am a servant of the prophet. As for you doctors, your ignorance is proverbial; you hide it by laying all to fate. If by chance your patient recovers, then you take all the credit of the cure to yourselves; should he die, you say, "God hath decreed thus. What can the efforts of man avail?" Go to, go to; when you have nearly killed your next patient, and then know not what more to ordain, send for me again, and I will cover your impudent ignorance by curing him as I have just done the druggist.'

" 'By my head, and by your death,' returned the doctor, 'I am not a man to hear this from anyone, much less from a dog of a dervish'; and immediately he got up, and approached me in a threatening attitude, making use of every epithet of abuse that he could think of.

"I received him with suitable expressions of contempt, and we very soon came to blows. He so effectually fastened upon my hair, and I upon his beard, that we plucked out whole handfuls from each other; we bit and spat, and fought with such fury, heedless of the sick man and the cries of the women, that the uproar became very great, and, perhaps, would have terminated in something serious, if one of the women had not run in to us, in great agitation, assuring us that the Darogah's officers[7] were then knocking at the door of the house, and inquiring whence proceeded all the disturbance.

"This parted us; and then I was happy to find that the bystanders were in my favor, for they expressed their contempt of the skill of the physician, whose only object was to obtain money without doing his patients any good, while they looked upon me in the light of a divine person, who in my handwriting alone possessed the power of curing all manner of disease.

"The doctor, seeing how ill matters were going for him, stole away with the best face he could; but before he left the room, he stooped down, and collecting as many of the hairs of his beard, which I had plucked from him, as he could find, to which he cunningly added some of my own hair, he brandished them in my face, saying, 'We shall see on whose side the laugh will be when you are brought before the qadi tomorrow, for beards are worth a ducat[8] per hair in Tehran; and I doubt, with all your talismans, whether you can buy these that I hold in my hand.'

"It was evident, that when his anger was cooled, out of regard to his own reputation, he would not put

[7]Policemen
[8]A beard is held so sacred in the East that every hair that grows upon a Mohammedan's chin is protected from molestation by a heavy fine.

his threat into execution; so the fear of being dragged before the justice gave me no uneasiness, and I therefore only considered how to make the most of the fortunate circumstance which had just taken place. The report that the druggist (who was the first in Tehran) had been brought to life, when on the point of death, by a newly arrived dervish, was soon spread about, and I became the object of general concern. From morning to night I was taken up in writing talismans, for which I made my customers pay according to their means, and in a short time I found myself the possessor of some hundreds of piasters. But, unfortunately for me, I did not meet with a dying druggist and a piece of his paper every day; and feeling myself reduced to live upon the reputation of this one miracle, which I perceived to my sorrow daily diminished, I made a virtue of necessity, and determining to make the tour of Persia, I immediately left Tehran. To whichsoever city I bent my steps, I managed matters so adroitly that I made my reputation precede my arrival there. The druggist had given me an attestation, under his seal, that he had been restored to life by virtue of a talisman written by my hand, and this I exhibited wherever I went, to corroborate the truth of the reports which had been circulated in my favor. I am now living upon this reputation: it supports me very tolerably for the present, but whenever I find that it begins to fail, I shall proceed elsewhere." The dervish here ended his history.

When the third dervish came to his turn to speak, he said, "My tale is short, although storytelling is my profession. I am the son of a schoolmaster, who, perceiving that I was endowed with a very retentive memory, made me read and repeat to him most of the histories with which our language abounds; and when he found that he had furnished my mind with a sufficient assortment, he turned me out into the world under the garb of a dervish, to relate them in public to such audiences as my talents might gather round me.

"My first essays were anything but successful. My auditors heard my stories, and then walked away without leaving me any reward for my pains. Little by little I acquired experience. Instead of being carried away, as I had at first permitted myself to be, by the interest of the story, I made a pause when the catastrophe drew near, and then, looking around me, said, 'All you who are present, if you will be liberal toward me, I will tell you what follows'; and I seldom failed in collecting a good handful of copper coin. For instance, in the story of the prince of Khatai and the princess of Samarkand, when the Ogre Hezar Mun seizes the prince, and is about to devour him; when he is suspended in the ogre's mouth, between his upper and lower jaw; when the princess, all disheveled and forlorn, is on her knees praying that he may be spared; when the attendants couch their lances, and are in dismay; when the horses start back in fright; when the thunder rolls, and the ogre growls; then I stop, and say, 'Now, my noble hearers, open your purses, and you shall hear in how miraculous a manner the Prince of Khatai cut the ogre's head off!' By such arts, I manage to extract a subsistence from the curiosity of men; and when my stock of stories is exhausted in one place, I leave it, travel to another, and there renew my labors."

The dervishes having finished their narratives, I thanked them for the entertainment and instruction which they had afforded me, and I forthwith resolved to learn as much from them as possible, in order to become a dervish myself, in case I should be obliged to abandon my present business.

Tit for Tat

Once I was a rabbiner. A rabbiner, not a rabbi. That is, I was called rabbi—but a rabbi of the crown.

To old-country Jews I don't have to explain what a rabbi of the crown is. They know the breed. What are his great responsibilities? He fills out birth certificates, officiates at circumcisions, performs marriages, grants divorces. He gets his share from the living and the dead. In the synagogue he has a place of honor, and when the congregation rises, he is the first to stand. On legal holidays he appears in a stovepipe hat and holds forth in his best Russian: *"Gospoda Prihozhane!"* To take it for granted that among our people a rabbiner is well loved— let's not say any more. Say rather that we put up with him, as we do a government inspector or a deputy sheriff. And yet he is chosen from among the people, that is, every three years a proclamation is sent us: *"Na Osnavania Predpisania . . ."* Or, as we would say: "Your Lord, the Governor, orders you to come together in the synagogue, poor little Jews, and pick out a rabbiner for yourselves . . ."

Then the campaign begins. Candidates, hot discussions, brandy, and maybe even a bribe or two. After which come charges and countercharges, the elections are annulled, and we are ordered to hold new elections. Again the proclamations: *"Na Osnavania Predpisania ..."* Again candidates, discussions, party organizations, brandy, a bribe or two ... That was the life!

Well, there I was—a rabbiner in a small town in the province of Poltava. But I was anxious to be a modern one. I wanted to serve the public. So I dropped the formalities of my position and began to mingle with the people—as we say: to stick my head into the community pot. I got busy with the Talmud Torah, the charity fund; interpreted a law, settled disputes, or just gave plain advice.

The love of settling disputes, helping people out, or advising them, I inherited from my father and my uncles. They—may they rest in peace—also enjoyed being bothered all the time with other people's business. There are two kinds of people in the world: those that you can't bother at all, and others whom you can bother all the time. You can climb right on their heads—naturally not in one jump, but gradually. First you climb into their laps, then onto their shoulders, then their heads—and after that, you can jump up and down on their heads and stamp on their hearts with your heavy boots—as long as you want to.

I was that kind, and without boasting I can tell you that I had plenty of ardent followers and plain hangers-on who weren't ashamed to come every day and fill my head with their clamoring and sit around till late at night. They never refused a glass of tea, or cigarettes. Newspapers and books they took without asking. In short, I was a regular fellow.

Well, there came a day . . . The door opened, and in
walked the very foremost men of the town, the sparkling
best, the very cream of the city. Four householders—men
of affairs—you could almost say: real men of substance.
And who were these men? Three of them were the Troika
—that was what we called them in our town because they
were together all the time—partners in whatever business any one of them was in. They always fought; they
were always suspicious of each other, and watched everything the others did; and still they never separated—
working always in this principle: if the business is a good
one and there is profit to be made, why shouldn't I have
a lick at the bone, too? And on the other hand, if it should
end in disaster—you'll be buried along with me, and lie
with me deep in the earth. And what does God do? He
brings together the three partners with a fourth one.
They operate together a little less than a year and end up
in a brawl. That is why they're here.

What had happened? "Since God created thieves,
swindlers, and crooks, you never saw a thief, swindler, or
crook like this one." That is the way the three old partners described the fourth one to me. And he, the fourth,
said the same about them. Exactly the same, word for
word. And who was this fourth one? He was a quiet little
man, a little innocent-looking fellow, with thick, dark eyebrows under which a pair of shrewd, ironic little eyes
watched everything you did. Everyone called him Nachman Lekach.

His real name was Nachman Noss'n, but everybody
called him Nachman Lekach, because as you know,
Noss'n is the Hebrew for "he gave," and *Lekach* means
"he took," and in all the time we knew him, no one had

ever seen him give anything to anyone—while at taking no one was better.

Where were we? Oh, yes . . . So they came to the rabbiner with the complaints, to see if he could find a way of straightening out their tangled accounts. "Whatever you decide, Rabbi, and whatever you decree, and whatever you say, will be final."

That is how the three old partners said it, and the fourth, Reb Nachman, nodded with that innocent look on his face to indicate that he, too, left it all up to me: "For the reason," his eyes said, "that I know that I have done no wrong." And he sat down in a corner, folded his arms across his chest like an old woman, fixed his shrewd, ironic little eyes on me, and waited to see what his partners would have to say. And when they had all laid out their complaints and charges, presented all their evidence, said all they had to say, he got up, patted down his thick eyebrows, and not looking at the others at all, only at me, with those deep, deep, shrewd little eyes of his, he proceeded to demolish their claims and charges—so completely, that it looked as if they were the thieves, swindlers, and crooks—the three partners of his—and he, Nachman Lekach, was a man of virtue and piety, the little chicken that is slaughtered before Yom Kippur to atone for our sins—a sacrificial lamb. "And every word that you heard them say is a complete lie; it never was and never could be. It's simply out of the question." And he proved with evidence, arguments, and supporting data that everything he said was true and holy, as if Moses himself had said it.

All the time he was talking, the others, the Troika, could hardly sit in their chairs. Every moment one or another of them jumped up, clutched his head—or his heart: "Of all things! How can a man talk like that! Such lies and falsehoods!" It was almost impossible to calm them down, to keep them from tearing at the fourth one's beard. As for me—the rabbiner—it was hard, very hard to crawl out from this horrible tangle, because by now it was clear that I had a fine band to deal with, all four of them swindlers, thieves, and crooks, and informers to boot, and all four of them deserving a severe punishment. But what? At last this idea occurred to me, and I said to them:

"Are you ready, my friends? I am prepared to hand down my decision. My mind is made up. But I won't disclose what I have to say until each of you has deposited twenty-five rubles—to prove that you will act upon the decision I am about to hand down."

"With the greatest of pleasure," the three spoke out at once, and Nachman Lekach nodded his head, and all four reached into their pockets, and each one counted out his twenty-five on the table. I gathered up the money, locked it up in a drawer, and then I gave them my decision in these words:

"Having heard the complaints and the arguments of both parties, and having examined your accounts and studied your evidence, I find according to my understanding and deep conviction, that all four of you are in the wrong, and not only in the wrong, but that it is a shame and a scandal for Jewish people to conduct themselves in such a manner—to falsify accounts, perjure yourselves and even act as informers. Therefore I have decided that since we have a Talmud Torah in our town with many children who have neither clothes nor shoes, and whose parents have nothing with which to pay their tuition, and since there has been no help at all from you gentlemen (to get a few pennies from you, one has to reach down into your very gizzards) therefore it is my decision that this hundred rubles of yours shall go to the Talmud Torah, and as for you, gentlemen, you can go home, in good health, and thanks for your contribution. The poor children will now have some shoes and socks and shirts and pants, and I'm sure they'll pray to God for you and your children. Amen."

Having heard the sentence, the three old partners— the Troika—looked from one to the other—flushed, unable to speak. A decision like this they had not anticipated. The only one who could say a word was Reb Nachman Lekach. He got up, patted down his thick eyebrows, held out a hand, and looking at me with his ironic little eyes, said this:

"I thank you, Rabbi Rabbiner, in behalf of all four of us, for the wise decision which you have just made known. Such a judgment could have been made by no one since King Solomon himself. There is only one thing that you forgot to say, Rabbi Rabbiner, and that is, What is your fee for this wise and just decision?"

"I beg your pardon," I tell him. "You've come to the wrong address. I am not one of those rabbiners who tax the living and the dead." That is the way I answered him, like a real gentleman. And this was his reply:

"If that's the case, then you are not only a sage and a rabbi among men, you're an honest man besides. So, if you would care to listen, I'd like to tell you a story. Say that we will pay you for your pains at least with a story."

"Good enough. Even with two stories."

"In that case, sit down, Rabbi Rabbiner, and let us have your cigarette case. I'll tell you an interesting story, a true one, too, something that happened to me. What happened to others I don't like to talk about."

And we lit our cigarettes, sat down around the table, and Reb Nachman spread out his thick eyebrows, and looking at me with his shrewd, smiling, little eyes, he slowly began to tell his true story of what had once happened to him himself.

All this happened to me a long time ago. I was still a young man and I was living not far from here, in a village near the railroad. I traded in this and that; I had a small tavern, made a living. A Rothschild I didn't become, but bread we had, and in time there were about ten Jewish families living close by—because, as you know, if one of us makes a living, others come around. They think you're shoveling up gold. . . . But that isn't the point. What I was getting at was that right in the midst of the busy season one year, when things were moving and traffic was heavy, my wife had to go and have a baby— our boy—our first son. What do you say to that? "Congratulations! Congratulations everybody!" But that isn't all. You have to have a bris, the circumcision. I dropped everything, went into town, bought all the good things I could find, and came back with the *Mohel* with all his instruments, and for good measure I also brought the *shammes* of the synagogue. I thought that with these two holy men and myself and the neighbors we'd have the ten men that we needed, with one to spare. But what does God do? He has one of my neighbors get sick—he is sick in bed and can't come to the bris, you can't carry him. And

another has to pack up and go off to the city. He can't wait
another day! And here I am without the ten men. Go do
something. Here it is—Friday! Of all days, my wife has
to pick Friday to have the bris—the day before the Sabbath. The *Mohel* is frantic—he has to go back right away.
The *shammes* is actually in tears. "What did you ever
drag us off here for?" they both want to know. And what
can I do?

All I can think of is to run off to the railroad station.
Who knows—so many people come through every day—
maybe God will send some one. And that's just what
happened. I come running up to the station—the agent
has just called out that a train is about to leave. I look
around—a little roly-poly man carrying a huge traveling
bag comes flying by, all sweating and out of breath,
straight toward the lunch counter. He looks over the
dishes—what is there a good Jew can take in a country
railroad station? A piece of herring—an egg. Poor fellow
—you could see his mouth was watering. I grab him by
the sleeve. "Uncle, are you looking for something to
eat?" I ask him, and the look he gives me says: "How did
you know that?" I keep on talking: "May you live to be
a hundred—God himself must have sent you." He still
doesn't understand, so I proceed: "Do you want to earn
the blessings of eternity—and at the same time eat a beef
roast that will melt in your mouth, with a fresh, white
loaf right out of the oven?" He still looks at me as if I'm
crazy. "Who are you? What do you want?"

So I tell him the whole story—what a misfortune had
overtaken us: here we are, all ready for the bris, the
Mohel is waiting, the food is ready—and such food!—and
we need a tenth man! "What's that got to do with me?"

he asks, and I tell him: "What's that got to do with you? Why—everything depends on you—you're the tenth man! I beg you—come with me. You will earn all the rewards of heaven—and have a delicious dinner in the bargain!" "Are you crazy," he asks me, "or are you just out of your head? My train is leaving in a few minutes, and it's Friday afternoon—almost sundown. Do you know what that means? In a few more hours the Sabbath will catch up with me, and I'll be stranded." "So what!" I tell him. "So you'll take the next train. And in the mean-time you'll earn eternal life—and taste a soup, with fresh dumplings, that only my wife can make. . . ."

Well, why make the story long? I had my way. The roast and the hot soup with fresh dumplings did their work. You could see my customer licking his lips. So I grab the traveling bag and I lead him home, and we go through with the bris. It was a real pleasure! You could smell the roast all over the house, it had so much garlic in it. A roast like that, with fresh warm twist, is a delicacy from heaven. And when you con-sider that we had some fresh dill pickles, and a bottle of beer, and some cognac before the meal and cherry cider after the meal—you can imagine the state our guest was in! His cheeks shone and his forehead glis-tened. But what then? Before we knew it the after-noon was gone. My guest jumps up; he looks around, sees what time it is, and almost has a stroke! He reaches for his traveling bag: "Where is it?" I say to him, "What's your hurry? In the first place, do you think we'll let you run off like that—before the Sab-bath? And in the second place—who are you to leave on a journey an hour or two before the Sabbath? And

if you're going to get caught out in the country somewhere, you might just as well stay here with us."

He groans and he sighs. How could I do a thing like
that to him—keep him so late? What did I have against
him? Why hadn't I reminded him earlier? He doesn't stop
bothering me. So I say to him: "In the first place, did I
have to tell you that it was Friday afternoon? Didn't you
know it yourself? And in the second place, how do you
know—maybe it's the way God wanted it? Maybe He
wanted you to stay here for the Sabbath so you could
taste some of my wife's fish? I can guarantee you, that
as long as you've eaten fish, you haven't eaten fish like
my wife's fish—not even in a dream!" Well, that ended
the argument. We said our evening prayers, had a glass
of wine, and my wife brings the fish to the table. My
guest's nostrils swell out, a new light shines in his eyes
and he goes after that fish as if he hadn't eaten a thing
all day. He can't get over it. He praises it to the skies. He
fills a glass with brandy and drinks a toast to the fish. And
then comes the soup, a specially rich Sabbath soup with
noodles. And he likes that, too, and the *tzimmes* also, and
the meat that goes with the *tzimmes,* a nice, fat piece of
brisket. I'm telling you, he just sat there licking his
fingers! When we're finishing the last course he turns to
me: "Do you know what I'll tell you? Now that it's all
over, I'm really glad that I stayed over for *Shabbes.* It's
been a long time since I've enjoyed a Sabbath as I've
enjoyed this one." "If that's how you feel, I'm happy," I
tell him. "But wait. This is only a sample. Wait till tomorrow. Then you'll see what my wife can do."

And so it was. The next day, after services, we sit
down at the table. Well, you should have seen the spread.

First the appetizers: crisp wafers and chopped herring, and onions and chicken fat, with radishes and chopped liver and eggs and *gribbenes*. And after that the cold fish and the meat from yesterday's *tzimmes*, and then the jellied neat's foot, or *fisnoga* as you call it, with thin slices of garlic, and after that the potato *cholent* with the *kugel* that had been in the oven all night—and you know what that smells like when you take it out of the oven and take the cover off the pot. And what it tastes like. Our visitor could not find words to praise it. So I tell him: "This is still nothing. Wait until you have tasted our borscht tonight, then you'll know what good food is." At that he laughs out loud—a friendly laugh, it is true—and says to me: "Yes, but how far do you think I'll be from here by the time your borscht is ready?" So I laugh even louder than he does, and say: "You can forget that right now! Do you think you'll be going off tonight?"

And so it was. As soon as the lights were lit and we had a glass of wine to start off the new week, my friend begins to pack his things again. So I call out to him: "Are you crazy? Do you think we'll let you go off, the Lord knows where, at night? And besides, where's your train?" "What?" he yells at me. "No train? Why, you're murdering me! You know I have to leave!" But I say, "May this be the greatest misfortune in your life. Your train will come, if all is well, around dawn tomorrow. In the meantime I hope your appetite and digestion are good, because I can smell the borscht already! All I ask," I say, "is just tell me the truth. Tell me if you've ever touched a borscht like this before. But I want the absolute truth!" What's the use of talking—he had to admit it: never before in all his life had he tasted a borscht like

this. Never. He even started to ask how you made the
borscht, what you put into it, and how long you cooked
it. Everything. And I say: "Don't worry about that! Here,
taste this wine and tell me what you think of *it*. After
all, you're an expert. But the truth! Remember—nothing
but the truth! Because if there is anything I hate, it's
flattery. . . ."

So we took a glass, and then another glass, and we
went to bed. And what do you think happened? My traveler overslept, and missed the early morning train. When
he wakes up he boils over! He jumps on me like a mur-
derer. Wasn't it up to me, out of fairness and decency, to
wake him up in time? Because of me he's going to have
to take a loss, a heavy loss—he doesn't even know himself how heavy. It was all my fault. I ruined him. I!
. . . So I let him talk. I listen, quietly, and when he's all
through, I say: "Tell me yourself, aren't you a queer sort
of person? In the first place, what's your hurry? What are
you rushing for? How long is a person's life altogether?
Does he have to spoil that little with rushing and hurry-
ing? And in the second place, have you forgotten that
today is the third day since the bris? Doesn't that mean
a thing to you? Where we come from, on the third day
we're in the habit of putting on a feast better than the one
at the bris itself. The third day—it's something to celebrate! You're not going to spoil the celebration, are you?"

What can he do? He can't control himself any more,
and he starts laughing—a hysterical laugh. "What good
does it do to talk?" he says. "You're a real leech!" "Just
as you say," I tell him, "but after all, you're a visitor,
aren't you?"

At the dinner table, after we've had a drink or two,

I call out to him: "Look," I say, "it may not be proper—
after all, we're Jews—to talk about milk and such things
while we're eating meat, but I'd like to know your honest
opinion: what do you think of *kreplach* with cheese?" He
looks at me with distrust. "How did we get around to
that?" he asks. "Just like this," I explain to him. "I'd like
to have you try the cheese *kreplach* that my wife makes
—because tonight, you see, we're going to have a dairy
supper . . ." This is too much for him, and he comes right
back at me with, "Not this time! You're trying to keep me
here another day, I can see that. But you can't do it. It
isn't right! It isn't right!" And from the way he fusses and
fumes, it's easy to see that I won't have to coax him too
long, or fight with him either, because what is he but a
man with an appetite, who has only one philosophy, which
he practices at the table? So I say this to him: "I give you
my word of honor, and if that isn't enough, I'll give you
my hand as well—here, shake—that tomorrow I'll wake
you up in time for the earliest train. I promise it, even if
the world turns upside down. If I don't, may I—you know
what!" At this he softens and says to me: "Remember,
we're shaking hands on that!" And I: "A promise is a
promise." And my wife makes a dairy supper—how can
I describe it to you? With such *kreplach* that my traveler
has to admit that it was all true: he has a wife too, and
she makes *kreplach* too, but how can you compare hers
with these? It's like night to day!

And I kept my word, because a promise is a promise.
I woke him when it was still dark, and started the samo-
var. He finished packing and began to say good-bye to me
and the rest of the household in a very handsome,
friendly style. You could see he was a gentleman. But I

interrupt him: "We'll say good-bye a little later. First, we have to settle up." "What do you mean—settle up?" "Settle up," I say, "means to add up the figures. That's what I'm going to do now. I'll add them up, let you know what it comes to, and you will be so kind as to pay me."

His face flames red. "Pay you?" he shouts. "Pay you for what?" "For what?" I repeat. "You want to know for what? For everything. The food, the drink, the lodging." This time he becomes white—not red—and he says to me: "I don't understand you at all. You came and invited me to the bris. You stopped me at the train. You took my bag away from me. You promised me eternal life." "That's right," I interrupt him. "That's right. But what's one thing got to do with the other? When you came to the bris you earned your reward in heaven. But food and drink and lodging—do I have to give you these things for nothing? After all, you're a businessman, aren't you? You should understand that fish costs money, and that the wine you drank was the very best, and the beer, too, and the cherry cider. And you remember how you praised the *tzimmes* and the puddings and the borscht. You remember how you licked your fingers. And the cheese *kreplach* smelled pretty good to you, too. Now, I'm glad you enjoyed these things; I don't begrudge you that in the least. But certainly you wouldn't expect that just because you earned a reward in heaven, and enjoyed yourself in the bargain, that *I* should pay for it?" My traveling friend was really sweating; he looked as if he'd have a stroke. He began to throw himself around, yell, scream, call for help. "This is Sodom!" he cried. "Worse than Sodom! It's the worst outrage the world has ever heard of! How much do you want?" Calmly I took a piece of paper and a pencil

and began to add it up. I itemized everything, I gave him
an inventory of everything he ate, of every hour he spent
in my place. All in all it added up to something like thirty-
odd rubles and some kopecks—I don't remember it exactly.

When he saw the total, my good man went green and
yellow, his hands shook, and his eyes almost popped out,
and again he let out a yell, louder than before. "What did
I fall into—a nest of thieves? Isn't there a single human
being here? Is there a God anywhere?" So I say to him,
"Look, sir, do you know what? Do you know what you're
yelling about? Do you have to eat your heart out? Here
is my suggestion: let's ride into town together—it's not
far from here—and we'll find some people—there's a rabbiner there—let's ask the rabbi. And we'll abide by what
he says." When he heard me talk like that, he quieted
down a little. And—don't worry—we hired a horse and
wagon, climbed in, and rode off to town, the two of us, and
went straight to the rabbi.

When we got to the rabbi's house, we found him just
finishing his morning prayers. He folded up his prayer
shawl and put his philacteries away. "Good morning," we
said to him, and he: "What's the news today?" The news?
My friend tears loose and lets him have the whole story
—everything from A to Z. He doesn't leave a word out.
He tells how he stopped at the station, and so on and so
on, and when he's through, he whips out the bill I had
given him and hands it to the rabbi. And when the rabbi
had heard everything, he says: "Having heard one side,
I should now like to hear the other." And turning to me,
he asks, "What do you have to say to all that?" I answer:
"Everything he says is true. There's not a word I can add.

Only one thing I'd like to have him tell you—on his word of honor: did he eat the fish, and did he drink the beer and cognac and the cider, and did he smack his lips over the borscht that my wife made?" At this the man becomes almost frantic, he jumps and he thrashes about like an apoplectic. The rabbi begs him not to boil like that, not to be so angry, because anger is a grave sin. And he asks him again about the fish and the borscht and the *kreplach*, and if it was true that he had drunk not only the wine, but beer and cognac and cider as well. Then the rabbi puts on his spectacles, looks the bill over from top to bottom, checks every line, and finds it correct! Thirty-odd rubles and some kopecks, and he makes his judgment brief: he tells the man to pay the whole thing, and for the wagon back and forth, and a judgment fee for the rabbi himself. . . .

The man stumbles out of the rabbi's house looking as if he'd been in a steam bath too long, takes out his purse, pulls out two twenty-fives, and snaps at me: "Give me the change." "What change?" I ask, and he says: "For the thirty you charged me—for that bill you gave me." "Bill? What bill? What thirty are you talking about? What do you think I am, a highwayman? Do you expect me to take money from you? I see a man at the railroad station, a total stranger; I take his bag away from him, and drag him off almost by force to our own bris, and spend a wonderful *Shabbes* with him. So am I going to charge him for the favor he did me, and for the pleasure I had?" Now he looks at me as if I really am crazy, and says: "Then why did you carry on like this? Why did you drag me to the rabbi?" "Why this? Why that?" I say to him. "You're a queer sort of person, you are! I wanted to show you what kind of man our rabbi was, that's all. . . ."

When he finished the story, my litigant, Reb Nach-man Lekach, got up with a flourish, and the other three partners followed him. They buttoned their coats and prepared to leave. But I held them off. I passed the ciga-rettes around again, and said to the storyteller:

"So you told me a story about a rabbi. Now maybe you'll be so kind as to let me tell you a story—also about a rabbi, but a much shorter story than the one you told."

And without waiting for a yes or no, I started right in, and made it brief:

This happened, I began, not so long ago, and in a large city, on Yom Kippur eve. A stranger falls into the town—a businessman, a traveler, who goes here and there, everywhere, sells merchandise, collects money . . . On this day he comes into the city, walks up and down in front of the synagogue, holding his sides with both hands, asks everybody he sees where he can find the rabbi. "What do you want the rabbi for?" people ask. "What business is that of yours?" he wants to know. So they don't tell him. And he asks one man, he asks another: "Can you tell where the rabbi lives?" "What do you want the rabbi for?" "What do you care?" This one and that one, till finally he gets the answer, finds the rabbi's house, goes in, still holding his sides with both hands. He calls the rabbi aside, shuts the door, and says, "Rabbi, this is my story. I am a traveling man, and I have money with me, quite a pile. It's not my money. It belongs to my clients—first to God and then to my clients. It's Yom

Kippur eve. I can't carry money with me on Yom Kippur, and I'm afraid to leave it at my lodgings. A sum like that! So do me a favor—take it, put it away in your strong box till tomorrow night, after Yom Kippur."

And without waiting, the man unbuttons his vest and draws out one pack after another, crisp and clean, the real red, crackling hundred ruble notes!

Seeing how much there was, the rabbi said to him: "I beg your pardon. You don't know me, you don't know who I am." "What do you mean, I don't know who you are? You're a rabbi, aren't you?" "Yes, I'm a rabbi. But I don't know *you*—who you are or what you are." They bargain back and forth. The traveler: "You're a rabbi." The rabbi: "I don't know who you are." And time does not stand still. It's almost Yom Kippur! Finally the rabbi agrees to take the money. The only thing is, who should be the witnesses? You can't trust just anyone in a matter like that.

So the rabbi sends for the leading townspeople, the very cream, rich and respectable citizens, and says to them: "This is what I called you for. This man has money with him, a tidy sum, not his own, but first God's and then his clients'. He wants me to keep it for him till after Yom Kippur. Therefore I want you to be witnesses, to see how much he leaves with me, so that later—you understand?" And the rabbi took the trouble to count it all over three times before the eyes of the townspeople, wrapped the notes in a kerchief, sealed the kerchief with wax, and stamped his initials on the seal. He passed this from one man to the other, saying, "Now look. Here is my signature, and remember, you're the witnesses." The kerchief with the money in it he handed over to his wife, had her lock it in a chest, and hide the keys where no one could find them. And he himself, the rabbi, went to *shul,* and prayed and fasted as it was ordained, lived through Yom Kippur, came home, had a bite to eat, looked up, and there was the traveler. "Good evening, Rabbi." "Good evening. Sit down. What can I do for you?" "Nothing. I came for my package." "What package?" "The money." "What money?" "The money I left with you to keep for me." "You gave *me* money to keep for you? When was that?"

The traveler laughs out loud. He thinks the rabbi is joking with him. The rabbi asks: "What are you laughing at?" And the man says: "It's the first time I met a rabbi who liked to play tricks." At this the rabbi is insulted. No one, he pointed out, had ever called him a trickster before. "Tell me, my good man, what do you want here?"

When he heard these words, the stranger felt his heart stop. "Why, Rabbi, in the name of all that's holy, do you want to kill me? Didn't I give you all my money? That is, not mine, but first God's and then my clients'? I'll remind you, you wrapped it in a kerchief, sealed it with wax, locked it in your wife's chest, hid the key where no one could find it. And here is better proof: there were witnesses, the leading citizens of the city!" And he goes ahead and calls them all off by name. In the midst of it a cold sweat breaks out on his forehead, he feels faint, and asks for a glass of water.

The rabbi sends the *shammes* off to the men the traveler had named—the leading citizens, the flower of the community. They come running from all directions. "What's the matter? What's happened?" "A misfortune. A plot! A millstone around our necks! He insists that he brought a pile of money to me yesterday, to keep over

Yom Kippur, and that you were witnesses to the act."

The householders look at each other, as if to say: "Here is where we get a nice bone to lick!" And they fall on the traveler: How could he do a thing like that? He ought to be ashamed of himself! Thinking up an ugly plot like that against their rabbi!

When he saw what was happening, his arms and legs went limp; he just about fainted. But the rabbi got up, went to the chest, took out the kerchief, and handed it to him.

"What's the matter with you! Here! Here is your money! Take it and count it, see if it's right, here in front of your witnesses. The seal, as you see, is untouched. The wax is whole, just as it ought to be."

The traveler felt as if a new soul had been installed in his body. His hands trembled and tears stood in his eyes.

"Why did you have to do it, Rabbi? Why did you have to play this trick on me? A trick like this."

"I just wanted to show you—the kind—of—leading citizens—we have in our town."

O. HENRY

Jeff Peters as a Personal Magnet

Jeff Peters has been engaged in as many schemes for making money as there are recipes for cooking rice in Charleston, S.C.

Best of all I like to hear him tell of his earlier days when he sold liniments and cough cures on street corners, living hand to mouth, heart to heart with the people, throwing heads or tails with fortune for his last coin.

"I struck Fisher Hill, Arkansas," said he, "in buckskin suit, moccasins, long hair and a thirty-carat diamond ring that I got from an actor in Texarkana. I don't know what he ever did with the pocket knife I swapped him for it.

"I was Dr. Waugh-hoo, the celebrated Indian medicine man. I carried only one best bet just then, and that was Resurrection Bitters. It was made of life-giving plants and herbs accidentally discovered by Ta-qua-la, the beautiful wife of the chief of the Choctaw Nation, while gathering truck to garnish a platter of boiled dog for the annual corn dance.

"Business hadn't been good at the last town, so I only had five dollars. I went to the Fisher Hill druggist, and he credited me for a half gross of eight-ounce bottles and corks. I had the labels and ingredients in my valise, left over from the last town. Life began to look rosy again after I got in my hotel room with the water running from the tap, and the Resurrection Bitters lining up on the table by the dozen.

"Fake? No, sir. There was two dollars' worth of fluid extract of cinchona and a dime's worth of aniline in that half gross of bitters. I've gone through towns years afterward and had folks ask for 'em again.

"I hired a wagon that night and commenced selling the bitters on Main Street. Fisher Hill was a low, malarial town; and a compound hypothetical pneumocardiac antiscorbutic tonic was just what I diagnosed the crowd as needing. The bitters started off like sweetbreads-on-toast at a vegetarian dinner. I had sold two dozen at fifty cents apiece when I felt somebody pull my coattail. I knew what that meant; so I climbed down and sneaked a five-dollar bill into the hand of a man with a German silver star on his lapel.

" 'Constable,' says I, 'it's a fine night.'

" 'Have you got a city license,' he asks, 'to sell this illegitimate essence of spooju that you flatter by the name of medicine?'

" 'I have not,' says I. 'I didn't know you had a city. If I can find it tomorrow, I'll take one out if it's necessary.'

" 'I'll have to close you up till you do,' says the constable.

"I quit selling and went back to the hotel. I was talking to the landlord about it.

" 'Oh, you won't stand no show in Fisher Hill,' says he. 'Dr. Hoskins, the only doctor here, is a brother-in-law of the Mayor, and they won't allow no fake doctors to practice in town.'

" 'I don't practice medicine,' says I, 'I've got a state

peddler's license, and I take out a city one wherever they demand it.'

"I went to the Mayor's office the next morning and they told me he hadn't showed up yet. They didn't know when he'd be down. So Doc Waugh-hoo hunches down again in a hotel chair and lights a jimpsonweed regalia, and waits.

"By and by a young man in a blue necktie slips into the chair next to me and asks the time.

" 'Half past ten,' says I, 'and you are Andy Tucker. I've seen you work. Wasn't it you that put up the Great Cupid Combination package on the Southern States? Let's see, it was a Chilian diamond engagement ring, a wedding ring, a potato masher, a bottle of soothing syrup and Dorothy Vernon—all for fifty cents.'

"Andy was pleased to hear that I remembered him. He was a good street man; and he was more than that— he respected his profession, and he was satisfied with 300 per cent profit. He had plenty of offers to go into the illegitimate drug and garden-seed business; but he was never to be tempted off of the straight path.

"I wanted a partner, so Andy and me agreed to go out together. I told him about the situation on Fisher Hill and how finances was low on account of the local mixture of politics and jalap. Andy had just got in on the train that morning. He was pretty low himself, and was going to canvass the town for a few dollars to build a new battle-ship by popular subscription at Eureka Springs. So we went out and sat on the porch and talked it over.

"The next morning at eleven o'clock when I was sitting there alone, an Uncle Tom shuffles into the hotel and asked for the doctor to come and see Judge Banks, who, it seems, was the Mayor and a mighty sick man.

" 'I'm no doctor,' says I. 'Why don't you go and get the doctor?'

" 'Boss,' says he. 'Doc Hoskin am done gone twenty miles in the country to see some sick persons. He's de only doctor in de town, and Massa Banks am powerful bad off. He sent me to ax you to please, suh, come.'

" 'As man to man,' says I, 'I'll go and look him over.' So I put a bottle of Resurrection Bitters in my pocket and goes up on the hill to the Mayor's mansion, the finest house in town, with a mansard roof and two cast-iron dogs on the lawn.

"This Mayor Banks was in bed all but his whiskers and feet. He was making internal noises that would have had everybody in San Francisco hiking for the parks. A young man was standing by the bed, holding a cup of water.

" 'Doc,' says the Mayor, 'I'm awful sick. I'm about to die. Can't you do nothing for me?'

" 'Mr. Mayor,' says I, 'I'm not a regular preordained disciple of S. Q. Lapius. I never took a course in a medical college,' says I. 'I've just come as a fellow man to see if I could be of any assistance.'

" 'I'm deeply obliged,' says he. 'Doc Waugh-hoo, this is my nephew, Mr. Biddle. He has tried to alleviate my distress, but without success. Oh, Lordy! Oh-ow-ow!!' he sings out.

"I nods at Mr. Biddle and sets down by the bed and feels the Mayor's pulse. 'Let me see your liver—your tongue, I mean,' says I. Then I turns up the lids of his eyes and looks close at the pupils of 'em.

" 'How long have you been sick?' I asked.

" 'I was taken down—ow-ouch—last night,' says the Mayor. 'Gimme something for it, Doc, won't you?'

" 'Mr. Fiddle,' says I, 'raise the window shade a bit, will you?'

" 'Biddle,' says the young man. 'Do you feel like you could eat some ham and eggs, Uncle James?'

" 'Mr. Mayor,' says I, after laying my ear to his right shoulder blade and listening, 'you've got a bad attack of superinflammation of the right clavicle of the harpsichord!'

" 'Good Lord!' says he, with a groan. 'Can't you rub something on it, or set it or anything?'

"I picks up my hat and starts for the door.

" 'You ain't going, Doc?' says the Mayor with a howl. 'You ain't going away and leave me to die with this—superfluity of the clapboards, are you?'

" 'Common humanity, Dr. Whoa-ha,' says Mr. Biddle, 'ought to prevent your deserting a fellow human in distress.'

" 'Dr. Waugh-hoo, when you get through plowing,' says I. And then I walks back to the bed and throws back my long hair.

" 'Mr. Mayor,' says I, 'there is only one hope for you. Drugs will do you no good. But there is another power higher yet, although drugs are high enough,' says I.

" 'And what is that?' says he.

" 'Scientific demonstrations,' says I. 'The triumph of mind over sarsaparilla. The belief that there is no pain and sickness except what is produced when we ain't feeling well. Declare yourself in arrears. Demonstrate.'

" 'What is this paraphernalia you speak of, Doc?' says the Mayor. 'You ain't a Socialist, are you?'

" 'I am speaking,' says I, 'of the great doctrine of psychic financiering—of the enlightened school of long-distance, sub-conscientious treatment of fallacies and meningitis—of that wonderful indoor sport known as personal magnetism.'

" 'Can you work it, Doc?' asks the Mayor.

" 'I'm one of the Sole Sanhedrims and Ostensible Hooplas of the Inner Pulpit,' says I. 'The lame talk and the blind rubber whenever I make a pass at 'em. I am a medium, a coloratura hypnotist, and a spirituous control. It was only through me at the recent seances at Ann Arbor that the late president of the Vinegar Bitters Company could revisit the earth to communicate with his sister Jane. You see me peddling medicine on the streets,' says I, 'to the poor. I don't practice personal magnetism on them. I do not drag it in the dust,' says I, 'because they haven't got the dust.'

" 'Will you treat my case?' asks the Mayor.

" 'Listen,' says I. 'I've had a good deal of trouble with medical societies everywhere I've been. I don't practice medicine. But, to save your life, I'll give you the psychic treatment if you'll agree as Mayor not to push the license question.'

" 'Of course I will,' says he. 'And now get to work, Doc, for them pains are coming on again.'

" 'My fee will be $250.00, cure guaranteed in two treatments,' says I.

" 'All right,' says the Mayor. 'I'll pay it. I guess my life's worth that much.'

"I sat down by the bed and looked him straight in the eye.

" 'Now,' says I, 'get your mind off the disease. You

ain't sick. You haven't got a heart or a clavicle or a funny-bone or brains or anything. You haven't got any pain. Declare error. Now you feel the pain that you didn't have leaving, don't you?'

" 'I do feel some little better, Doc,' says the Mayor, 'darned if I don't. Now state a few lies about my not having this swelling in my left side, and I think I could be propped up and have some sausage and buckwheat cakes.'

"I made a few passes with my hands.

" 'Now,' says I, 'the inflammation's gone. The right lobe of the perihelion has subsided. You're getting sleepy. You can't hold your eyes open any longer. For the present the disease is checked. Now, you are asleep.'

"The Mayor shut his eyes slowly and began to snore.

" 'You observe, Mr. Tiddle,' says I, 'the wonders of modern science.'

" 'Biddle,' says he. 'When will you give Uncle the rest of the treatment, Dr. Pooh-pooh?'

" 'Waugh-hoo,' says I. 'I'll come back at eleven to-morrow. When he wakes up, give him eight drops of turpentine and three pounds of steak. Good morning.'

"The next morning I went back on time. 'Well, Mr. Riddle,' says I, when he opened the bedroom door, 'and how is Uncle this morning?'

" 'He seems much better,' says the young man.

"The Mayor's color and pulse was fine. I gave him another treatment, and he said the last of the pain left him.

" 'Now,' says I, 'you'd better stay in bed for a day or two, and you'll be all right. It's a good thing I happened to be in Fisher Hill, Mr. Mayor,' says I, 'for all the reme-

dies in the cornucopia that the regular schools of medicine use couldn't have saved you. And now that error has
flew and pain proved a perjurer, let's allude to a cheer-
fuler subject—say the fee of $250. No checks, please. I
hate to write my name on the back of a check almost as
bad as I do on the front.'

" 'I've got the cash here,' says the Mayor, pulling a
pocketbook from under his pillow.

"He counts out five fifty-dollar notes and holds 'em
in his hand.

" 'Bring the receipt,' he says to Biddle.

"I signed the receipt, and the Mayor handed me the
money. I put it in my inside pocket careful.

" 'Now do your duty, officer,' says the Mayor, grinning much unlike a sick man.

"Mr. Biddle lays his hand on my arm.

" 'You're under arrest, Dr. Waugh-hoo, alias Peters,'
says he, 'for practicing medicine without authority under
the state law.'

" 'Who are you?' I asks.

" 'I'll tell you who he is,' says the Mayor, sitting up
in bed. 'He's a detective employed by the State Medical
Society. He's been following you over five counties. He
came to me yesterday, and we fixed up this scheme to
catch you. I guess you won't do any more doctoring
around these parts, Mr. Fakir. What was it you said I had,
Doc?' The Mayor laughs. 'Compound—well it wasn't softening of the brain, I guess, anyway.'

" 'A detective,' says I.

" 'Correct,' says Biddle. 'I'll have to turn you over to
the sheriff.'

" 'Let's see you do it,' says I, and I grabs Biddle by

the throat and half throws him out the window, but he pulls a gun and sticks it under my chin, and I stand still. Then he puts handcuffs on me, and takes the money out of my pocket.

" 'I witness,' says he, 'that they're the same bills that you and I marked, Judge Banks. I'll turn them over to the sheriff when we get to his office, and he'll send you a receipt. They'll have to be used as evidence in the case.'

" 'All right, Mr. Biddle,' says the Mayor. 'And now, Doc Waugh-hoo,' he goes on, 'why don't you demonstrate? Can't you pull the cork out of your magnetism with your teeth and hocus-pocus them handcuffs off?'

" 'Come on, officer,' says I, dignified. 'I may as well make the best of it.' And then I turns to old Banks and rattles my chains.

" 'Mr. Mayor,' says I, 'the time will come soon when you'll believe that personal magnetism is a success. And you'll be sure that it succeeded in this case, too.'

"And I guess it did.

"When we got nearly to the gate, I says: 'We might meet somebody now, Andy. I reckon you better take 'em off, and—' Hey? Why, of course it was Andy Tucker. That was his scheme; and that's how we got the capital to go into business together."

DAVID FLETCHER

The Spoils of Sacrilege

Bunny was to be discovered one afternoon, prudently enveloped in a strong apron, oiling Raffle's bat. As he did so, he delivered himself of a monologue:

"I don't in the least mind oiling your bat for you! I don't mind whitening your boots for you, when you want to be a special swell at Lord's! I don't mind running errands for you as if I was your fag at Uppingham all over again! I said I don't mind! And I don't! Not in the least!" On the avowal Bunny paused. He had spoken the last claims in a loud voice, directed at Raffles's bedroom. Now he waited for some response. There was none. He continued. "But what I do mind is that you won't let me do anything more useful. When we go burgling, it's you who decides everything. And who does everything! I'm just the plumber's mate. I hand you your tools, and go back for anything you've forgotten—except you're so clever you never forget anything. I don't have to go back." Again the young man paused, glaring toward the bedroom.

Raffles, to his consternation, now entered the room from the hall and politely inquired as to where Bunny was going back.

"Didn't you hear what I was saying?" said Bunny, more surprised than angry.

"I thought you were talking to yourself," explained Raffles. "And I thought it wasn't polite to listen."

"I was talking to you," Bunny firmly informed him.

"Oh, I'm sorry. Was it interesting?"

"I was saying, you have no reason to split everything you make down the middle, and give me half!"

"It's so simple," Raffles said cheerfully. "I was never any good at arithmetic."

"Simply because it's simple . . . It's not a good enough reason in the first place . . . ," Bunny began to protest.

"Ah," Raffles interrupted, "In the first place it was to save you from dishonor, Bunny. I thought that seemed a good enough reason."

"Yes," agreed Bunny in a softened manner, touched as always to be reminded of that original act of kindness, kindness which he had never and could never forget. "And I'm eternally grateful to you."

"Then what are you moaning about?" asked Raffles, picking up and inspecting his bat.

"You've gone on doing it since!" Bunny cried.

"Friend and partner—what else could I do?"

"But half! The same as yourself!" To Bunny the injustice of this arrangement required no further elucidation.

Raffles set down the bat and said:

"You eat as much as I do. You drink as much as I do. You smoke as many Sullivans as I do. You . . ."

"But I don't do as much of the work as you do!"

Bunny interrupted with the air of one who is hitting the nail resoundingly on the head.

"Ah," said Raffles again, recognizing familiar conversational ground. "The work . . . Burgling?"

"Yes," confirmed Bunny.

"You want to do more of the burgling?"

"Yes," Bunny repeated, with undiminished firmness.

"It's a very skilled job cracking cribs," Raffles said modestly; "I happen to be good at it, from a kind of natural cunning—as I happen to be good at spinning a cricket ball."

"I don't insist on cracking cribs," said Bunny, "but if I'm to get half of the proceeds, I do insist on earning it, one way or another."

"By the exercise of your natural talents?"

"Yes, if I have any."

"You have at least one great talent, Bunny," Raffles assured him. "For looking innocent. The whole of Scotland Yard could stare at you closely and every man jack of them would be deeply ashamed of himself for having even suspected you. And because you are innocent, I, your friend, am innocent, too."

Bunny digested this familiar argument, but was in no mood to be persuaded by it.

"I'm sorry, but my innocent looks do not entitle me to half the proceeds," he insisted.

"Are you," inquired Raffles pessimistically, "going to make an argument of it?"

"Yes," vowed Bunny.

And so he did. Over sherry at the dear Old Bohemian where they had repaired for dinner, Bunny complained that Raffles never took his advice on the planning and execution of their adventures. During dinner itself, Raffles discovered that the disproportion between Bunny's efforts and his rewards was making him feel guilty. This, Raffles admitted, was not to be tolerated but how might the situation be remedied?

"I mean," he said, "if I think of enough places to burgle and things to steal, and I'm the expert at actually cracking the cribs in question, and I'm the one who knows the fences who'll give us money for whatever we steal. . . . Well, what's left for you to specialize in?"

It was a good question and a pertinent one. It occupied Bunny throughout the brandy and the pleasant stroll to the Turkish Baths in Northumberland Avenue afterward. It was not, in fact, until the two friends were rather hotly ensconced in the steam room of that estimable establishment, that he made an answer to the question.

"I could draw plans," he announced with confidence.

"What?" asked Raffles, whose mind had been elsewhere.

"I said I could draw plans. I used to be good at drawing."

"I'm sure you were," agreed Raffles. "Plans of what?"

"Plans of houses you were going to burgle."

At this Raffles looked alarmed. It was not the matter of plans that caused him disquiet, but their public situation.

"It's all right," Bunny assured him casually. "There's nobody else here. I looked."

"In this steam . . . ," said Raffles dubiously, peering at an impenetrable fog.

"You like working things out on plans," Bunny reminded him.

"Which houses do you know well enough to draw plans of?" asked Raffles, sensing that nothing else would deter his friend. "I mean plans showing details like the window fastenings? And the bolts on the doors?" he added.

"I . . . er . . . well . . . er. . . ." None sprang to mind. Bunny heaved a sigh. "None, I suppose. Except my own flat," he conceded unhappily.

"When you want me to burgle your place, Bunny, just say the word," Raffles said, giving himself up to the relaxing and beneficial effects of the steam, and thinking that he had now successfully put an end to Bunny's ambitions as a draftsman.

This, however, was not the case. Bunny did think of a house, and a very suitable one at that. Pinfield Park some forty miles from the metropolis, and conveniently close to the Brighton line, had been Bunny's boyhood home. There, indulgent parents had allowed their boy the run of the mansion. Every nook and cranny was engraved upon his mind, and for the next few days Bunny, although keeping to his Mount Street flat, constantly revisited that house in memory, translating his tender childhood recollections onto paper. The result was as fine a set of detailed plans as any architect or cracksman could require, and surveying his handiwork, Bunny felt truly useful at last. He could scarcely wait to show them to Raffles. His walk became a skip, his run a dance that would have delighted Terpsichore herself as he hurried to the Albany and Raffles. With a flourish he unrolled the plans and proudly explained them. Raffles gave them a glance, no more, and mildly inquired why he should be interested in these admirable details of Pinfield Park.

"To burgle it, of course!" cried Bunny, frustrated and disappointed by this cool response.

"And why should I do that?" asked Raffles in the same tone.

"Because you're a burglar!" Bunny shouted.

"A burglar but not a thief, Bunny," Raffles spoke quietly, with a dignified hint of reproof in his voice. "At least not a thief who steals anything and everything, out of habit, whenever the opportunity presents itself. That is a vice and a crime and deserves to be punished. I, on the other hand, steal only to remain virtuous, to pay my bills like a respectable member of society. I admit, there are times when I am tempted by a particular object, a necklace, a tiara, or by the difficulty of a particular task; the risk; the challenge. Then perhaps I go a-burgling; but I don't really think that entitles you to call me a burglar, as if I were Bill Sykes and wore a striped jersey and carried a bag over my shoulder marked 'Swag.' "

Bunny hung his head, partly in shame but, it must be admitted, mostly out of disappointment. At Raffles's command, he rolled up the plans.

"It's the most marvelous opportunity," he grumbled sadly.

"But not a challenge," Raffles insisted.

"And we're not hard up?" asked Bunny, clutching at straws.

"Not at the moment."

"And there's no particular object to tempt you?"

"None that I know of. Might there be one?" Raffles's eyes contained, as he asked this question, a glimmer of that gleam which always lit his countenance when a challenge or temptation presented itself.

"They're stinking rich," said Bunny. "The Osbornes. The people who bought the house."

"What kind of rich?" asked Raffles, still interested.

"Made their money in South American railways. Run hundreds of horses. Hunt all winter, then the point-to-point at the end of the season, then polo all summer long. Never off the back of one horse or another. And I think they wear pink for dinner every blessed night of their lives."

"Not your style," agreed Raffles.

"Nor yours," agreed Bunny. "You don't know one end of a horse from another."

"And even if I did, I wouldn't know which end to aim at."

"If the Osbornes heard you say that, they'd have you hanged for treason," Bunny laughed.

"I know the kind. What are they like apart from that?"

"He's a huge, beefy, red-faced fellow. Eats like a horse and drinks like one, too. His wife doesn't eat like a horse, but she looks like one."

"You miss the point," Raffles said impatiently. "What does the wife wear?"

"Oh, clothes. Like a normal person," said Bunny obtusely.

"No, you ninny. What does she wear round her neck?"

"Oh, necklaces and so on."

Bunny was being deliberately evasive, having glimpsed a way to rouse Raffles's enthusiasm for the task he held so dear. He turned to the mantelpiece and idly inspected the impressive row of invitation cards. He picked up one, a duplicate of which rested on his own mantelpiece, and inquired if Raffles were planning to accept. His friend confirmed that he was, adding:

"Don't evade the question, Bunny. What sort of necklaces?"

"Oh, diamonds and that sort of thing," Bunny replied, as though such stones were of no particular interest.

"And that sort of thing!" echoed Raffles, shocked at this entirely unprofessional interest in their staple means of making a living.

"Yes, *you* know," continued Bunny in the same careless fashion. "Big as pigeons' eggs. I mean, with her husband so rich, she can afford it."

In fact, Bunny had lost none of his regard for diamonds. On the contrary, he saw in them the means to persuade Raffles to put his plans to good use. Accordingly, Bunny employed all his innocent charm to cajole their mutual hostess into inviting Mrs. Osborne to the dinner to which Raffles had said he meant to go. This accomplished, he crossed his fingers—which was all he could do to encourage Mrs. Osborne to wear her fabled diamonds on that occasion. She did so, and though perhaps not quite so large as pigeons' eggs, the stones were of sufficient weight and circumference to put that steely gleam in Raffles's eyes. So much Bunny was able to observe from the opposite end of the table. Time and again Raffles's gaze strayed from the face of the charming lady on his right to the dazzling array of jewels that adorned Mrs. Osborne. Bunny, highly pleased with himself, awaited the psychological moment before offhandedly remarking to Raffles that the lady was in fact the mistress of Pinfield Park.

"You deliberately got her invited, so that I could see that necklace and be tempted by it," Raffles accused him as soon as they had reached the Albany.

"I thought it was rather a good idea," smiled Bunny.

"Did you?"

"Well, I mean, it does get rather monotonous, you being the clever one," he said.

"So you thought you'd try it?"

"Yes."

"And you are very pleased with the result?"

"Well," admitted Bunny, "it did what I wanted."

"Tempted me."

"Yes."

"Satan!" cried Raffles, who was secretly rather pleased with Bunny's display of initiative.

"It's not that I *want* you to be a burglar, Raffles," Bunny hastened to explain. "It's just that if you *are* a burglar, then I want to help you. Really help you. I want to do my share."

"And so you shall," promised Raffles.

"You mean that?" Bunny's face was the very portrait of joy.

"I'll take charge of getting down to the place, but when we're in sight of the house, you take command."

Bunny could scarcely believe his ears.

"You'll bring your tools, of course?" he asked.

"But I shall use them only under your control and direction," Raffles asserted.

"By Jove!" cried Bunny, who was as thrilled as it was possible for him to be.

"A big responsibility, Bunny," Raffles warned.

"Yes, my word!"

"We have to decide what night it's going to be. We don't want to go on a night when Mrs. Osborne is wearing the necklace in London."

But Bunny had already made inquiries, and now with jubilant pride he set about informing Raffles of his discoveries. On the following Friday week the Osbornes were giving their annual dinner to the hunt. It was certain to be, according to Bunny's information, a lively night and therefore a good one for burglars.

"Still," mused Raffles, "if it's a dinner party, the hostess won't leave her jewels upstairs. She'll wear them, my boy."

"Not all of them, Raffles. She might wear her rope of pearls and, of course, a ring or two, or three. I gather Mrs. Osborne is generally the only woman there. Now no woman is going to clap on all sail in jewels for a roomful of drunken fox hunters."

"True enough, Bunny." Raffles agreed, making a mental note of Bunny's rapidly developing powers of observation and deduction.

He proposed a toast to the venture, and the pair settled down to finalize the details. Since Bunny was no stranger to the area, Raffles, who occupied his usual position as commander until the house was reached, insisted that he travel to a railway station some distance beyond Pinfield and rendezvous with Raffles at a suitably late hour. Reluctantly, Bunny agreed to this proposal and resigned himself to a two-mile trudge through the byways of Sussex before his moment of glory began.

And so it was. The rendezvous accomplished on a fine, moonlit night, the pair walked together to a point at the edge of Pinfield Park which gave them a fine view of the house. It stood imposingly amid the parkland, four anachronistic towers rising from its corners, and shining with celebratory lights. The two friends gazed at their target for some minutes.

"Well, Bunny," Raffles said at last. "From this moment on. . . ."

"Raffles," began Bunny, his tone positively thick with second thoughts, "do you think . . . ?"

"It is not my business to think, Bunny. You are in charge, and I am in your hands," Raffles said firmly.

For a moment Bunny wished, quite devoutly, that it were not so, but he put a brave face on it.

"They're having dinner," he said, pointing out the blazing dining room.

"Let's have a look at them," said Raffles, taking a step forward. Instantly he stopped, and turned apologetically to Bunny. "I beg your pardon. *You* must say what we shall do."

"Well . . . let's have a look at them, shall we?" suggested Bunny.

"Good. I hoped you'd say that," smiled Raffles. "Lead on."

Moments later, the young commander and his willing accomplice were surveying the company at dinner through the convenient slats of a venetian blind. It was indeed a riotous gathering of pink-coated men in the midst of which sat Mrs. Osborne, resplendent, as Bunny had predicted, in her rope of pearls and a quantity of rings. Swiftly and quietly, Bunny pointed out the florid-faced bulk of Mr. Osborne, the son of the house, and other members of the party. Raffles was quick to congratulate his friend on the prediction concerning Mrs. Osborne's ornaments, and drew the inevitable conclusion that her diamonds must be upstairs.

"Shall we go and see?" he added.

"If you like," said Bunny.

"I beg your pardon. I meant, do you command that we shall go and see?"

"Yes."

"I obey, O master!" Raffles grinned impishly.

Bunny led the way to the back of the house and quietly indicated the door he had already marked on his plan as being the best means of access for burglars. It led, as he reminded Raffles, to the back stairs from whence it would take but a moment to reach the bedrooms.

"Am I to use my tools?" inquired Raffles, approaching the door.

"Yes," said Bunny resolutely.

Raffles reached out and turned the handle of the door. It opened noiselessly.

"First rule of burgling," he whispered. "Don't break in unless you have to."

Bunny was eager to proceed. He pressed close behind Raffles, who paused, however.

"May I not command but suggest," he suggested, "that we put our masks on at this point?"

"Yes, right," agreed Bunny impatiently.

"Since your face is known in the neighborhood, and mine is not entirely unknown to readers of the newspapers. . . ."

"Yes. All right. I'm putting it on," said Bunny sharply.

Suitably masked, Bunny led the way into the house and up the back stairs. These divided at a landing. A second flight went up into one of the four towers. The landing itself gave access to a long corridor which led to the main bedrooms. Bunny hurried down this corridor which was divided into two by a baize door. This he shouldered with familiarity, knowing it to be of the swing-hinged variety. He recoiled in surprise, clutching his shoulder. He gave the door a sharp push. It did not swing.

"Damn the thing!" Bunny exclaimed.

"May I look?" asked Raffles politely.

"Do." Bunny stepped back haughtily.

Raffles applied his eye to a crack between the stubborn door and its solid jamb.

"Locked on the other side," he announced.

"Blast!"

"Any way round it?"

"No."

"What do we do?"

"Er . . ."

"Shall I have a go with my tools?"

"Yes, would you?" said Bunny with relief.

Raffles produced his slim, compact box of tools and selected therefrom a long daggerlike instrument with a serrated edge. Tearing a portion of baize from the paneling, he swiftly began to saw a hole in the wood, close to the lock, explaining as he did so that though slower than a jimmy this method had the advantage of being considerably less noisy.

"Sorry about this, Raffles," said Bunny stiffly.

"The great thing about the burglar's life is, you keep

coming up against the unexpected," commented Raffles, busily cutting away.

At that moment, on the other side of the door, Mrs. Osborne's personal maid emerged from her employer's bedroom and saw the protruding point of a cutting tool appearing through the baize door. At once she realized the import of what she saw and, on tiptoe, hurried to the main staircase.

No sooner had she disappeared than Raffles was able to knock free the rough circle of wood he had cut from the door. He slipped his hand through the hole and turned the key. Once again Bunny took command, conducting Raffles to the master bedroom. Once there, he turned up the gas and announced that he left it to Raffles to unearth the jewels. The latter immediately approached another door which led into a small dressing room. This contained yet a third door, giving access to the corridor, which was securely bolted. Experience told Raffles that this was the repository of the jewels, and his keen, professional eyes quickly spied a handsome antique chest, which bore a stout modern lock. To this he applied his jimmy. The lock yielded with a sharp crack.

"Eureka!" he whispered. "Go and see if I've roused anybody, Bunny," he said as he lifted the lid.

Bunny did as he was bid. All seemed well, but he took the precaution of stepping out into the corridor to make absolutely sure. At the head of the main staircase a large, ornate mirror was fixed to the wall, and what Bunny saw therein caused his heart to stand still. The male members of the hunt, resplendent in their pink coats and grasping riding crops with unmistakable determination, were creeping in stockinged feet up the stairs. Bunny turned on his heel and fled back to Raffles. The latter immediately handed Bunny two jewel cases which, out of long habit, he obediently pocketed while blurting out his terrible news.

"Did they see you?" hissed Raffles, rising at once and concealing two more cases in his pockets.

"No."

"Come on then."

He was already running, and Bunny hastened to follow him. In the corridor they dashed for the baize door just as the hunt appeared at the top of the stairs. At once this formidable pack of gentlemen gave cry.

"Gone away! Gone away!"

"Yoick, yoick!"

"Yonder they go!"

Raffles and Bunny hurtled through the baize door which swung to behind them.

"Hold on," called Raffles, "I'll lock it."

The delay, though destined to be brief, might prove to their advantage. He pushed his hand through the hole he had cut and turned the key, but before he could withdraw, his hand was seized by Mr. Osborne himself with a yell of bloodcurdling triumph.

"What's up?" said Bunny, hopping from one foot to the other.

"My hand's held. They've got me tight. It's no good. I'm done," Raffles whispered.

"Got your revolver?" asked Bunny.

"In my pocket."

"Blaze away through the door."

"No."

"Or let me."

"No. You might hit someone."

"What you going to do?"

"I'm done," Raffles repeated. "You get out while you can. Never mind me."

"I'm not going without you," said Bunny with resolution.

At this, despite the pain in his hand which was being cruelly twisted by the baying huntsmen, Raffles managed a ghost of a smile.

"Good pal," he said. "Feel in my pocket."

"Revolver?" said Bunny, his hopes reviving.

"No. Oil bottle. With my tools. Just a chance. Run the oil down my arm, to the wrist."

Bunny located the bottle and, forcing himself to be calm, began to trickle the oil as Raffles had instructed. Raffles began to twist and wriggle. The commotion beyond the door increased, indicating that the oil was having the desired effect. At last, with a grimace of pain, Raffles twisted his hand free and pulled it through the hole. Immediately the clamor on the other side of the door became more ferocious. A hunting horn added its raucous brays to the din. Bunny and Raffles ran as fast as they could along the corridor but, on reaching the landing, found their route blocked. Some members of the hunt, anticipating Raffles's escape, had made a detour and were already climbing up the back stairs. At the same time, the remainder of the pack, led by the formidable figure of Mr. Osborne, burst through the baize door.

"Up here," shouted Bunny, making a dash for the second flight of stairs.

Raffles panted at his heels, and the two friends emerged breathless in an attic room. Bunny did not pause but made straight for an ancient wooden ladder which led to a trapdoor. Up he went, as agile as a monkey, forcing the trapdoor open. He threw himself into the room above, swiftly followed by Raffles. With great presence of mind, Bunny recovered himself and slammed the trapdoor shut, just as the bald pate of Mr. Osborne appeared. With a cry, the stout gentleman fell back onto his followers. Bunny planted his feet firmly on the trapdoor. From below came the cries:

"Gone to earth! Gone to earth!"

"Where's the terrier?"

"Dig 'em out!"

Raffles struggled to his feet and, seeing a chair, pulled it forward onto the trapdoor. He sat down at once and, with a rueful expression, looked at his painful and damaged hand.

"Near thing," said Bunny quietly.

"Too close for comfort," agreed Raffles. He pulled off his mask and returned again to the contemplation of his hand. "Don't think I'll be doing any slow bowling for a week or two," he said.

"Don't say they've damaged your spinning finger?" cried Bunny in alarm, stripping off his own mask and bending in the gloom for a sight of the injury.

"Not permanently. But, yes, they have."

"The brutes!"

"It was when I wrenched my hand away," Raffles explained. "Lucky I did, though. There's no cricket team in Wormwood Scrubs."

Bunny shuddered at the mention of that penal institution.

"Strike a light, Bunny, will you?" asked Raffles.

Bunny did so and held the match aloft. By its flickering imperfect light he espied the stubs of two candles in dusty holders on a table a few feet away. He groped his way toward the table and soon had both candles burning. By their light Raffles saw that they were in an oddly shaped, neglected room at the very top of one of the four towers which adorned Pinfield Park. Three of the windows looked on to the empty sky. The fourth gave a view of the tiled roof of the building.

"I must have left those candles here a dozen years ago," said Bunny in an odd voice. "Osborne never comes up here, I suppose. And his son's too old. But this was my sanctum sanctorum when I was a boy."

"Was it?" said Raffles gently.

"I smoked my first pipe here. I wrote my first verses here."

"Who to?" asked Raffles with an indulgent smile.

"The Rector's daughter. She was called Phillida."

"Did she flout you?"

"Yes," Bunny said sadly.

From below, Raffles's sharp ears heard the withdrawal of the hunt.

"They've given up hope of getting in from underneath," he said, interrupting Bunny's reverie. "So they're going to try some other way. What other ways are there?"

"Er . . ."

Bunny gazed about him blankly, his mind still clouded by memories of his vanished childhood.

"Come on, Bunny," said Raffles testily. "The whole reason for our coming here was you know the place backward."

"Yes, I do. I was just working it out."

"Sorry, Bunny," said Raffles. "I don't mean to be sharp with you, but I'm blessed if I can see how we can get out of here."

"The roof," said Bunny quietly.

"What good is the roof to me?" snapped Raffles.

"No, I mean, the only other way they can get at you. Up through one of the skylights and across the roof."

"Ah," said Raffles, getting up and walking to the window from which could be seen the moonlit roof of Pinefield Park. The grey slates gleamed eerily in the cold light. The stone chimneys rose into the sky, offering no help.

"Bunny," said Raffles quietly.

"Yes?"

"What are we going to do?"

Bunny said nothing. Raffles watched his face on which were etched lines of sadness and defeat.

"I ask," said Raffles after a long silence, "because you're in charge. We agreed. I simply do what you tell me to. So I'm waiting to be told."

Bunny looked at his feet. He rocked on his heels. He said nothing.

"Frankly," said Raffles, his voice betraying a slight edge, "I'm getting tired of waiting."

"Yes," said Bunny.

"What are we going to do? You must decide."

"Would you mind taking command, Raffles?" said Bunny in a low emotional voice.

"Now?"

"Now and always."

"Do you mean that?" asked Raffles.

"I was a fool ever to think I could do it," confessed Bunny miserably. "The whole thing's my fault. I was a blithering idiot to lead you up here."

"Nonsense, Bunny," Raffles said. "There was no other way to run."

"But that damned door in the corridor. I didn't know about that."

"Of course you didn't. How could you have known?"

"Getting your hand caught in that hole. . . ."

"That was my fault, not yours."

"I'll never forgive myself if you've damaged your spinning finger."

"I'll bowl left-handed. And I've done that before now."

"It's no good, Raffles. You can try and make me feel all right, but whatever you say, I know very well I'm simply not cut out to be in charge of things. I'm cut out to be a helper, that's all."

"A most loyal helper," Raffles smiled at him. "Who else would have stayed with me when I was trapped?"

"I couldn't have run. It wasn't possible," Bunny said with a firm shake of his head.

"That's what I mean. It wasn't possible—for you. It would have been possible for lots of other people."

"Oh . . ." said Bunny, understanding but not feeling any better.

"So I take command again?" asked Raffles.

"Please."

"And our motto is, Victory or Wormwood Scrubs?"

"Hear, hear," said Bunny unhappily.

Just then he spotted a dim figure climbing through one of the skylights. It stood for a moment, a shadow silhouetted against the night sky. Bunny drew Raffles's attention to it. Instantly Raffles drew his revolver from his pocket, smashed the window, and fired a shot toward the figure.

"You didn't hit him?" cried Bunny, craning over Raffles's shoulder.

"Of course I didn't. I damaged the slates a yard to the right of him. Near enough to give him a bit of a fright, that's all."

"Good man," said Bunny with relief.

But Raffles knew that no one but Bunny would believe that he had not fired to kill. Should they be apprehended, and just at that moment this seemed to be extremely likely, the shot would add ten years to the sentence he would receive. All this passed through his mind as he scanned the roof for some possible means of escape.

"Is that a working flagstaff out there?" he asked, pointing to the distant pole.

"It always used to be."

"Then there'll be halyards," said Raffles, hope stirring in him.

"They were as thin as clothes lines," said Bunny.

"And they're sure to be rotten. And we should be seen cutting them down." Raffles thus dismissed his hope. "No, Bunny, that won't do." He stared again at the grey and dismal roof. "Wait a minute," he said. "Is there a lightning conductor?"

"There was," said Bunny, leaning out of the broken window toward the nearest chimney. "Yes. There still is. On that chimney stack."

"How thick?" asked Raffles.

"As I remember it, it was rather thicker than a lead pencil. Why?"

"Lightning conductors have wires that run to earth," said Raffles sagely. "Which is where we want to be."

"What?" said Bunny, his mouth becoming dry with alarm.

"They sometimes bear you," Raffles informed him. "The difficulty is to keep a grip. But I've been up and down them before tonight. And anyway it's our only chance."

With grim determination, Raffles took from his pocket a pair of white kid gloves. He pulled them on and stuffed his handkerchief into the palm of the right.

"You're going to go down the wire?" asked Bunny, his voice trembling.

"And you're going to come after me," Raffles said. "If I get down all right."

"But if you don't?" cried Bunny in a panic. "Supposing it comes away from the chimney?"

"Then I shall get to earth even faster. And you'll have to stay here and face the music without me."

"Suppose it breaks . . . ," persisted Bunny.

"Suppose it doesn't," replied Raffles. "Don't say, 'Be careful'; say 'Good luck.' "

With all his heart Bunny said:

"Good luck."

"Give me a couple of minutes, then you come."

So saying, Raffles opened the window and climbed out onto the roof. For a moment he paused, a wide grin on his face.

"Victory or Wormwood Scrubs!" he whispered to

Bunny, adding to himself as he climbed across the slippery tiles toward the chimney, "Or, of course, heaven or hell."

Bunny stood at the window holding his breath. He saw Raffles reach the chimney stack and locate the wire. He seized it purposefully, adjusted his grip and, letting the wire take most of his weight, began to walk slowly backward toward the edge of the roof. Before he reached that perilous point, however, Bunny had hidden his face in his hands. It seemed an age that he stood there, his ears straining for the scream, the sickening thud that would announce the end of his dearest, his most valued friend. No sound came. At last he lowered his hands and stared out of the window. The wire lay limp and intact on the roof. Raffles had made it! The joy this certainty brought him was almost immediately dampened by the realization that now it was his turn. Bunny looked around him. He did not want to risk the wire. He had such fond memories of this room. In the flickering candlelight he could almost see himself as he had been—a young, untainted, innocent boy. What a long and tortuous way he had traveled since then! What dishonor had been his lot! What a burden of guilt he bore! Bunny moved to the window, and there, contemplating the journey he was about to make, he had another, a much clearer vision. He was lying at the foot of the walls of Pinfield Park. He was most surely dead, and spilling from his pockets was the incriminating evidence of his shame. No, he would not do it. He turned back into the room and took from his pockets the two jewel cases Raffles had thrust into his hands. He opened them sadly. The candlelight struck pure, innocent fire from the gems of Mrs. Osborne's necklace and her matching tiara. A cleansing, purifying fire, Bunny thought, placing these objects on the table. He would go to his death; he would be identified as Mr. Manders who had once been young and happy in this very house, but he would not be branded, even in death, a thief. To take these ornaments, he thought, fumbling the empty boxes back into his pockets, would be tantamount to an act of sacrilege, and that, at least, was not in Bunny's style.

With a strange calmness now, Bunny pulled on his gloves and padded the palm of his right hand with his handkerchief. Briefly, he said farewell to the room, to his youth, and climbed out onto the tiles. He reached the chimney stack, took up the wire, and tugged it experimentally. It held. He positioned his hands carefully and, closing his eyes, began to walk backward to his fate.

Below, in one of the well-tended flower beds, Raffles stared anxiously upward. He had traveled a very long and dangerous way. Now where was Bunny? He did not care to think of the drop had the wire not held. He only hoped it would hold as fast for Bunny. A slight sound caught his attention. Bunny, reduced to an indistinct black shape appeared at the edge of the roof, came over and began the last part of the descent, his feet braced against the sheer wall of Pinfield Park. He continued steadily downward until he reached a spot some twenty feet above the ground. From above him there was a rending sound, the clatter of mortar on the tiles. With a thundering heart, Raffles just had time to flatten himself against the wall as the lightning conductor flew past him, followed seconds later by Bunny. The latter landed with a dull sound in the soft part of the flower bed. Masonry and mortar showered around him.

"You all right?" asked Raffles.

"Knocked all the wind out of me," panted Bunny, sitting up and not quite believing that he had survived.

"Legs all right?"

Bunny felt them tentatively. They seemed all right. He stood up. He was a bit wobbly, but upright.

"All right to run?" whispered Raffles.

"Yes."

"Come on. On the grass."

Raffles set off at a brisk trot, round behind the house and away over the parkland. Bunny did his best to keep up and to keep low. Suddenly he collided with Raffles who had come to a sudden stop on the bank of a small boating lake.

"Where are we now?" asked Raffles.

"The lake," panted Bunny.

"Obviously."

"My father had it dug when we first came here," supplied Bunny. "I learned to row on it. Wonder if they still have . . . No. Mr. Osborne may be a sporty man, but I doubt if he's a boaty man."

Raffles looked around him in the gloom.

"There's a punt," he said, making toward the partially concealed boat which was drawn up close under some reeds.

"For the ladies, perhaps," said Bunny irrelevantly.

"For us," Raffles corrected him, stepping into the frail and swaying craft and picking up the pole from the bottom. "Come on. I'll try to remember how we used to do it on the Backs," he said.

Bunny clambered in, noting as he did so that Raffles was intending to punt from the front of the boat. He

pointed this out as Raffles plunged the pole deep into the
dark water.

"Good heavens, Bunny," he said with an offended air,
"you don't suppose I was at Oxford? Where they do everything from the wrong end!"

Bunny could think of no answer to this. The punt slid
smoothly out toward the center of the lake, Bunny peering into the dark to locate the boathouse he remembered
so clearly on the opposite bank.

Meanwhile, the Osborne hunt, not a whit deterred by
Raffles's warning shot, had retreated, regrouped, and
now prepared themselves for a final offensive on the
tower room. Armed with unsportsmanlike shotguns, Mr.
Osborne led his baying pack up the ladder, threatening to
blast the burglars to pieces at the least show of opposi-
tion. The trapdoor yielded, the huntsman and his followers climbed into the room. The candles guttered in the
breeze from the smashed and open window, striking fire
from Mrs. Osborne's most prized jewels which made a
sort of still life on the table.

Now, for all it may seem otherwise, Mr. Osborne was
a genuine sportsman. The recovery of the diamonds satisfied him, and his friends and family agreed with him
that the "foxes" had given them a jolly good run for their
money. It was decided, therefore, to dispatch but one man
to inform the police of the incident—this being their duty
as good country gentlemen—but to call off any further
pursuit. A toast was proposed to the wily foxes, and Mrs.
Osborne was persuaded to don her treasures that all
might see the spoils.

It was the sound of that lone horse galloping away
from the house that reached Raffles's ears as he and

Bunny arrived at the comparative safety of the neglected boathouse. Raffles surmised that what they had heard was only the front-runner of the pack, sent to summon the police. He confidently predicted a full hue and cry at any moment. Bunny insisted that he did not wish to be hunted anymore, and Raffles assured him that he should not be. The pack would be off across country, scouring all roads that led to railway stations. It would not occur to them to seek their quarry in their very own park. But Bunny wanted to be off anyway.

"The very closeness is our safety," Raffles argued.

"I wish I thought so," said Bunny morosely.

"Even if you don't," Raffles ticked him off, "remember that I am in command, and you do what I tell you."

"Yes, all right, Raffles. I remember," Bunny said. "But how long are we going to stay here?"

"Until the uproar dies down," replied Raffles.

Bunny kept silence. Tiny wavelets lapped from the lake against the sides of the punt. Apart from that and the quiet sounds of their own breathing, the silence was complete.

"Raffles?" said Bunny.

"Yes?"

"There isn't any uproar."

"No," agreed Raffles. "Strange."

"Very," Bunny assented.

"Just one man gone for the police and the hunt aren't turning out at all," Raffles mused. "I'm going to see what's happening," he said with determination.

With warnings to be careful, not to be seen, Bunny watched Raffles glide once more across the stygian lake. He felt useless and he felt depressed. He also felt very tired. He sat down, leaning his back against the wooden wall of the boathouse and prepared himself for a long wait.

In no time at all Raffles reached the bank and sped softly across the park to the still gaily illumined house. He drew close to the dining-room window and peeked again through the venetian blind. All was jollity and carousing within. The flushed, pink-coated men drank toast after toast, with loud bays of laughter and impromptu calls on the hunting horn. Raffles simply could not understand it. He frowned and shifted his point of vantage. Then he understood. Peering now between Mr. Osborne and a similarly well-fleshed comrade, he saw the unmistakable flash and gleam of diamonds. The two men obligingly drew apart. Mrs. Osborne beamed almost as brightly as her tiara and her necklace.

Raffles did not need to observe any longer. He retraced his steps, deep in thought, and, for the third time, made the crossing of the lake. Bunny heard his approach and leapt forward eagerly to steady the incoming vessel and to make her fast.

"I simply don't understand," said Raffles, stepping out of the punt. "They're as jolly as ever. They don't seem to be doing anything about us. Can you think of an explanation, Bunny?"

"No," said Bunny, his face wearing a less than usually innocent expression.

Raffles pondered in silence. The sound of carriage wheels on gravel carried to them across the still lake.

"Well," said Raffles, "there go their wheels on the drive, bearing the departing guests. There must be some explanation of why they gave up." He continued to wrack his brains.

"The influence of liquor, I should think," said Bunny.

"You think it made them kindly disposed toward us?" wondered Raffles.

"I think it made them do nothing more than want to go to bed."

"I suppose you're right," Raffles conceded after a moment. "Well, I'm going back."

"What for?" demanded Bunny with a start.

Raffles heaved a sigh.

"To get back to London we have to go to the railway station. We must suppose that there will be a policeman at the railway station, looking for two gentlemen in evening dress and toppers, with or without black masks. If he sees two such gentlemen, he will undoubtedly arrest them—and they'll deserve it for being so stupid!"

Bunny avoided his friend's eyes. Once again Raffles stepped into the punt and signaled to Bunny to shove off. This he did, watching Raffles silhouetted against the lightening sky. The water looked grey now, and wisps of mist, like tatters of chiffon, swirled around his friend and leader, his mentor in all things, and soon swallowed him up. Miserably Bunny made himself as comfortable as possible on an old bench, and, in a short space of time, was sound asleep. But it was a sleep without rest, a sleep haunted by images. Himself as a boy falling from the high, high roof of Pinfield Park, jewels scattering from his pockets. The inescapable figure of a dark and angry man drifting out of the mists of a black and bubbling lake. The man reached toward him. He sought, Bunny knew, explanations which he trembled to give.

Bunny woke with a start to find Raffles standing over him, his arms filled with clothing. These he dropped onto the floor and straightened up. He was transformed by breeches and a black hacking jacket, both several sizes too large for him. On his head a smart bowler and the whole bizarre rig covered by a gargantuan riding mackintosh.

"Steady on, Bunny," Raffles laughed as Bunny started up. "Don't you recognize me now I've gone all horsey? Here, I've got some things for you."

"You've been in the house again," cried Bunny.

"I had to. We'd never have got away as we were."

While Bunny struggled into a similar outfit, also too large but somewhat padded out by his own clothes underneath, Raffles outlined his latest exploit, concluding with a graphic imitation of Mr. Osborne's stentorian snoring.

"Ouch!" said Bunny as he pulled off his evening shoe.

"What's the matter?"

"I did something to my ankle when I fell, and it's gone a bit swollen," he explained, gently probing the injured limb.

"We'll make a virtue of your unsteady gait," Raffles said, putting stones into Bunny's patent-leather shoes. "Write it into your character," He dropped the weighted shoes into the lake and watched them sink happily.

Careful of his ankle, Bunny put on a pair of stout brown brogues and stood up, leaning heavily upon his friend. Thus it was that two decidedly unsteady gentlemen of an equally decidedly horsey character reached Pinfield Halt in time for the milk train to London. Their lively speech and uncertain gait attracted the amused attention of a constable who was patrolling there. He was, however, used to such sights in the environs of the Osborne residence and did no more than to advise the gentlemen to go steady. He even helped them into the

London train where, with relief, they exchanged tired smiles.

"Now," said Raffles, "as soon as we get off this train . . ."

"At Victoria," Bunny interrupted happily.

"No." Raffles shook his head solemnly. "We get off this train at Clapham Junction. And then we take a cab . . ."

"To the Albany, I hope," said Bunny. "I'm longing for a glass of your Scotch whisky."

"We shall take a cab to Chelsea," Raffles informed him. "A second to Whitehall, and a third to the Albany. I'm like you. Bunny. I never feel safe until I'm home again, but I like to confuse my trail in getting there."

Bunny's face fell, but Raffles promised him a generous Scotch whisky as soon as they arrived. And that they did before nine o'clock. Having furnished Bunny with the promised beverage, Raffles withdrew to his bedroom and removed his riding clothes. He returned to the sitting room, fastening the belt of an elegant silk dressing gown, and helped himself to stimulating refreshment.

"I'll drink a toast to the expedition," he cried, raising his glass. "I've never been on one that ran so close to the edge of disaster, or that ended in such a glorious triumph."

"I hope you're right about the triumph," Bunny said levelly. "It's enough for me that we're safe."

"Well, let's see. I've got two jewel cases," Raffles remarked, taking them from the pockets of the discarded mackintosh. "I gave you two, didn't I?"

"Yes," said Bunny, squirming slightly in his chair.

"Unfortunately, there's nothing in mine. I looked while I was waiting for the Osbornes to go to sleep." He tossed the empty cases onto a settee. "But you must have something in yours." He rubbed his hands together in eager anticipation.

"I'm very much afraid," said Bunny, who was, "that I'm in the same unlucky state as you." He produced the two jewel cases from his pockets. "These are empty, too."

"What?" cried Raffles, snatching one. "But they can't be!"

"I'm afraid they are."

Raffles opened the case he held and tossed it aside.

"By Jove! What a sell," he said. "Absolute swizz."

"Yes," agreed Bunny.

"Not a triumph at all, but a frost," complained Raffles.

"That's right," sighed Bunny.

"We put in all that effort for exactly nothing. Or more precisely," he bitterly corrected himself, "for four empty jewel cases."

"That's so," sighed Bunny.

Raffles paused, picked up the case he had taken from Bunny, and examined it.

"But this one must have held that magnificent necklace," he said. "And this one was obviously made to hold a tiara," he continued, inspecting the second case which Bunny had placed on the table.

Bunny agreed that, very likely, those priceless objects had indeed rested in those worthless receptacles.

"And she wasn't wearing either of them," Raffles went on relentlessly. "We saw that through the window. So where could they have been?"

Bunny forced himself to meet Raffles's puzzled gaze.

"Raffles," he said, steeling himself. "I'll be frank with you. I meant you never to know, but it's easier than going on telling lies. The items were in the cases all right. I left them behind me in the tower room."

"Why, Bunny?" Raffles asked in the most quiet and neutral of voices.

As best he could, Bunny related to Raffles the awful vision he had experienced in the tower room and his attendant feelings of shame and dishonor. Raffles listened in attentive silence.

"It was unbearable. It was sacrilege," Bunny said with emotion. "You may say that I ought to have thought of all this before, but I didn't. I only thought of it then, and that's all that there is to it."

"You were always a bad liar, Bunny," Raffles commented.

"Hopeless," agreed the young man despairingly.

"Will you think *me* one when I tell you that I can understand what you felt, and what you did? As a matter of fact, I have understood for several hours now," he confessed.

"What I felt, Raffles?" Bunny asked, not quite understanding.

"And what you did." Raffles confirmed with a nod. "I guessed it in the boathouse. You were in such a mood of just wanting to get away from the place, whatever the cost, and Osborne and his friends were so slow to come after us—they who'd been so keen on the chase—it seemed as though they'd found something that took the edge off their keenness. And then I went back to the house and took another look through the venetian blinds.

And what do you think I saw?' he asked, plunging his hands into his dressing-gown pockets.

"I've no idea," said Bunny with complete truth.

"The whole lot of them, prematurely gloating over the recovery of these two pretty things."

With a simple flourish, Raffles drew from his pockets the diamond tiara and its complementary necklace. The morning sun struck an arpeggio of light from their many-faceted surfaces. Bunny gaped.

"I went back into their bedroom, Bunny," Raffles reminded him, putting the jewels on the table. "They'd left all their jewelry simply lying on the dressing table, for anyone to take. It seemed a shame not to. After all, we had risked life, limb, and liberty. And I had not your sentimental scruples," he added gently. "Why should I go empty away?"

"You stole them a second time!" gasped Bunny.

"I took back what had once, however briefly, been mine," Raffles asserted.

"I admit there is a logic in it, and a kind of poetic justice," said Bunny.

"If you want to hear the full story of my second visit to the Osbornes' bedroom, drive home for a fresh kit, and meet me at the Turkish Baths in twenty minutes," said Raffles with sudden vivacity. "I feel more than a little grubby after my night on the tiles. And we can have breakfast in the cooling gallery."

"Done," said Bunny instantly, his heavy spirits suddenly lightening. He took a step towards the door but a thought, an important thought, made him pause. "Just one thing, Raffles. I have been no use to you tonight, and worse than no use. I shall be delighted to have breakfast with you, to celebrate your exploit, but I shall absolutely and definitely not take any share of tonight's proceeds. I didn't earn any."

Bunny had spoken with great dignity, and Raffles was duly impressed.

"I agree with you, Bunny. And I had already considered this very question. I came to the conclusion that your share of the loot should be only the small stuff I picked up at the same time." With a broad grin of irrepressible happiness, Raffles delved again into his pockets. "The rope of pearls, the rings . . ." These and other small costly items he rumbled onto the table. Bunny stared at them with renewed astonishment, and before he could protest, Raffles said: "A fair price for the pleasure of your company, Bunny."

Bunny, of course, accepted. What else could he do? He had learned a lesson that night more precious even than the life he had feared to lose. He had learned that his own qualities, although definitely not those of a leader, were yet valued and understood by one naturally equipped to lead. Through Raffles, to whom he had turned in desperation, Bunny had regained his honor and was concerned to retain it, even in death. But more, he had learned to value justly his own innate innocence, as Raffles had always done. He left the Albany that morning with a new sense of self-respect, and he faced the future, whatever adventures it might bring, with a stout heart, knowing that Raffles would always bring him through.

P. G. WODEHOUSE

Uncle Fred Flits By

In order that they might enjoy their after-luncheon coffee in peace, the Crumpet had taken the guest whom he was entertaining at the Drones Club to the smaller and less frequented of the two smoking rooms. In the other, he explained, though the conversation always touched an exceptionally high level of brilliance, there was apt to be a good deal of sugar thrown about.

The guest said he understood.

"Young blood, eh?"

"That's right. Young blood."

"And animal spirits."

"And animal, as you say, spirits," agreed the Crumpet. "We get a fairish amount of those here."

"The complaint, however, is not, I observe, universal."

"Eh?"

The other drew his host's attention to the doorway, where a young man in form-fitting tweeds had just appeared. The aspect of this young man was haggard. His eyes glared wildly and he sucked at an empty cigarette holder. If he had a mind, there was something on it. When the Crumpet called to him to come and join the party, he merely shook his head in a distraught sort of way and disappeared, looking like a character out of a Greek tragedy pursued by the Fates.

The Crumpet sighed.

"Poor old Pongo!"

"Pongo?"

"That was Pongo Twistleton. He's all broken up about his Uncle Fred."

"Dead?"

"No such luck. Coming up to London again tomorrow. Pongo had a wire this morning."

"And that upsets him?"

"Naturally. After what happened last time."

"What was that?"

"Ah!" said the Crumpet.

"What happened last time?"

"You may well ask."

"I do ask."

"Ah!" said the Crumpet.

Poor old Pongo (said the Crumpet) has often discussed his Uncle Fred with me, and if there weren't tears in his eyes when he did so, I don't know a tear in the eye when I see one. In round numbers the Earl of Ickenham, of Ickenham Hall, Ickenham, Hants, he lives in the country most of the year, but from time to time has a nasty way of slipping his collar and getting loose and descending upon Pongo at his flat in the Albany. And every time he does so, the unhappy young blighter is subjected to some soul-testing experience. Because the trouble with this uncle is that, though sixty if a day, he becomes on arriving in the metropolis as young as he feels—which is, apparently, a youngish twenty-two. I don't know if you happen to know what the word "excesses" means, but those are what Pongo's Uncle Fred from the country, when in London, invariably commits.

It wouldn't so much matter, mind you, if he would confine his activities to the club premises. We're pretty broad-minded here, and if you stop short of smashing the piano, there isn't much that you can do at the Drones that will cause the raised eyebrow and the sharp intake of breath. The snag is that he will insist on lugging Pongo out in the open and there, right in the public eye, proceeding to step high, wide, and plentiful.

So when, on the occasion to which I allude, he stood pink and genial on Pongo's hearth rug, bulging with Pongo's lunch and wreathed in the smoke of one of Pongo's cigars, and said: "And now, my boy, for a pleasant and instructive afternoon," you will readily understand why the unfortunate young clam gazed at him as he would have gazed at two-penn'orth of dynamite, had he discovered it lighting up in his presence.

"A what?" he said, giving at the knees and paling beneath the tan a bit.

"A pleasant and instructive afternoon," repeated Lord Ickenham, rolling the words round his tongue. "I propose that you place yourself in my hands and leave the program entirely to me."

Now, owing to Pongo's circumstances being such as to necessitate his getting into the aged relative's ribs at intervals and shaking him down for an occasional much-needed tenner or what not, he isn't in a position to use the iron hand with the old buster. But at these words he displayed a manly firmness.

"You aren't going to get me to the dog races again."

"No, no."

"You remember what happened last June."

"Quite," said Lord Ickenham, "quite. Though I still think that a wiser magistrate would have been content with a mere reprimand."

"And I won't—"

"Certainly not. Nothing of that kind at all. What I propose to do this afternoon is to take you to visit the home of your ancestors."

Pongo did not get this.

"I thought Ickenham was the home of my ancestors."

"It is one of the homes of your ancestors. They also resided rather nearer the heart of things, at a place called Mitching Hill."

"Down in the suburbs, do you mean?"

"The neighborhood is now suburban, true. It is many years since the meadows where I sported as a child were sold and cut up into building lots. But when I was a boy, Mitching Hill was open country. It was a vast, rolling estate belonging to your great-uncle, Marmaduke, a man with whiskers of a nature which you with your pure mind would scarcely credit, and I have long felt a sentimental urge to see what the hell the old place looks like now. Perfectly foul, I expect. Still, I think we should make the pious pilgrimage."

Pongo absolutely-ed heartily. He was all for the scheme. A great weight seemed to have rolled off his mind. The way he looked at it was that even an uncle within a short jump of the loony bin couldn't very well get into much trouble in a suburb. I mean, you know what suburbs are. They don't, as it were, offer the scope. One follows his reasoning, of course.

"Fine!" he said. "Splendid! Topping!"

"Then put on your hat and rompers, my boy," said Lord Ickenham, "and let us be off. I fancy one gets there by omnibuses and things."

Well, Pongo hadn't expected much in the way of mental uplift from the sight of Mitching Hill, and he didn't get it. Alighting from the bus, he tells me, you found yourself in the middle of rows and rows of semidetached villas, all looking exactly alike, and you went on and you came to more semidetached villas, and those all looked exactly alike, too. Nevertheless, he did not repine. It was one of those early spring days which suddenly change to midwinter and he had come out without his overcoat, and it looked like rain and he hadn't an umbrella, but despite this his mood was one of sober ecstasy. The hours were passing and his uncle had not yet made a goat of himself. At the dog races the other had been in the hands of the constabulary in the first ten minutes.

It began to seem to Pongo that with any luck he might be able to keep the old blister pottering harmlessly about here till nightfall, when he could shoot a bit of dinner into him and put him to bed. And as Lord Ickenham had specifically stated that his wife, Pongo's Aunt Jane, had expressed her intention of scalping him with a blunt knife if he wasn't back at the Hall by lunchtime on the morrow, it really looked as if he might get through this visit without perpetrating a single major outrage on the public weal. It is rather interesting to note that, as he thought this, Pongo smiled, because it was the last time he smiled that day.

All this while, I should mention, Lord Ickenham had been stopping at intervals like a pointing dog and saying that it must have been just about here that he plugged the gardener in the trousers seat with his bow and arrow and that over there he had been sick after his first cigar, and he now paused in front of a villa which for some unknown reason called itself The Cedars. His face was tender and wistful.

"On this very spot, if I am not mistaken," he said, heaving a bit of a sigh, "on this very spot, fifty years ago come Lammas Eve, I . . . Oh, blast it!"

The concluding remark had been caused by the fact that the rain, which had held off until now, suddenly began to buzz down like a shower bath. With no further words, they leaped into the porch of the villa and there took shelter, exchanging glances with a grey parrot which hung in a cage in the window.

Not that you could really call it shelter. They were protected from above all right, but the moisture was now falling with a sort of swivel action, whipping in through the sides of the porch and tickling them up properly. And it was just after Pongo had turned up his collar and was huddling against the door that the door gave way. From the fact that a female of general-servant aspect was standing there, he gathered that his uncle must have rung the bell.

This female wore a long mackintosh, and Lord Ickenham beamed upon her with a fairish spot of suavity.

"Good afternoon," he said.

The female said good afternoon.

"The Cedars?"

The female said yes, it was The Cedars.

"Are the old folks at home?"

The female said there was nobody at home.

"Ah? Well, never mind. I have come," said Lord Ickenham, edging in, "to clip the parrot's claws. My assistant, Mr. Walkinshaw, who applies the anesthetic," he
added, indicating Pongo with a gesture.

"Are you from the bird shop?"

"A very happy guess."

"Nobody told me you were coming."

"They keep things from you, do they?" said Lord
Ickenham sympathetically. "Too bad."

Continuing to edge, he had got into the parlor by
now, Pongo following in a sort of dream and the female
following Pongo.

"Well, I suppose it's all right," she said. "I was just
going out. It's my afternoon."

"Go out," said Lord Ickenham cordially. "By all
means go out. We will leave everything in order."

And presently the female, though still a bit on the
dubious side, pushed off, and Lord Ickenham lit the gas
fire and drew a chair up.

"So here we are, my boy," he said. "A little tact, a
little address, and here we are, snug and cozy and not
catching our deaths of cold. You'll never go far wrong if
you leave things to me."

"But, dash it, we can't stop here," said Pongo.

Lord Ickenham raised his eyebrows.

"Not stop here? Are you suggesting that we go out
into that rain? My dear lad, you are not aware of the
grave issues involved. This morning, as I was leaving

home, I had a rather painful disagreement with your aunt. She said the weather was treacherous and wished me to take my woolly muffler. I replied that the weather was not treacherous and that I would be dashed if I took my woolly muffler. Eventually, by the exercise of an iron will, I had my way, and I ask you, my dear boy, to envisage what will happen if I return with a cold in the head. I shall sink to the level of a fifth-class power. Next time I came to London, it would be with a liver pad and a respirator. No! I shall remain here, toasting my toes at this really excellent fire. I had no idea that a gas fire radiated such warmth. I feel all in a glow."

So did Pongo. His brow was wet with honest sweat. He is reading for the bar, and while he would be the first to admit that he hasn't yet got a complete toehold on the law of Great Britain, he had a sort of notion that oiling into a perfect stranger's semidetached villa on the pretext of pruning the parrot was a tort or misdemeanor, if not actual barratry or soccage in fief or something like that. And apart from the legal aspect of the matter, there was the embarrassment of the thing. Nobody is more of a whale on correctness and not doing what's not done than Pongo, and the situation in which he now found himself caused him to chew the lower lip and, as I say, perspire a goodish deal.

"But suppose the blighter who owns this ghastly house comes back?" he asked. "Talking of envisaging things, try that one over on your pianola."

And, sure enough, as he spoke, the front doorbell rang.

"There!" said Pongo.

"Don't say 'There!' my boy," said Lord Ickenham

reprovingly. "It's the sort of thing your aunt says. I see no reason for alarm. Obviously this is some casual caller. A ratepayer would have used his latchkey. Glance cautiously out of the window and see if you can see anybody."

"It's a pink chap," said Pongo, having done so.

"How pink?"

"Pretty pink."

"Well, there you are, then. I told you so. It can't be the big chief. The sort of fellows who own houses like this are pale and shallow, owing to working in offices all day. Go and see what he wants."

"You go and see what he wants."

"We'll both go and see what he wants," said Lord Ickenham.

So they went and opened the front door, and there, as Pongo had said, was a pink chap. A small young pink chap, a bit moist about the shoulder blades.

"Pardon me," said this pink chap, "is Mr. Roddis in?"

"No," said Pongo.

"Yes," said Lord Ickenham. "Don't be silly, Douglas —of course I'm in. I am Mr. Roddis," he said to the pink chap. "This, such as he is, is my son Douglas. And you?"

"Name of Robinson."

"What about it?"

"My name's Robinson."

"Oh, *your* name's Robinson? Now we've got it straight. Delighted to see you, Mr. Robinson. Come right in and take your boots off."

They all trickled back to the parlor, Lord Ickenham pointing out objects of interest by the wayside to the chap, Pongo gulping for air a bit and trying to get himself abreast of this new twist in the scenario. His heart was becoming more and more bowed down with weight of woe. He hadn't liked being Mr. Walkinshaw, the anesthetist, and he didn't like it any better being Roddis junior. In brief, he feared the worst. It was only too plain to him by now that his uncle had got it thoroughly up his nose and had settled down to one of his big afternoons, and he was asking himself, as he had so often asked himself before, what would the harvest be?

Arrived in the parlor, the pink chap proceeded to stand on one leg and look coy.

"Is Julia here?" he asked, simpering a bit, Pongo says.

"Is she?" said Lord Ickenham to Pongo.

"No," said Pongo.

"No," said Lord Ickenham.

"She wired me she was coming here today."

"Ah, then we shall have a bridge four."

The pink chap stood on the other leg.

"I don't suppose you've ever met Julia. Bit of trouble in the family, she gave me to understand."

"It is often the way."

"The Julia I mean is your niece Julia Parker. Or, rather, your wife's niece Julia Parker."

"Any niece of my wife is a niece of mine," said Lord Ickenham heartily. "We share and share alike."

"Julia and I want to get married."

"Well, go ahead."

"But they won't let us."

"Who won't?"

"Her mother and father. And Uncle Charlie Parker and Uncle Henry Parker and the rest of them. They don't think I'm good enough."

"The morality of the modern young man is notoriously lax."

"Class enough, I mean. They're a haughty lot."

"What makes them haughty? Are they earls?"

"No, they aren't earls."

"Then why the devil," said Lord Ickenham warmly, "are they haughty? Only earls have a right to be haughty. Earls are hot stuff. When you get an earl, you've got something."

"Besides, we've had words. Me and her father. One thing led to another, and in the end I called him a perishing old—Coo!" said the pink chap, breaking off suddenly.

He had been standing by the window, and he now leaped lissomely into the middle of the room, causing Pongo, whose nervous system was by this time definitely down among the wines and spirits and who hadn't been expecting this *adagio* stuff, to bite his tongue with some severity.

"They're on the doorstep! Julia and her mother and father. I didn't know they were all coming."

"You do not wish to meet them?"

"No, I don't!"

"Then duck behind the settee, Mr. Robinson," said Lord Ickenham, and the pink chap, weighing the advice and finding it good, did so. And as he disappeared, the doorbell rang.

Once more Lord Ickenham led Pongo out into the hall.

"I say!" said Pongo, and a close observer might have

noted that he was quivering like an aspen.

"Say on, my dear boy."

"I mean to say, what?"

"What?"

"You aren't going to let these bounders in, are you?"

"Certainly," said Lord Ickenham. "We Roddises keep open house. And as they are presumably aware that Mr. Roddis has no son, I think we had better return to the old layout. You are the local vet, my boy, come to minister to my parrot. When I return, I should like to find you by the cage, staring at the bird in a scientific manner. Tap your teeth from time to time with a pencil and try to smell of iodoform. It will help to add conviction."

So Pongo shifted back to the parrot's cage and stared so earnestly that it was only when a voice said, "Well!" that he became aware that there was anybody in the room. Turning, he perceived that Hampshire's leading curse had come back, bringing the gang.

It consisted of a stern, thin, middle-aged woman, a middle-aged man, and a girl.

You can generally accept Pongo's estimate of girls, and when he says that this one was a pippin, one knows that he uses the term in its most exact sense. She was about nineteen, he thinks, and she wore a black beret, a dark-green leather coat, a shortish tweed skirt, silk stockings, and high-heeled shoes. Her eyes were large and lustrous, and her face like a dewy rosebud at daybreak on a June morning. So Pongo tells me. Not that I suppose he has ever seen a rosebud at daybreak on a June morning, because it's generally as much as you can do to lug him out of bed in time for nine-thirty breakfast. Still, one gets the idea.

"Well," said the woman, "you don't know who I am, I'll be bound. I'm Laura's sister Connie. This is Claude, my husband. And this is my daughter Julia. Is Laura in?"

"I regret to say, no," said Lord Ickenham.

The woman was looking at him as if he didn't come up to her specifications.

"I thought you were younger," she said.

"Younger than what?" said Lord Ickenham.

"Younger than you are."

"You can't be younger than you are, worse luck," said Lord Ickenham. "Still, one does one's best, and I am bound to say that of recent years I have made a pretty good go of it."

The woman caught sight of Pongo, and he didn't seem to please her, either.

"Who's that?"

"The local vet, clustering round my parrot."

"I can't talk in front of him."

"It is quite all right," Lord Ickenham assured her. "The poor fellow is stone-deaf."

And with an imperious gesture at Pongo, as much as to bid him stare less at girls and more at parrots, he got the company seated.

"Now, then," he said.

There was silence for a moment, then a sort of muffled sob, which Pongo thinks proceeded from the girl. He couldn't see, of course, because his back was turned and he was looking at the parrot, which looked back at him—most offensively, he says, as parrots will, using one eye only for the purpose. It also asked him to have a nut.

The woman came into action again.

"Although," she said, "Laura never did me the honor

to invite me to her wedding, for which reason I have not communicated with her for five years, necessity compels me to cross her threshold today. There comes a time when differences must be forgotten and relatives must stand shoulder to shoulder."

"I see what you mean," said Lord Ickenham. "Like the boys of the old brigade."

"What I say is, let bygones be bygones. I would not have intruded on you, but needs must. I disregard the past and appeal to your sense of pity."

The thing began to look to Pongo like a touch, and he is convinced that the parrot thought so, too, for it winked and cleared its throat. But they were both wrong. The woman went on.

"I want you and Laura to take Julia into your home for a week or so, until I can make other arrangements for her. Julia is studying the piano, and she sits for her examination in two weeks' time, so until then she must remain in London. The trouble is, she has fallen in love. Or thinks she has."

"I know I have," said Julia.

Her voice was so attractive that Pongo was compelled to slue round and take another look at her. Her eyes, he says, were shining like twin stars and there was a sort of Soul's Awakening expression on her face, and what the dickens there was in a pink chap like the pink chap, who even as pink chaps go wasn't much of a pink chap, to make her look like that, was frankly, Pongo says, more than he could understand. The thing baffled him. He sought in vain for a solution.

"Yesterday, Claude and I arrived in London from our Bexhill home to give Julia a pleasant surprise. We stayed, naturally, in the boardinghouse where she has been living for the past six weeks. And what do you think we discovered?"

"Insects."

"Not insects. A letter. From a young man. I found to my horror that a young man of whom I knew nothing was arranging to marry my daughter. I sent for him immediately, and found him to be quite impossible. He jellies eels!"

"Does what?"

"He is an assistant at a jellied eel shop."

"But surely," said Lord Ickenham, "that speaks well for him. The capacity to jelly an eel seems to me to argue intelligence of a high order. It isn't everybody who can do it, by any means. I know if someone came to me and said, 'Jelly this eel!' I should be nonplussed. And so, or I am very much mistaken, would Ramsay MacDonald and Winston Churchill."

The woman did not seem to see eye to eye.

"Tchah!" she said. "What do you suppose my husband's brother Charlie Parker would say if I allowed his niece to marry a man who jellies eels?"

"Ah!" said Claude, who, before we go any further, was a tall, drooping bird with a red soup-strainer moustache.

"Or my husband's brother, Henry Parker."

"Ah!" said Claude. "Or Cousin Alf Robbins, for that matter."

"Exactly. Cousin Alfred would die of shame."

The girl Julia hiccuped passionately, so much so that Pongo says it was all he could do to stop himself nipping across and taking her hand in his and patting it.

"I've told you a hundred times, Mother, that Wilberforce is only jellying eels till he finds something better."

"What is better than an eel?" asked Lord Ickenham, who had been following this discussion with the close attention it deserved. "For jellying purposes, I mean."

"He is ambitious. It won't be long," said the girl, "before Wilberforce suddenly rises in the world."

She never spoke a truer word. At this very moment, up he came from behind the settee like a leaping salmon.

"Julia!" he cried.

"Wilby!" yipped the girl.

And Pongo says he never saw anything more sickening in his life than the way she flung herself into the blighter's arms and clung there like the ivy on the old garden wall. It wasn't that he had anything specific against the pink chap, but this girl had made a deep impression on him, and he resented her gluing herself to another in this manner.

Julia's mother, after just that brief moment which a woman needs in which to recover from her natural surprise at seeing eel-jelliers pop up from behind sofas, got moving and plucked her away like a referee breaking a couple of welterweights.

"Julia Parker," she said, "I'm ashamed of you!"

"So am I," said Claude.

"I blush for you."

"Me, too," said Claude. "Hugging and kissing a man who called your father a perishing old bottle-nosed Gawd-help-us."

"I think," said Lord Ickenham, shoving his oar in, "that before proceeding any further we ought to go into that point. If he called you a perishing old bottle-nosed

Gawd-help-us, it seems to me that the first thing to do is to decide whether he was right, and frankly, in my opinion . . ."

"Wilberforce will apologize."

"Certainly I'll apologize. It isn't fair to hold a remark passed in the heat of the moment against a chap . . ."

"Mr. Robinson," said the woman, "you know perfectly well that whatever remarks you may have seen fit to pass don't matter one way or the other. If you were listening to what I was saying, you will understand . . ."

"Oh, I know, I know. Uncle Charlie Parker and Uncle Henry Parker and Cousin Alf Robbins and all that. Pack of snobs!"

"What!"

"Haughty, stuck-up snobs. Them and their class distinctions. Think themselves everybody just because they've got money. I'd like to know how they got it."

"What do you mean by that?"

"Never mind what I mean."

"If you are insinuating—"

"Well, of course, you know, Connie," said Lord Ickenham mildly, "he's quite right. You can't get away from that."

I don't know if you have ever seen a bullterrier embarking on a scrap with an Airedale and just as it was getting down nicely to its work suddenly having an unexpected Kerry blue sneak up behind it and bite it in the rear quarters. When this happens, it lets go of the Airedale and swivels round and fixes the butting-in animal with a pretty nasty eye. It was exactly the same with the woman Connie when Lord Ickenham spoke these words.

"What!"

"I was only wondering if you had forgotten how Charlie Parker made his pile."

"What are you talking about?"

"I know it is painful," said Lord Ickenham, "and one doesn't mention it as a rule, but, as we are on the subject, you must admit that lending money at two hundred and fifty percent interest is not done in the best circles. The judge, if you remember, said so at the trial."

"I never knew that!" cried the girl Julia.

"Ah," said Lord Ickenham. "You kept it from the child? Quite right, quite right."

"It's a lie!"

"And when Henry Parker had all that fuss with the bank, it was touch and go they didn't send him to prison. Between ourselves, Connie, has a bank official, even a brother of your husband, any right to sneak fifty pounds from the till in order to put it on a hundred-to-one shot for the Grand National? Not quite playing the game, Connie. Not the straight bat. Henry, I grant you, won five thousand of the best and never looked back afterwards, but, though we applaud his judgment of form, we must surely look askance at his financial methods. As for Cousin Alf Robbins . . ."

The woman was making rummy stuttering sounds. Pongo tells me he once had a Pommery Seven which used to express itself in much the same way if you tried to get it to take a hill on high. A sort of mixture of gurgles and explosions.

"There is not a word of truth in this," she gasped at length, having managed to get the vocal cords disentangled. "Not a single word. I think you must have gone mad."

Lord Ickenham shrugged his shoulders.

"Have it your own way, Connie. I was only going to say that, while the jury were probably compelled on the evidence submitted to them to give Cousin Alf Robbins the benefit of the doubt when charged with smuggling dope, everybody knew that he had been doing it for years. I am not blaming him, mind you. If a man can smuggle cocaine and get away with it, good luck to him, say I. The only point I am trying to make is that we are hardly a family that can afford to put on dog and sneer at honest suitors for our daughters' hands. Speaking for myself, I consider that we are very lucky to have the chance of marrying even into eel-jellying circles."

"So do I," said Julia firmly.

"You don't believe what this man is saying?"

"I believe every word."

"So do I," said the pink chap.

The woman snorted. She seemed overwrought.

"Well," she said, "goodness knows I have never liked Laura, but I would never have wished her a husband like you!"

"Husband?" said Lord Ickenham, puzzled. "What gives you the impression that Laura and I are married?"

There was a weighty silence, during which the parrot threw out a general invitation to the company to join it in a nut. Then the girl Julia spoke.

"You'll have to let me marry Wilberforce now," she said. "He knows too much about us."

"I was rather thinking that myself," said Lord Ickenham. "Seal his lips, I say."

"You wouldn't mind marrying into a low family,

would you, darling?" asked the girl, with a touch of anxiety.

"No family could be too low for me, dearest, if it was yours," said the pink chap.

"After all, we needn't see them."

"That's right."

"It isn't one's relations that matter: it's oneselves."

"That's right, too."

"Wilby!"

"Julia!"

They repeated the old-ivy-on-the-garden-wall act. Pongo says he didn't like it any better than the first time, but his distaste wasn't in it with the woman Connie's.

"And what, may I ask," she said, "do you propose to marry on?"

This seemed to cast a damper. They came apart. They looked at each other. The girl looked at the pink chap, and the pink chap looked at the girl. You could see that a jarring note had been struck.

"Wilberforce is going to be a very rich man some day."

"Some day!"

"If I had a hundred pounds," said the pink chap, "I could buy a half share in one of the best milk walks in South London tomorrow."

"If!" said the woman.

"Ah!" said Claude.

"Where are you going to get it?"

"Ah!" said Claude.

"Where," repeated the woman, plainly pleased with the snappy crack and loath to let it ride without an encore, "are you going to get it?"

"That," said Claude, "is the point. Where are you going to get a hundred pounds?"

"Why, bless my soul," said Lord Ickenham jovially, "from me, of course. Where else?"

And before Pongo's bulging eyes he fished out from the recesses of his costume a crackling bundle of notes and handed it over. And the agony of realizing that the old bounder had had all that stuff on him all this time and that he hadn't touched him for so much as a tithe of it was so keen, Pongo says, that before he knew what he was doing he had let out a sharp, whinnying cry which rang through the room like the yowl of a stepped-on puppy.

"Ah," said Lord Ickenham. "The vet wishes to speak to me. Yes, vet?"

This seemed to puzzle the cerise bloke a bit.

"I thought you said this chap was your son."

"If I had a son," said Lord Ickenham, a little hurt, "he would be a good deal better-looking than that. No, this is the local veterinary surgeon. I may have said I *looked* on him as a son. Perhaps that was what confused you."

He shifted across to Pongo and twiddled his hands enquiringly. Pongo gaped at him, and it was not until one of the hands caught him smartly in the lower ribs that he remembered he was deaf and started to twiddle back. Considering that he wasn't supposed to be dumb, I can't see why he should have twiddled, but no doubt there are moments when twiddling is about all a fellow feels himself equal to. For what seemed to him at least ten hours, Pongo had been undergoing great mental stress, and one can't blame him for not being chatty. Anyway, be that as it may, he twiddled.

"I cannot quite understand what he says," announced Lord Ickenham at length, "because he sprained a finger this morning and that makes him stammer. But I gather that he wishes to have a word with me in private. Possibly my parrot has got something the matter with it which he is reluctant to mention even in sign language in front of a young unmarried girl. You know what parrots are. We will step outside."

"*We* will step outside," said Wilberforce.

"Yes," said the girl Julia. "I feel like a walk."

"And you?" said Lord Ickenham to the woman Connie, who was looking like a female Napoleon at Moscow. "Do you join the hikers?"

"I shall remain and make myself a cup of tea. You will not grudge us a cup of tea, I hope?"

"Far from it," said Lord Ickenham cordially. "This is Liberty Hall. Stick around and mop it up till your eyes bubble."

Outside, the girl, looking more like a dewy rosebud than ever, fawned on the old buster pretty considerably.

"I don't know how to thank you!" she said. And the pink chap said he didn't, either.

"Not at all, my dear, not at all," said Lord Ickenham.

"I think you're simply wonderful."

"No, no."

"You are. Perfectly marvelous."

"Tut, tut," said Lord Ickenham. "Don't give the matter another thought."

He kissed her on both cheeks, the chin, the forehead, the right eyebrow, and the tip of the nose, Pongo looking on the while in a baffled and discontented manner. Everybody seemed to be kissing this girl except him.

Eventually the degrading spectacle ceased, and the girl and the pink chap shoved off, and Pongo was enabled to take up the matter of that hundred quid.

"Where," he asked, "did you get all that money?"

"Now, where did I?" mused Lord Ickenham. "I know your aunt gave it to me for some purpose. But what? To pay some bill or other, I rather fancy."

This cheered Pongo up slightly.

"She'll give you the devil when you get back," he said, with not a little relish. "I wouldn't be in your shoes for something. When you tell Aunt Jane," he said, with confidence, for he knew his Aunt Jane's emotional nature, "that you slipped her entire roll to a girl, and explain, as you will have to explain, that she was an extraordinarily pretty girl—a girl, in fine, who looked like something out of a beauty chorus of the better sort, I should think she would pluck down one of the ancestral battle-axes from the wall and jolly well strike you on the mazzard."

"Have no anxiety, my dear boy," said Lord Ickenham. "It is like your kind heart to be so concerned, but have no anxiety. I shall tell her that I was compelled to give the money to you to enable you to buy back some compromising letters from a Spanish demimondaine. She will scarcely be able to blame me for rescuing a fondly loved nephew from the clutches of an adventuress. It may be that she will feel a little vexed with you for a while, and that you may have to allow a certain time to elapse before you visit Ickenham again, but then I shan't be wanting you at Ickenham till the ratting season starts, so all is well."

At this moment, there came toddling up to the gate

of The Cedars a large red-faced man. He was just going in when Lord Ickenham hailed him.

"Mr. Roddis?"

"Hey?"

"Am I addressing Mr. Roddis?"

"That's me."

"I am Mr. J. G. Bulstrode from down the road," said Lord Ickenham. "This is my sister's husband's brother, Percy Frensham, in the lard and imported-butter business."

The red-faced bird said he was pleased to meet them. He asked Pongo if things were brisk in the lard and imported-butter business, and Pongo said they were all right, and the red-faced bird said he was glad to hear it.

"We have never met, Mr. Roddis," said Lord Ickenham, "but I think it would be only neighborly to inform you that a short while ago I observed two suspicious-looking persons in your house."

"In my house? How on earth did they get there?"

"No doubt through a window at the back. They looked to me like cat burglars. If you creep up, you may be able to see them."

The red-faced bird crept, and came back not exactly foaming at the mouth but with the air of a man who for two pins would so foam.

"You're perfectly right. They're sitting in my parlor as cool as dammit, swigging my tea and buttered toast."

"I thought as much."

"And they've opened a pot of my raspberry jam."

"Ah, then you will be able to catch them red-handed. I should fetch a policeman."

"I will. Thank you, Mr. Bulstrode."

"Only too glad to have been able to render you this little service, Mr. Roddis," said Lord Ickenham. "Well, I must be moving along. I have an appointment. Pleasant after the rain, is it not? Come, Percy."

He lugged Pongo off.

"So that," he said, with satisfaction, "is that. On these visits of mine to the metropolis, my boy, I always make it my aim, if possible, to spread sweetness and light. I look about me, even in a foul hole like Mitching Hill, and I ask myself, How can I leave this foul hole a better and happier foul hole than I found it? And if I see a chance, I grab it. Here is our omnibus. Spring aboard, my boy, and on our way home we will be sketching out rough plans for the evening. If the old Leicester Grill is still in existence, we might look in there. It must be fully thirty-five years since I was last thrown out of the Leicester Grill. I wonder who is the bouncer there now."

Such (concluded the Crumpet) is Pongo Twistleton's Uncle Fred from the country, and you will have gathered by now a rough notion of why it is that when a telegram comes announcing his impending arrival in the great city Pongo blanches to the core and calls for a couple of quick ones.

The whole situation, Pongo says, is very complex. Looking at it from one angle, it is fine that the man lives in the country most of the year. If he didn't, he would have him in his midst all the time. On the other hand, by living in the country he generates, as it were, a store of loopiness which expends itself with frightful violence on his rare visits to the center of things.

What it boils down to is this: Is it better to have a

loopy uncle whose loopiness is perpetually on tap but spread out thin, so to speak, or one who lies low in distant Hants for three hundred and sixty days in the year and does himself proud in London for the other five? Dashed moot, of course, and Pongo has never been able to make up his mind on the point.

Naturally, the ideal thing would be if someone would chain the old hound up permanently and keep him from Jan. one to Dec. thirty-one where he wouldn't do any harm—viz, among the spuds and tenantry. But this, Pongo admits, is a Utopian dream. Nobody could work harder to that end than his Aunt Jane, and she has never been able to manage it.

No Petty Thief

Maybe it was the coming of the rains that caused the thing to happen. For the rains came early that November to the mountains. They were cold rains as well as I remember, dropping from the black clouds that raced over the mountaintops like thin-bellied foxhounds. Driven by high mountain winds, they lashed at the treetops, stripping them bare long before it was time to shed their leaves. It was these early rains that stopped the work on the highway they were building through the mountains.

I guess I ought to 've been ashamed of myself, too, for it was the first road ever to be built in our county. It was a real road they were making. They were going down into the deep valleys and around the rocky-walled mountains and over the mountains. Of course we had several jolt-wagon roads, log roads, cowpaths, goat paths, fox paths, rabbit paths, and footpaths. But you couldn't drive an automobile over one of these. And if the contractors could've only finished the big road and covered it with loose gravel before November, we'd a-had a real road that people could've driven automobiles over. It would've been a real road like I've heard a few counties in the mountains already had. I've only heard about these roads. I've never seen one of 'em.

And because we didn't have automobiles in our county, nice spring wagons and hug-me-tight buggies, and a lot of fancy vehicles like they had in other counties and in Edensburg, the county-seat town of our county, maybe that is what caused me to do what I did. For I'd stood in the Edensburg streets many times and watched the automobiles roll over the dirt streets and out of town a little ways as far as the turnpikes went. And I watched the buggies, hug-me-tights, and the fancy express wagons. I loved to watch their wheels roll. It was a lot better than the sleds we used, pulled by a team of skinny mules on our hilly farm. The sled slid over the ground on runners winter and summer. And it wasn't any fun watching runners slide and hearing the green dogwood runners grit on the rocks and the hard dry dirt. But it was fun to watch wheels roll. I'd stand and watch them for hours, and what I wanted most in this world was to own something with wheels. Whether I could find level ground enough around our house or not for the wheels to roll, if I had just had something with wheels I could have sat and looked at it for hours, admiring the wheels and the machinery.

Now if it wasn't the rains coming early or my love for wheels and machinery, I don't know what made me do it. I do know that I was raised in a decent home. My pa never used the word "raised" when he spoke about one of his ten young'ins. He allus said he he didn't raise young'ins but he "jerked 'em up by the hair on the head." And Pa was about right in a way. He did jerk us up by the hair on the head, but he didn't use any monkey business. He was a strict man in a fashion, belonging to the

Old Fashion Church, and when he jerked us up by the hair on the head, he did it in decency and order. That's why I hate what I've done on account of Pa and Ma. They never learned us to lie, steal, gamble, cuss, smoke, and drink. And when I tell you what happened to me, I don't want you to blame Ma and Pa. They had nothing to do with it. And I'll regret what I done to my dying day just because of Ma and Pa.

As I have said, the rains came early to the mountains in that November. And before the Big Road got too muddy, the men got the machinery out. I mean they drove the dump trucks, the caterpillar tractors, and big graders back to Edensburg where they had started the road from in the first place. But one piece of machinery they didn't take back with 'em was the big steam shovel. Maybe it was because it couldn't go back over the muddy road under its own power, and maybe it was too big for a caterpillar tractor to pull. Maybe they were afraid it would bog down even if pulled under its own power and with a tractor helping it. Anyway, they left it a-settin' there lonesomelike in the November rain.

I didn't work on the road. I had too much work at home to do. For I raised light burley terbacker on the steep mountain slope, where it was too steep to plow with mules but I dug the ground up with a hoe. And every time I had a chance to leave the terbacker, say fer a few hours, I would hurry over the mountain to watch 'em build the Big Road. I liked to watch a piece of machinery working like a man and I liked to watch the wheels roll. One of the pieces of machinery I loved most of all was the big steam shovel. And when it was left alone sitting in the rain, an idear popped into my head. And I went back home to get my monkey wrench.

You may think it was a hard job. But it wasn't too hard. I started taking off the little pieces first. I started stripping it like the wind and rain was stripping a big tree of leaves. Only I had a warm feeling for the steam shovel, and the wind and the rain didn't have any feeling fer the tree. There was something about this steam shovel that I loved. It was a beautiful thing to me. I had the same love touching it that a lot of the mountain boys have fer their pistols. It was the touch of ownership; yet I knew it didn't belong to me. But it would belong to me. It would belong to me even fer a little while. I knew that it was mine. Fer I was going to take it. And I was taking it to a place where I didn't think it would ever be found. And if it was found, it would be a place that it couldn't move out under its own power plus a dozen caterpillar tractors pulling at it.

After I'd taken it apart, I started carrying the little pieces over the mountain. Maybe I'd better tell you what kind of strength I have. I'm not a little weakling what you might think. I'm not what you'd call a real tall man. I just measure a bit over twelve hands high, which is a little over six feet. But I'm almost six hands across the shoulders. And my legs above my knees are about the size of tough-butted white oaks big enough for banks timbers and below my knees they are big as gnarled locust fence posts. My wrists are big as handspikes, tapering up to my arm muscles, which are pretty powerful and I'm not a-lying. When I swell my arm muscles, they're nigh as big as half-a-gallon lard buckets.

If Brother John was alive today, he could tell you the time when I lifted the back end of a jolt wagon from a chughole when it was loaded with corn. Eif Porter could tell you the time when ten woodchoppers, one at a time, tried to lift the butt end of a sawlog and I was the only one that could come up with it. I didn't even get red in the face lifting it, either. I ain't a-saying that I'm the biggest and the stoutest man in the hills, but I ain't a-lyin' when I tell you I'm powerful on a lift. And everybody around home could tell you that I couldn't get a pair of boots big enough to fit me. My legs wouldn't go down into 'em. Too much calf on my leg. I was pretty well fitted fer the task that I was a-going to do.

So I started carrying my steam shovel up over the mountain and down the other side to my terbacker barn that was built on the steep slope with a high lower side and a short upper side. And I arranged my terbacker that was a-curing on terbacker sticks on the tierpoles all around the sides and the ends of the barn. I had a big open space in the middle of my barn with big brown terbacker walls all around that no human eye could see through. Right in the middle of my barn, I shoveled off a level place to set up my steam shovel.

You'd be surprised how many parts there are to a steam shovel. The best way to find this out is to start taking one apart. It's a lot of work. And it would be awfully hard if a body had to do a lot of watching out fer somebody a-trying to catch him. But I guess the road builders thought a steam shovel would be safe to leave where they had stopped working on the road. They even guarded their trucks and tractors in Edensburg, but they didn't bother to guard the steam shovel or even send anybody back to look about it. So I didn't have anybody around to bother me. And I got in some good time.

If I's to tell you how long it took me to take it down and take the parts apart, it would surprise you. I had it down in less than three days and had taken it apart. And I didn't let any dead leaves gather under my feet when I started carrying it over the mountain. I'd take a big load, and I'd never set it down to wind a minute. I'd carry it right to the barn and take it back under the bright wall of terbacker to the place I'd prepared for it.

Believe it or not, I rolled the wheels, one at a time, over the mountain. A steam shovel's wheels ain't too big a thing but they are powerfully heavy. And the beam that holds the shovel is one of the pieces I couldn't carry. So I hitched my mules to it and dragged it like I's a-snakin' a big crosstie up over the mountain. I took all the parts loose from the engine I could, but the main body of the engine I hauled on my sled across the mountain. And the shovel was as big a load as any man would want to carry, but the worst thing about it was the durned shovel was so unhandy fer a body to get on his back. So I hauled that over on a sled, too. I carried all of it or rolled it but these three pieces. And I got it in the terbacker barn by myself because I didn't want to let anybody in on the secret. I carried so many loads over the mountain that I made a path from where the steam shovel used to be to my barn. My shoe heels had sunk into the earth since I carried such heavy loads on my back. But I knew the sun would come out and dry the leaves, and the wind would blow the leaves over the mountain again and kiver up all the trail. I knew it was too much of a job for me to go back with a stick or a rake and kiver up the path that I had made with my heavy brogans. So I left it to the wind, sun, and the rain to kiver the trail of evidence I'd left behind me.

Then came the happiest hours I ever spent in my life. I was putting my steam shovel back together. I'd laid out all the parts careful not to get them mixed. First I put the wheels on good foundations and got up the framework. And then I used a block and tackle that I used at hog-killing time to swing up the beam and the shovel. For I couldn't get up steam and let it work under its own power in my terbacker barn. I would have set the barn on fire and lost my terbacker crop and my steam shovel. I had to do it myself just with the help of the block and tackle. And I had by the end of November one of the prettiest things in my barn that ever my eyes looked upon when it come to machinery.

It was hard for me to believe that I had it. Sometimes it seemed like a dream. But I would pinch myself as I went to my barn to look at it again, again, and again to see if I were asleep and dreaming or if I were wide awake. But I wasn't dreaming. I was very much awake. Even my wife knew something was wrong with me, since I spent so much time at the barn. But I told her my terbacker was in "case" and I was taking it down and handing it off. She had allus helped me at this busy season with the terbacker, but she felt good and thought I loved her more when I told her that I would be able to take care of the terbacker this season. Since she was slender as a bean-pole and I was such a mountain of a man, she had allus climbed up on the tierpoles and handed the terbacker down fer me to strip. She was allus afraid that a tierpole would come unnailed when I swung onto it a-climbin' up in the barn. But she didn't have all this worry about me now.

I would go to my barn in the morning and just stand

and look at my steam shovel. And I'd think of the power it had. I'd think about the way I'd seen it bite into the dirt and rocks easier than I could sink my teeth into a piece of squirrel or possum. And how it would lift a big bite of dirt and rocks onto the trucks. How graceful the long beam would swing around just by pulling a little lever, and then there was another little lever a body pulled and it would unload its bite into the truck. And how it puffed, blew, and steamed, but it never sweated no matter how much dirt and rocks it moved. All day long it worked and it never tired. I guessed it could do the work of a hundred men with picks and shovels. And after it had dug a slice of road, how it would move with huffs and puffs under its own powerful power to a new place and start work. And now I loved to put my hand onto it and I had a sense of ownership and power, a feeling that nearly lifted me to the skies.

But the November rains stopped falling. The winter sun had come out again, making the day bright and warm. Though the ground froze a little at night, it wasn't enough to have stopped my steam shovel's eating away the earth. For the bright sunlight and the crisp wind had made the weather good again for road building. And as I had expected, the road builders came back and brought their machinery. Naturally, they didn't find the steam shovel.

There was a lot of excitement. They had expected it to be right where they left it. And the day I sauntered over where I had dismantled the shovel, I found a crowd gathered around and I joined them to listen to their talk. I never saw a crowd of men so confused. Nearly every man on this road gang said the steam shovel had to be

taken off under its own power and there wasn't any road
for it to get out except going back through Edensburg.

They had all been living in Edensburg, and not one
had seen a steam shovel rolling through the streets of
this little mountain town. Besides, when it had passed
through on its way to build us a road, all the young'ins
in the town had followed it. And the old people who had
never seen a steam shovel had come out to watch it, too.
It was the biggest thing that had ever gone through the
town. And now the road builders argued with each other
how the shovel had ever been taken back through the
town, popular as it was among the people, without someone a-seeing it. One man laughed, said it had grown
wings big enough to fly it over the mountain back to
"civilization." The men said a lot of foolish things like
that. But one of the old men with hard, cold, blue eyes
said he didn't think it was impossible for a man to carry
it away on his back and that was the only way he believed
it could have got away. When he said these words, he
looked me over. He looked at my shoulders and my big
hands, forearms, and my legs that were cased in my
overalls, stretching them like full meal sacks. Then he
pointed out that the steam-shovel tracks didn't leave the
spot, and the ground had been tramped down like a floor
around where the steam shovel had once been. But when
he said these words, everybody laughed and said that
was impossible, but I could tell from the way this old man
acted that he believed it had been carried away.

I didn't feel comfortable any longer around these
men. And when I snuck away, they were talking about
bringing in an "expert" to find the steam shovel. I didn't
go back the way I'd carried the steam shovel fer I

thought they might get suspicy and come over the path to my barn. I went down another path and circled out of my way a couple of miles like a fox. Instead of going down to my barn from the north, I came in from the west. And I went in to look at my shovel again. There it was, safe, pretty, and dry. And it was in a place that I didn't think it would ever be found. Even if they had to buy a new steam shovel or stop building the road that we needed so much, I didn't care. It was a toy I loved to fondle, and something I wanted to keep forever.

I guess I did neglect my wife and my two young'ins since in these last days I spent so much time at the barn. Rhoda thought my work with the terbacker was coming along mighty slow. She even tried to hurry me to get it off to the market before Christmas. But Christmas or no Christmas, I still fondled my toy. I looked at its beauty and thought of its power and forgot about Christmas although the terbacker was in case and the season was wonderful. Rhodie even threatened coming to the barn and helping me. But I told her not to mind for I had the work well under hand and that I could easily do it myself.

And I guess I would have gotten along someway if it hadn't been for the "expert" the boss man of the road gang went out somewhere and got to help him find the shovel. And maybe it was the wind and the sun of that early December that were against me. Maybe it was the rain had failed to do its part. I could have laid it onto several things when I heard voices upon the mountain and peeped through a crack in the barn. I saw a big man in front, dressed in good clothes, whose face I'd never seen with the road builders before. He was leading the men like a pack of hounds. He was out in front on my

tracks. He was following the path I had made. The rain
had never erased my deep shoe prints in the dirt, and if
the leaves had once kivered them, the sun had dried the
leaves and the wind had blown them off again, leaving my
path clean as a whistle fer 'em to follow. And that old man
with the cold, hard, blue eyes must have put the "expert"
wise that a man could carry off a steam shovel. For they
found it clean, dry, and purty in my terbacker barn.

No use to tell you more about it. Naturally I was
arrested and tried in Edensburg. And people came in
great droves to hear the trial. There was a lot in the
papers about it. They even had my picture in the papers.
And everybody wondered how I had carried away a
steam shovel. Even the jurymen would hardly believe it
until I told them the truth. When they swore me to God
that I could tell the truth, that is just what I done. I told
'em I wasn't no petty thief. I told 'em I'd never stole
anything in my life before. I told them the whole story
how I'd carried it all but three pieces and that I thought
I could've carried two of them. Even I had a time convinc-
ing the jury against my lawyer's advice that I had done
it. But I finally convinced them after the whole jury went
to the spot. They followed me over the path to my barn
where I showed them the shovel.

If you know the people and the laws in our state, it
would've been better fer me to 've kilt a man. I would
have stood a better chance of coming clear. Anyway I
wouldn't have got but one or two years in the pen even
if I hadn't done it in self-defense. But when you steal
something, even if it's just a chicken, let alone a steam
shovel, you're a gone gosling. Why they let me off with
only seven years and a day was, I was honest enough to

tell the truth after they found the shovel in my barn. If I'd a-tried to got outen it, I'd been given life. The road builders fit me hard, too, fer they had to build a road to my barn to get the shovel. Not a one of the whole gang was man enough to carry it back.

DILLON ANDERSON

The Weather Prophet

"Listen, Claudie," I said, "I'd about as soon be plumb out of money as to have only five dollars."

"I druther have this here five dollars, Clint," he answered.

"But what I'm trying to tell you is this," I went on. "We've got to get our car fixed, and that five dollars won't do it. You know what the man at the garage said; he won't touch the burnt-out bearing for less than twenty dollars."

Claudie just stood there on the docks looking at a battered-up old shrimper nudging its way into the pier. It was late in the afternoon; the hot Texas sun was beginning to ease up on us a little, and the mosquitoes were moving in. We'd been watching the fishing boats for an hour or so as they came in from the Gulf of Mexico to unload their catch at the Rockport wharf.

"Remember, Claudie," I said, "we've been here on the waterfront for three days now, and nobody has offered us any kind of a job at all. You know that. The only thing we've been asked to since we broke down here is the crap game on that big yacht tonight. Who worked up that invitation? Me or you?"

"You did," Claudie admitted, "but you didn't have to tell the man on the yacht that you was a friend of the Governor of Texas. He'd have asked you anyhow."

"Well," I said, "I can't figure how I'm going to get even one roll with the dice if I haven't got any money."

"You shoulda thought of that last night before you tried to break all them pinball machines," he answered.

"Listen, Claudie," I went on, "do you know what happened to the man in the Bible with five talents?"

"No. What?"

"I'll tell you," I said. "He put the talents to work, that's what; and in the long run he turned out better than the fellow that just sat on what he had."

Claudie's stubborn look was softening up around the edges.

"Another thing, Claudie," I went on, "you might have noticed how I've been watching the birds in the sky all day."

"What have they got to do with it?" Claudie wanted to know as he kicked against a rotten pile on the docks and watched the splinters fall among some jellyfish that were squooching around there in the water.

"Plenty," I told him. "It's in the sky that changes in a man's luck first begin to show up. You can tell it first in the flight of the birds—the gulls mainly, but now I can feel it in my bones, too. This is my lucky day with the dice."

"Trouble is," Claudie fussed, "you've felt it before and been wrong."

"Tell you what I'll do, Claudie," I said. "You keep four dollars and let me have one. If I'm wrong, the whole five wouldn't last long; but if I'm right, that'll be enough to get me started. I'll give you exactly half of what I win, and your dollar back to boot."

That got him; he fished out an old dollar bill and turned it over to me, and I said, "Thank you, Claudie. Now I want you to come along to the crap game with me. You might bring me even more luck."

When we got down to the private docks about dusk, we found the yacht we were looking for. The name was printed in gold letters on the rear end: *The Pride of Texas, III.* It was the biggest of eight nice long shiny boats tied up there. The lights were already burning inside, and we could see how fine it was fixed up in there: big comfortable chairs and sofas, a radio, and pretty rugs on the floor.

The man that had asked me to the crap game stuck his head through a window and said, "Come aboard, men," and we climbed on the boat's rear end, where it was like a porch with a big awning over it.

I said to the man, "I didn't get your name this morning, Captain."

"Hinder," he said, "but they call me Squatty," and I could see why. He wasn't much over five feet tall, and he was nearly square. His jaw set out a little like a bulldog's, but he had nice, friendly little eyes. He was wearing a blue cap with some gold palms on the front.

"Clint Hightower is the name," I told him, "and this big guy here is my associate, Claudie Hughes. He came to bring me luck." Claudie grinned, and we went inside.

While we waited for the other crapshooters to come along, Squatty told us *The Pride of Texas, III,* belonged to a rich oilman named Easley, who lived in Fort Worth.

Squatty said he was pretty sure that Mr. Easley was still in Canada on a vacation, and that, he explained, was why the crap game was going on in the owner's cabin that night.

Squatty told us he lived on the boat and kept it shipshape all the time. He was real proud of the way it looked, too, and he should have been. All the brass was shining, the windows were clean, and you couldn't see a speck of dust anywhere.

It wasn't long before the other crapshooters came along. I remember one was a San Antonio plumber with one eye; there was a fat shrimp-boat captain that they called Fishmouth; there was a Mexican, too, and a Bible salesman with a peculiar motto tattooed on his arm. It said, "Oh hell, what's the use?" There was another one, too; a very grubby-looking character that came late, lost his money, and left early. His name was "Bird Dog" something. I noticed they all called Squatty "Captain Squatty."

That owner's cabin was something! There were two big bunks, wide almost as beds, a dresser with real drawers and a mirror above it, and bright lights all around. A nice smooth rug covered the floor—perfect for dice—and there was plenty of room to move around on it.

We all got right down on the rug and went to work with the dice. The first time I rolled I shot a half and ran it up to five dollars before I fell off. It looked like my lucky day, but Claudie just sat there on one of the bunks with a droopy look on his face. Then I faded some of the others, as the dice went around, and when it came my turn again, I was down to about where I had started. But I put down a dollar and made four passes before I fell off again. I almost didn't drag in time, but I came out with three dollars.

It went along like this for three or four hours; several times I was up, but not much; other times I got down to nearly even. Along about midnight people started to gape and stretch, and it began to look like the game was about over. The luck had been pretty even all around, except I could tell from the ugly looks they were giving Fishmouth that he had been stashing some money away.

I figured it was time for me to hit a big lick if I had one in my system, so when I got the dice I counted out and put down all I had—eight dollars and a half. They covered it, and I rolled two big, ugly sixes—boxcars. They gathered up my money and yelled, "Go ahead, Clint; you've still got the dice."

I looked at Claudie, and he was sound asleep there on the bunk. "Wake up, Claudie," I said. "I need another dollar." Claudie woke up, but he did not give me another dollar. I whispered to him that I still had the dice and told him it was the unluckiest thing in the world for a man to pass a roll he had coming to him, but Claudie just sat there blinking. Everybody was looking at me, and I had to do something right away. It is at such times as this that a man may have his best ideas. The best one I had was to say, "Gents, my associate here, Claudie, will shoot for me. I've got a little cramp in my right arm." Nobody said no, so I said, "Go ahead, Claudie, and shoot a dollar."

He was still too drowsy to argue, so he put a dollar down. Somebody covered it, and Claudie rolled the dice out on the rug. He made a neat seven.

"Fade it, men," I said. "We shoot the two dollars." The two got to be four, the four got to be eight, and when it was sixteen, Claudie said he wanted to drag it and quit.

"Are you crazy?" I asked him. "I knew I'd seen luck for somebody in the sky today. It wasn't me. It was you. Let it all ride!"

Claudie let it ride and passed again. Next he made two hard points: a nine and then a ten. We had sixty-four dollars won, and they had to dig deep to cover it, but they did. Claudie came out with eight for a point, and on the very next roll he made it the hard way—two fours. His luck was in the light of the moon.

"Eighter," I yelled, "from Decatur, the county seat of Wise," and all I got was some black looks. Then I said, "We let it all ride. A hundred and twenty-eight dollars is begging."

Captain Squatty went through a little door in the front of the owner's cabin and came back with a roll of bills you could have wadded a cannon with. He counted them out, and with what Fishmouth dug out of his jeans, they finally got our pile of money covered. There on the cabin floor was two hundred and fifty-six dollars—half ours and half theirs—and one more pass was all we needed to break up the game. I looked at Claudie, and I could see he was ready. He was lightning ready to strike, and he did! He rolled a great big sparkling eleven, and it got so quiet we could hear the oysters clapping their shells together on the bottom of Rockport Bay.

Captain Squatty spoke up first; he said he was out of cash, but he had a government bond in the bank at Port Lavaca; he wondered if he could put in his I.O.U. to cover the two hundred and fifty-six dollars.

"Sure. Let's have it," I told him, so he wrote it out on the back of an envelope and put it on top of the pile of bills there on the cabin floor. By this time Claudie had a wild, rich look in his eyes, like a trapeze artist taking a bow. He was blowing on the dice and whispering soft words to them.

Captain Squatty was pale as a ghost, and little beads of sweat were cropping out all over his face, but he said, "Go ahead, Claudie, and shoot; but you'd better roll them hard against the bulkhead."

"Against the what?" Claudie asked.

"The door to the head, right there in front of you," the Captain told him. He was almost fussy with Claudie, I thought.

Claudie snorted like a mule colt as he came out with the dice. "Come seven," he said in a hoarse voice. The bones bounced against the door and settled back on the soft rug—a six and an ace.

"Seven it is," I said as I picked up the pile of bills and Captain Squatty's I.O.U. "You can't beat a shooter that is in tune with the sky."

After all the others left, I and Claudie stayed on the boat a little while to speak with Captain Squatty alone about the I.O.U.; but before we could, he went to the icebox and got out three bottles of cold beer. A little color came back to Captain Squatty's face as he swigged the beer, and he licked his lips where they'd been drying up after Claudie's last roll; then he said, "Gents, I am worried about that I.O.U. you've got there."

"We're not, Captain Squatty," I told him. "You can get your I.O.U. back in the morning when you cash the bond."

He swallowed, and his face got the color of the underside of a raw oyster. "Trouble is," he said, "the bond ain't enough to do it. It's only a twenty-five dollar bond."

Claudie began to count on his fingers, and I said, "Captain, I wouldn't worry a minute about the difference. It ain't but two hundred and thirty-one dollars."

He lit a cigarette and took a drag that burnt it about halfway down before he said, "That's what I figure it, but I haven't got the money."

"Think nothing of it, Captain," I said. "I and Claudie can take it out in board and room on this yacht. We'll use this room right here and credit you with ten dollars every day we stay. Before long it'll be paid out."

Captain Squatty said, "But this is the owner's cabin—"

Then I cut in, "And now I wonder if you could pass us another couple of bottles of that nice cold beer. We're going to like it here fine."

The next morning it was cloudy and a little cooler, so I and Claudie slept late. As I was waking up, I thought what a shame and a waste it was for those lovely mattresses not to be used every night of the world. When Captain Squatty came from the little room in the front of the boat where he had his bunk, I told him that I and Claudie had one weakness we hoped he could get used to.

"What's that?" he asked.

"We like our breakfast in bed. The other meals we get up and dress for."

Without a word, Captain Squatty went into the kitchen and started pumping away on the alcohol stove.

"Claudie," I said, "would you like a little coffee first, or with your breakfast?"

"I like coffee first thing, Clint," Claudie answered.

"Hear that, Captain Squatty?" I yelled. "I and Claudie like coffee first; one lump for me and two for him. No cream, please; we like it hot and black."

After breakfast we got dressed, and I sent Claudie up to the garage to get the burnt-out bearing on our car fixed. "See about a new battery, too, Claudie," I told him as he left. "I like for a battery to turn the starter over fast, and you might want a coon or fox tail for the radiator cap. Get it if you like."

While Captain Squatty cleaned up the kitchen and washed the dishes, I went out on the rear end of the boat and stood under the awning to study the sky. Higher up it was solid gray, and dark clouds were rolling in low from the gulf. The gusty air had the feel of worse weather coming, and I called Captain Squatty out to speak with him about it.

"Tell me, Captain," I said, "what do you make of this weather?"

"The glass is low, Clint," he answered.

"The what?" I asked.

"The barometer," he said. "It's below twenty-nine. There's a hurricane somewhere out there in the gulf."

"Don't tell Claudie," I said. "He's always been afraid of storms."

But when Claudie came back to the yacht around noon, he had already heard about it. In fact, he said, the town was pretty full of hurricane talk. The storm was still way down in the Gulf of Mexico, close to Yucatán, they were saying, but it could blow in anywhere along the Gulf coast.

The next day the sky looked a lot better, and there

was almost no wind at all. The talk along the waterfront was that the hurricane was about to peter out down around Mexico somewhere. Captain Squatty said the glass was higher, and told me he liked the feel of the weather. I said, "Couldn't we fire up this here yacht, Captain, and go out there in the bay and catch ourselves a nice mess of fish?"

"I can't do it," he answered.

"I don't know why," I said. "We'll credit you ten dollars on the I.O.U. for every fishing trip we make."

"Mr. Easley's orders are not to move *The Pride of Texas* from this dock except for a hurricane."

"What?" I asked him. "You mean you would go right out in a hurricane?"

"Sure," he said. "In case of a big blow, *The Pride of Texas* would be bashed all to hell against this dock here if I left it tied up. Out in the bay you can anchor a boat and ride it out. That's part of my job; to pull out in the bay if there's a hurricane coming."

The next morning our car was ready to run again, so we left Claudie to watch the boat and the weather while I drove Captain Squatty over to Port Lavaca to get our bond. We cashed it for twenty-five dollars, and I marked up the Captain's payment on the I.O.U. I gave him credit for another twenty dollars to cover the two days we had lived on the boat and another five dollars on account of the Captain's fine cooking. That cut it down to two hundred and six dollars.

On the way back from Port Lavaca, the sun broke through the clouds, and Captain Squatty said he believed that old hurricane must have blown itself out somewhere.

"Don't be too sure," I answered; "the sky don't look too good, and the air don't feel right to me yet."

The Captain grunted and said, "I just think you want to go fishing, Clint, but you wouldn't get me in any more trouble with Mr. Easley than I'm already in, would you?"

"The last thing I'd want to do," I told him, "would be to get you in trouble with Mr. Easley."

The next morning there wasn't a cloud in the sky, the water was clear and blue, and the air felt fresh and clean. A lot of fishing boats shoved off early. I and Claudie got up and dressed for breakfast. Captain Squatty served it to us on the rear end of the boat under the awning. While he was bringing us toothpicks, I credited him with ten more dollars for another day; then, while I was at it, I credited him with another ten dollars for the next day and said, "Captain, from here on we're going to pay in advance every day. See here, this I.O.U. is down now to a hundred and eighty-six dollars."

Captain Squatty only nodded his head and chewed a while on one of his thumbnails.

After breakfast Claudie went to get us some cards and cigars and bring Captain Squatty's mail back from the post office. We smoked and played pitch all morning on the deck while the Captain freshened up the boat. He wiped all the windows with a chamois skin; he swept the boat out from one end to the other and waxed the floors and the wood inside; then he hosed and mopped the outside of the boat and polished all the brass on it. By noon there wasn't anything about the boat that wasn't shining, except our cigarette trays, and Captain Squatty emptied them and wiped the ashes out inside. Then he went to the store where Mr. Easley had a charge account and bought provisions for the day.

When Captain Squatty came back with a big basket full of groceries and things, I asked him how the glass was, and he said, "Rising; the hurricane must be gone."

"That's what I want to speak to you about, Captain," I told him. "I have a feeling about the weather."

"The glass is good enough for me," he answered as he went down to the kitchen with the food. I followed him down there and left Claudie at the card table.

"Captain Hinder." I spoke very serious and firm. "Suppose you got warned that a hurricane was coming and you didn't take *The Pride of Texas, III,* out in the bay to ride it out. Then if a hurricane did come, you'd really be in trouble with Mr. Easley, wouldn't you?"

"I'll say I would," he answered.

"Well," I said, "I'm warning you, Captain; there may be a hurricane. Don't tell Claudie—he's afraid of storms —but I figure we'd better get this yacht out in the bay."

The Captain's jaw tightened up, and his eyes seemed to get smaller, but he didn't say a word.

"Of course," I went on, "we can fish until it comes up. We'll give you an extra sixteen dollars' credit for the trip. That'll cut the I.O.U. down to a hundred and seventy dollars. I'll bet you never thought you'd work it off so fast!"

"I'll do it if you credit me with twenty-six dollars for the trip," he answered, and I took him up in a hurry.

I pulled out the I.O.U., wrote the credit on the back, and showed it to him. "See?" I said. "Paid in advance."

Captain Squatty fired up the motors while Claudie untied us from the docks, and we took off. As we hummed along through the water with the motors singing together, I and Claudie sat back in the deck chairs on the rear end smoking cigars and feeding bread crumbs to the gulls.

"Claudie," I said, "this is the way a man should live every day of his life. A lot of people get themselves so tangled up in work that they never take time to pleasure themselves; they get old before they learn to enjoy the finer things in this great big world. Take Mr. Easley; I'll bet he's up there in Canada bothering himself about taxes and expenses the way the government is spending money all the time."

"I shore feel sorry for Mr. Easley," Claudie said.

When we got out in the middle of Copano Bay, we saw a big bunch of gulls working above the water, close to a little green island, and the Captain said that was a very good sign: the gulls were eating mullet that had been driven to the top of the water by a school of bigger fish. We circled the island and found that the gulls were working above a long, narrow reef where the water was light green and so shallow that the waves broke and splashed in a line along the surface. Captain Hinder said it was an oyster reef where the fishing was sometimes good. He eased the boat across the blue channel that lay betwixt the island and the reef and backed us up to the edge of the green water. He showed Claudie how to throw the anchor over, and we settled down to fish from the rear end of the boat.

Mr. Easley had the fanciest hooks and lines and winding reels I ever saw anywhere. Captain Squatty rigged our tackle and baited our hooks with shrimp, and from the first the fishing was fine. We caught speckled trout, gaff-top catfish, croakers, whiting, and a few little sharks that we threw back. Claudie caught a stingray about the size of a catcher's mitt, and that long stinger whipping around scared Claudie aplenty. I stepped inside the boat and watched Claudie dodge and dance away from the stingray until Captain Squatty got it back in the water.

The sun was slipping behind a big blue cloud bank in the west, and we had the fish box half full when Captain Squatty pointed out that the other fishing boats were leaving.

"We better get back to Rockport, Clint," he said. "It'll take us an hour or more."

"You must be forgetting my warning, Captain Hinder," I said, looking him straight in the eye. He looked down.

"What warning?" Claudie wanted to know.

"Never mind, Claudie," I said. "We'll be on the reef at daylight, and that's when fishing is always best."

The Captain moved the boat away from the edge of the reef into the deeper water, and Claudie threw the anchor in the water. He was getting very handy with it. Captain Squatty fried us a mess of fresh fish in cornmeal, and we had a big supper on the yacht. We washed it down with cold beer. The slap, slap of the water against the sides and the easy sway of the boat back and forth made us sleepy on top of all that food and beer, so we turned in early.

When a man has got himself used to the finer things in life, it jolts him to be roused in the middle of a deep sleep. This thought bruised my mind way in the middle of

the night when I felt the boat take a big sway that batted
my face up against the magazine rack next to my bunk.
I wondered why they couldn't put shock absorbers
around the owner's cabin to save him from such rough
movements of the boat. Then Claudie said, "What the hell
was that we hit?"

Captain Squatty came in and turned on the lights. He
said that a big wave had hit the boat.

"It ain't gonna sink, is it?" Claudie wanted to know
as he got up and started buttoning his shirt.

"No, Claudie," I told him, "it ain't gonna sink," but
I wasn't too sure, since by this time the yacht was rolling
and swaying around more than ever. Then another wave
hit us, and a lot of water flew in the porthole by my bunk
and sprinkled me all over. It tasted salty.

"Captain Hinder," I said, "take a look at the glass."
He did and said it was low and falling.

"Here's your hurricane," I told him. "I'm glad your
dad-gummed glass has found out about it."

Then another wave hit and slammed us all down on
one side of the owner's cabin. It broke loose the pots and
pans below, and you couldn't have matched the racket
they made if you'd beaten a tow sack full of tin cans
against the bottom of a washtub.

We went out on the rear end, and sure enough, it was
blowing hard, and the rain was coming down in sheets.
The awning was flapping around back there, popping in
the wind like a buggy whip, until Captain Squatty finally
got it down and brought it inside. Then the hurricane
really got into high gear.

I've seen the wind blow the wash right off a clothes-
line, and I've seen it blow knotholes out of pine fences,

but that was on dry land. It's worse on the water. The wind was coming in gusts—hard, howling gusts, each one stronger and longer and louder, until I had a feeling deep in my insides that something had to give somewhere; then it would ease up a little before it came again, harder each time than the time before, until *The Pride of Texas, III,* was bobbing around like a dead fly in a churn.

I told Claudie how the yacht was better off where we were, and he tried to believe me, but all he could say was, "I've allus been scared of storms." He began to gulp and swallow like an old tomcat with a fish bone in his throat, and a light skim came over his eyes. He turned green around his mouth and chin like the sticky, gummy green of scums that form on stagnant water. He said he might be a little sick if the wind didn't die down pretty soon. It didn't, but as it went on and on, howling and screaming and whining out there, we got down on the floor of the boat and tried to get used to it—as used to it, that is, as a man can get to that much wind. For a long time nothing happened except a whole lot more of the same thing, and Captain Squatty told us that was about all there'd be to riding out the hurricane. Claudie said he figured that was enough.

When daylight came, it made us feel better to see that we were still where we'd been the night before and not away off somewhere in the middle of a stormy ocean. The little island was right where it had been, and on the other side the waves were still piling up and breaking over the reef, but the water wasn't green any more; it was muddy gray. The gusts were getting easier by the time it was broad-open day, and the rain was pouring almost straight down in between them. In an hour it was dead calm, and Claudie was looking more like himself. He said his liver was still bothering him some, though, and he believed he'd go back to bed.

"I wouldn't," Captain Squatty told him. "It's only half over. The center is passing us now. In a little while we'll have the other half."

He was a man who knew his hurricanes all right, and pretty soon the wind started to blow again—but from the other direction. The yacht swung around on the anchor rope so that the rear end was pointed toward the reef and the island was up ahead. We drank some coffee while we could, and by the time we were through, the hurricane was up to full steam again—and then some. It was raining harder again, and it was raining plumb sideways— that's how hard the wind was blowing.

"Two halves of a hurricane is all they is, ain't they?" Claudie asked once between gusts.

"Certainly, Claudie," I told him. "You got that far in arithmetic, I know."

I don't know what made me glance out in front of the boat as it swung back and forth against the anchor and rolled in the wind, but when I did I saw that something awful had happened to the island. It was a long way off. First I thought it had moved, and then I knew it must have been the yacht moving. Captain Squatty saw it at almost the same time that I did; then we looked back of us, and there were the waves piling up on the reef not fifty feet away. The Captain's little eyes got big, and he said, "Good God, we're dragging anchor!"

"How's that?" Claudie asked.

"We're dragging anchor," he said. "If we pile up on that oyster reef, there won't be a piece of this here yacht big enough to pick your teeth with. Get up on the bow and get ready to raise the anchor. I'll start the motors."

I said, "Who? Me?" as Squatty ran to start the motors and yelled, "Both of you, or it'll be too late."

I looked at Claudie, and Claudie looked ready. We went through Captain Squatty's cubbyhole to the lid that opened on the front of the boat where the anchor rope was tied.

"Go on, Claudie," I said. "I'm coming behind you." He opened the lid, and when he did, a gust of wet wind swept through it and slapped us down on the floor.

"Go ahead," I urged him, "we haven't got much time," and somehow Claudie got his six-and-a-half-foot bulk through the hatch. Then I got out, and we both held onto the little stob on the front of the boat where the anchor rope was tied. We were in a long, high gust that got harder and stronger, until I felt like it would buckle in my eardrums if it got any worse.

Finally, we both got a good hold on the anchor rope. It was tight, and I could feel a quiver in it as the anchor would give and drag a little. I knew that anchor was plowing a furrow there on the bottom of the bay. I looked back once and saw that on one of our long swings against the anchor the rear end of the yacht was nearly even with the breakers on the reef. I figured we might clear it once more; but I figured if we did, it would be the last time. When the wind slacked between gusts, I knew it was our last time to get her away before all hell broke loose on the rear end. By this time the motors were whining and groaning, and we could feel the whole boat throb as they fought against the wind. We eased forward a little, and I and Claudie pulled the rope in and kept it tight, coiling up the slack behind us. Finally, we were right over the anchor, and the rope went straight down from the front of the boat.

"It's now or never, Claudie," I yelled, and we heisted hard on it, but the anchor wouldn't budge.

Claudie reached down and got another hold on the rope; I got one just behind him, and we pulled with everything we had. I could see the big veins standing out on his neck like chicken guts, and it seemed that new muscles rose up around his eyes and ears as he strained to lift it. But the anchor was stuck solid in the bottom of Copano Bay. Captain Squatty was yelling something at us, but it wasn't any use. You couldn't hear anything above the roar of another gust that was building up, and by that time we were pulling as hard as we knew how, just to hold our own. Then we weren't holding our own; we had to pay out some rope or go over with it, and I yelled, "Latch it onto the stob, Claudie, or we'll be back where we started."

Claudie wrapped the anchor rope several times around the stob there, as the gust blew out, and then the boat was pitching and rolling hard against the tight rope. That was what broke the anchor out, and as soon as it gave way, we pulled the rope in until the anchor was out of the water. I could see we were moving forward, away from the reef, with both motors screaming and straining down in the heart of *The Pride of Texas, III.*

In a few minutes we were clear out in the deep water, a hundred yards or more away from the reef, and Captain Squatty was yelling and motioning for us to drop the anchor again. We did, and this time it held. We got back down into the boat and closed the lid as another gust came and grew into full flow. Then Claudie was sick—very sick—but Captain Squatty said it was all right, since he'd cleaned up after seasick people before.

The hurricane petered out almost as fast as it had come. In an hour or so the yacht settled down to an easy roll, and the rain slacked up, but none of this cured Claudie. He was stretched out on the floor of the owner's cabin, blinking his eyes and swallowing.

Around noon we pulled up the anchor and started back. As we left Copano Bay and headed south for Rockport, the water was plumb smooth again. I got out Captain Squatty's I.O.U., and gave him credit for another day's room and board, and showed him how this cut it down to a hundred and fifty dollars.

Then I went down to the owner's cabin to check up on Claudie. He was still on the floor, and he had laid beside him some things out of his pockets—wet matches, cigars, a deck of cards, and a letter. When I saw the letter was addressed to Captain Earl Hinder and postmarked Fort Worth, I said, "Where the hell did you get that, Claudie?"

"At the post office, whenever it was I went to get the mail," he answered and rolled over on his stomach. "I must have forgot to give it to Captain Squatty."

I took it up to the Captain, and as he read it, the muscles started working and quivering around his jawbones. He said, "It's from Mr. Easley. He will be here Tuesday night with two guests."

"Tuesday night was last night," I reminded him.

"Oh, my God!" he yelled. "I'm ruined."

"Ruined?" I said. "What do you mean ruined? Suppose you hadn't taken *The Pride of Texas, III,* out on Tuesday?"

By this time we were getting close to Rockport, and we could see what an awful mess the hurricane had made there. Tree limbs and chunks of wood were floating all around in the water. Four of the other yachts were partly sunk, and the back end of another one was battered and busted plumb out. There wasn't a one of them that wasn't bashed in one way or the other. One yacht, a blue one nearly as big as ours, was turned over and half sunk. There was a hole in the bottom a horse could have walked through.

A crowd of people stood there on the docks looking at all the damage, and as we eased up to the place where *The Pride of Texas, III,* belonged, they all came over toward us. They grabbed our ropes and helped us tie up, and we climbed back onto dry land.

Mr. Easley was there to meet us. He was a nice little gray-haired man, all macked out in sport clothes. He shook hands with Captain Squatty and shook hands with us.

"Any damage to *The Pride of Texas, III?*" he asked.

"None, sir," Captain Squatty said, standing straight and looking Mr. Easley in the eye.

"Hinder," he said, "you are a real skipper. I knew you could smell out a blow if anybody could."

Squatty said, "Mr. Easley, I couldn't have done it without the help of these two fine seamen here, Clint and Claudie."

Mr. Easley beamed on us and took out a big green roll. He peeled off a hundred-dollar bill and handed it to me. He gave Claudie one, too, and said he wondered if it was a big enough tip at that.

"Mr. Easley," I stated, "this is your change," and I gave him fifty dollars out of the roll we'd won in the crap game.

"I don't get it, fellows," he said.

"I and my associate, Claudie, are professional men," I said. "We do not work for tips. A hundred and fifty is all we are due, and that is all we will take. If you feel like it, you might want to give that extra fifty to Captain Squatty, though. He's a fine skipper."

CHARLES EINSTEIN

The New Deal

Rafferty was not the only one losing at the blackjack table, but he had been there the longest. He had been sitting there since ten in the morning; now it was after three, and the waitresses of the Wanderlust, Las Vegas' fanciest and newest hotel, had offered him drinks on the house half-a-dozen times at least. The hotel could well afford buying him a drink to keep him where he was.

But he was not drinking; he was only losing. Losers are, by profession, doubters. This was Las Vegas and the Wanderlust was a brand-new hotel and the dealers' faces were not familiar.

The dealer gave Rafferty two fives. He himself had a six showing. Rafferty had bet forty dollars. He put eight more five-dollar chips on the line to double his bet and took one card face down. He sneaked a look under the corner: a queen. Rafferty had twenty going for him.

The dealer turned up his down card: a seven. Now he had thirteen. Then, an ace. Fourteen. He hit himself again: a two. Sixteen. He hit himself for the last time. A five. Twenty-one. His practiced side-hand motion swept away all of Rafferty's chips.

"I want a new deck," Rafferty said.

"What's that?"

"I said I want a new deck."

"We just broke this one ten minutes ago."

"And it's breaking me. I want a new deck." Rafferty moistened his lips. "And a new dealer."

The two other men who were playing at the table shifted uneasily. They were losing, too, and perhaps secretly they shared Rafferty's spoken sentiments, but they did not want to be drawn in on this.

They were drawn in on it. The dealer drew them in: "Either of you gentlemen want to complain?"

The two men looked down at the green of the table, studying the pattern and the arc inscription: DEALER MUST HIT 16 & STAND ON ALL 17S.

"Don't drag anybody else into it," Rafferty said coldly to the dealer. "It only takes one man to make a complaint. I'm making it."

Out of nowhere, the pit boss appeared. That is not a definitive statement; all pit bosses appear from nowhere. This one was small, cushion-footed, leathery-faced, black-haired. He said to the dealer: "And?"

The dealer nodded toward Rafferty.

"Yes, Mr. Rafferty?" the pit boss said. They knew his name. He had cashed three checks so far today.

"I don't like the cards."

The dealer said, "New deck ten minutes ago."

"Spread 'em," the pit boss said to him.

The dealer spread the deck faceup.

"No," Rafferty said. "You're wasting your time. If I knew what to look for I'd be on your side of the table."

"All right," the pit boss said. "New deck."

"Ah, what for?" Rafferty said. He sighed. "They all

come out of the same box, don't they?"

"Well, then," the pit boss said, "what can we do?"

Rafferty sighed again. "You know," he said, "it'd be terrible for a new place like this to get into trouble. Take away your gambling license, you're dead. You know that, don't you?"

"He asked for a new deck," the dealer said defensively to the pit boss. "You offer him one and now he says 'no.' Maybe he's got a little case of loser's fatigue."

"Oh, I want a new deck," Rafferty said. "But not out of the box backstage. Suppose I told you I had a deck upstairs in my room. Would you play with my cards?"

The pit boss laughed. Then he looked at Rafferty's face and stopped laughing. He said, "You know better than that, Mr. Rafferty. The house supplies the cards."

"I bought them at the cigar counter over there," Rafferty said. "They're the same brand the house uses, aren't they?"

"We didn't see you buy them," the dealer said. "We don't know what you did upstairs."

"Shut up," the pit boss said to him.

"And I don't know what you do downstairs," Rafferty said to the dealer. "All I know is, there's a lot of fives in your deck."

"Nobody's making you play," the dealer said to him. "You don't like the game, nobody's making you sit there."

"I told you, shut up," the pit boss said to him. Four or five people had gathered behind Rafferty and the other players to listen. "Mr. Rafferty, can I talk to you for a minute?"

"We can talk here," Rafferty said. But there was

something in the way the pit boss looked at him. He shrugged and stood up. "All right." He moved away from the playing area, and the pit boss ducked under the rope and joined him.

"How much are you out?" the pit boss said in a low voice.

"I don't know exactly," Rafferty said. "Couple of thousand, maybe. Does it make any difference?"

"Look," the pit boss said, "on the one hand, we run an honest game. On the other hand, we don't want any trouble. We'll do anything reasonable to prove we're on the level."

"You won't play with my cards, will you?"

"I said anything reasonable," the pit boss said.

"But they're the same cards you use. I bought them right over there."

The pit boss shook his head patiently. "Nobody would call that reasonable, Mr. Rafferty. The dealer had it right. Nobody knows you bought them here. And nobody knows how long ago it was. If you were to buy a deck right now and we played them fresh, that would be another thing."

"All right," Rafferty said.

"I beg your pardon?"

"I said all right. They're your terms. I accept."

"I don't understand."

"I will walk with you this minute to the cigar counter," Rafferty said, "and I will buy a deck of cards, and then we will walk back to the table and play blackjack with those cards."

"Ah, Mr. Rafferty," the pit boss said. "Don't be ridiculous."

"Ridiculous?" Rafferty's voice went up and the other man looked uncertainly around. "All I've just done is agree to something you yourself proposed."

"But it isn't worked that way," the pit boss said. "Suppose everybody came in wanting to play with his own cards or his own dice. We'd have to make a career out of checking up on people."

"I'm not everybody," Rafferty said. "You proposed something, and the minute I agree, you change your mind. You say the cards over here are the same as the cards over there. So I'm not playing with my cards. I'm playing with your cards."

"Then what difference does it make?"

"The difference is that you said they were the same cards; I didn't. I'd like to see if the cards you sell over the counter to the public are the same as the ones you play with. Call it an experiment."

Rafferty grinned coldly, then suddenly turned and walked the few steps to the cigar counter. The pit boss followed him. He said, "What are you going to do?"

"Just buy a deck of cards," Rafferty said. He nodded at the girl behind the counter. "Cards?"

"A dollar, sir," the girl said and slid a deck across the glass top of the counter.

Rafferty set a silver dollar on the counter. He turned and held out the deck to the pit boss. "Here," he said. "You hold them. Just to make sure I'm not cheating."

The pit boss took the deck and stared at him. "You figure we're sensitive, so you're trying to make trouble, aren't you?"

"No," Rafferty said. "You're the one who's looking for trouble. All I'm looking for is an even shake. To repeat, all I'm doing is taking up your offer."

The pit boss swallowed. "Suppose you have a run of luck."

"Then I have a run of luck."

"Then you can go around saying this proves we're crooked."

"If you're not, you don't have anything to worry about."

"And if you keep on losing? What then? Do you hang it on the dealer?"

"There'll be people watching," Rafferty said. "I'm not worried about card tricks. Not this time around."

"You could still sit there and complain and cause us more trouble."

"Not really," Rafferty said. "A deck lasts about an hour in play, doesn't it? And if I went back to the counter for another deck, that *would* be unreasonable, wouldn't it? No, I've made my play. I'm truly interested in whether you think it's asking too much."

The pit boss looked down at his shoes. "This doesn't prove a thing, you know. If we were dishonest, the easiest thing in the world now would be to rig it so you win."

"I'd be delighted," Rafferty said. "Except that doing that would make you look really bad."

"Then what do you want?"

"A fresh start with a new deck of cards."

"Mr. Rafferty," the pit boss said, "I . . ." He paused. "All right. You've got an hour."

"Thank you," Rafferty said, and they went back to the table. A new dealer was called over. The pit boss himself broke the seal and spread the cards.

Rafferty played for an hour, while the pit boss and

an ever-growing crowd of onlookers watched.

At the end of the hour, Rafferty stood up. He had won eighteen thousand dollars.

"Are you satisfied?" the pit boss said to him.

"Not quite," Rafferty said smoothly. "I'm out a dollar."

"You're out a . . . ?"

"For the cards."

"I see," the pit boss said. His voice struggled for control. "But that's not a dollar, Mr. Rafferty, because the cards at this point aren't worth a dollar anymore. They're used. So here are the cards, Mr. Rafferty, and you sell them for what you can get for them. And I'm not supposed to say this, but I'm going to say it anyway— don't come back here, Mr. Rafferty. It costs us too much to prove to you we're honest, and I'm not talking just about money. We like people who take our word for it, because we *are* honest, and we have their good will and the only way we can stay in business is to stay honest and settle for the house edge. You understand, Mr. Rafferty?"

"Perfectly," Rafferty said. "You don't have to worry about me coming back. It's unlikely I'd ever have another run like this one."

He nodded, fended his way through the group of onlookers, and went to the elevators and up to his room. When he got there, he found there was a young woman seated at the writing table. She had an extremely thin artist's pen in her hand, and she was marking the backs of a new deck of cards. The package the cards came in had been opened so that the seal was left unbroken.

"Hi," she said to Rafferty. "How'd you do?" She was

the girl who had been behind the cigar counter downstairs.

"Fifteen net," Rafferty said, "and I told you not to
be seen up here. And lay off the cards for now. Wait till
we get to Reno."

ROBERT TRAVER

The Great Uranium Hoax

One beautiful October day I was sitting disconsolately in my office way up on the second floor of the local Woolworth tower working on a trial brief. I confess an acute allergy to the preparation of trial briefs. I paused and sighed and wished I were out partridge hunting. Then Donna came in and interrupted my reverie.

"Walter Holbrook's outside," she said. "In person— not a movie."

I sat up. Walter Holbrook was the big wheel of the Peninsula Land and Timber Company, one of the biggest owners of mining and timber lands in the entire Lake Superior district. What could *he* possibly want with the local D.A.? Maybe, I thought, his company was at last coming to its senses and was about to retain me. I grew as fluttery and expectant as a debutante facing her first stag line.

"If he's sober, Donna, show him in," I said. Donna and I are always full of little private jokes. Our days are one dizzy round of gaiety and fun.

Mr. Holbrook was an efficient operator. He wasted no time. "Mr. Traver," he said, briefly pumping my hand

and sitting across the desk from me, "our company has a problem that our attorneys advise us may require the attention of your office."

"Oh, yes," I answered rather inanely, ruefully admiring the swift smoothness with which he had got across the idea that he was consulting me purely in my capacity as D.A. "What is your problem?"

As Walter Holbrook paused to light a cigarette, I studied him with considerable interest. I had never moved extensively in the rarefied atmosphere inhabited by big-business executives, and this was my first traffic with one as D.A. I was rather curious to observe a member of the species at work. When Walter Holbrook finally went on speaking, I quickly found myself recognizing the type: brisk, dominant, self-assured, persuasive—the kind heavily favored by the dream merchants of Hollywood. Yes, here was a man who knew precisely what he wanted to say—and said it like a Scotchman dictating a cablegram. A prepaid cablegram, I should perhaps add, to labor my little joke.

"Ah," he breathed, exhaling a thin cloud of cigarette smoke. "Well—" He seemed to be mentally assuming the role I was giving him. "It's this way, Mr. Traver," he began. "It all started last month. Stranger called at our main local office. Man by the name of Robbins—Kurt Robbins. Insisted on seeing me. Refused to state his business to the receptionist. Accordingly refused to see him." He shrugged. "Got to do it, you know. All manner of creeps and crackpots call on me every day. Couldn't ever get anything done otherwise."

"Yes," I said, recalling that *he* had not stated *his*

business to Donna. (But then I also recalled that D.A.s were elected to sit there and take it.) "Then what happened?"

Walter Holbrook resumed the composition of his cablegram. "The next day he was back. Same result. Then he left and telephoned from a pay station. Mysterious as hell. Told my secretary that he had to see me. Matter of the utmost importance to my company. Something about a mineral discovery. Had to discuss it on the highest local level. Said I would really appreciate the necessity for secrecy and strict confidence when I talked with him."

"You saw him?" I said, pondering the qualities—and lack of them—that apparently made up a successful executive.

He smiled briefly. "Yes," he said. "Guess my curiosity got the best of me. That phrase 'mineral discovery' threw me, I guess. He was back at my office in five minutes. Ellen—that's my secretary—showed him in. He was a tall, lean, outdoor-type sort of man of about thirty-eight to forty. Kind of resembled what's-his-name—him—that strong, silent, hard-riding Western movie actor, I forget his name. Anyway, he introduced himself.

" 'My name's Kurt Robbins,' he said. 'I'm a prospector. I've prospected everywhere for everything, I guess. Practically all over the world. This past summer I've been doing a little prospecting in this Lake Superior area. Very interesting country.' Then he glanced over his shoulder. 'May I close your office door?'

" 'As you wish,' I said, as he went and stealthily shut my door. I half expected him to suddenly wheel on me with an old six-shooter—the kind with the cadaver score nicked on the handle. 'But just how do your interesting international prospecting activities affect our company?' I sparred.

" 'I'll try to show you,' he said. He was carrying a bulging and battered leather case—more like an old saddlebag. He must have lugged it along on his first prospecting trip. He now opened it and produced not a six-shooter but several rock samples—all about the size of my fist—and plumped them down on my desk blotter. 'These grab samples came from land owned by your company,' he announced, giving me one of those piercing, faraway, open-range looks of his. 'Beautiful, aren't they?'

" 'What are they?' I asked Robbins, growing a trifle impatient with his juvenile air of mystery. 'The damned stuff looks like a poor grade of coal to me. We're exclusively in the business of handling timber and iron and copper mining rights, in case you didn't know.'

"He laughed coolly and said, 'You're also primarily in the business of making money, Mr. Holbrook. If the stuff in these samples is what I think it is, perhaps both of us can make a bundle of money—that is, if the idea doesn't cause you excessive pain.' [The trapped and listening D.A. was beginning to develop a sneaking regard for Prospector Robbins. Walter Holbrook went on with his story.]

" 'What do you think it is?' I asked Robbins.

" 'Well, I haven't run an assay on it yet,' Robbins said, 'but from the way it kicks hell out of my Geiger counter, I know that these rock samples are pieces of a highly radioactive mineral. I'm sure of that. However, if it's radioactive thorium, it's commercially valueless, as even a slave to iron and copper doubtless knows.' He was quite a sarcastic dude, you see. 'But if it's uranium—' He paused and shrugged.

" 'But whichever it is, thorium or uranium, it would still be on *our* land,' I told Robbins, thinking it was time to remind him of this minor detail.

" 'Precisely. That's why I came to see you,' he replied dryly. 'If it's uranium, I want to make a deal with your company.'

" 'What's your proposition?' I asked.

" 'Fifty percent of the net profit,' he answered, as cool as a cucumber. He even smiled. Yes, Mr. Traver, this —this common trespasser sat there in my office, never batting an eye—and demanded half of the profits on our own stuff." Walter Holbrook paused and shook his head in wonder. He finally composed himself, following the contemplation of such heresy, and went on with his story. "At that point I also told him that I did not believe my company would agree to pay such a high percentage for the mining of its own minerals from its own land. 'In fact,' I told him, 'I'm not sure that they will be willing to make any "deal," as you call it, in any event.'

"Here Robbins rose abruptly, still smiling, ready to leave. 'Well, will you at least put it up to your company?' he said. Then he added, with that mocking smile of his: 'Only Uncle Joe and his Russian rangers would be apt to reward you for flatly turning down a possible new American uranium mine. Will you put my proposition up to your company's top brass, Mr. Holbrook?'

" 'Even that is a question,' I frankly answered him. 'You admit you're not sure yourself what the stuff is. Before I can be bothering our head office at Wilmington with a slim prospect like this, I'll have to know that it's uranium; and, equally important, that it is of sufficiently high grade and quantity to be worth mining. The only way we can determine this last point is for you to tell me where on our land you found the stuff—so that our consulting geologist and his staff can go out and look it over. How about it?'

"Robbins walked to my office door and put his hand on the knob and turned to me, smiling. 'Relax, my generous friend. *That* will come after you boys have signed on the dotted line—fifty percent.'

" 'Suppose—just suppose, of course—that we get a little greedy and go out and find it ourselves—without you?' I suggested, testing him out a little.

"He continued to smile—a lofty, superior sort of smirk. 'Greed is of course every man's privilege,' he said. 'And I have lived long enough never to discount its possible presence in others. But I'll take a chance on that. I guess I like the look in your steady little eyes. And after all, you've only got about one—or is it two?—hundred thousand odd acres of land to comb over. My guess is that in about, say, thirty years your geologist might stumble onto it. Both you and I would be a little on the ripe side by then.' Then he opened my door, ready to leave.

" 'Aren't you going to take your precious samples?' I said, pointing to the rocks on my desk. I really had no intention of giving them up. 'Or perhaps I should keep them, since you admit that you trespassed on our land to get them.'

"He quickly closed the door and stood facing me. 'You're welcome to the samples, Mr. Holbrook. Take them with the blessings of the copyright infringer.

There're a lot more where they came from. Really quite an unusual outcrop. As for our "deal," as you seem not to like to call it, I'll be back in two weeks for my answer. Right now I must take a little business flight to New York. Remember, fifty percent is my proposition. No less. If the stuff's thorium, I apologize for wasting your time —and for trespassing on your property. In the meantime, you will of course understand that it is to our mutual advantage to keep this discovery in the utmost confidence. But, as I have said, I trust you to keep my secret. Good day, sir'—and he was gone."

Walter Holbrook paused and lit another cigarette. First he carefully rolled it and tapped it and fitted it into a long amber holder. During this elaborate ritual I packed and lit my pipe, glanced furtively at my watch, and saw my evening's partridge hunt flying out the window. But at least I'd still try for it.

"Did he ever come back?" I gently prodded.

"In two weeks to the hour he was back at our office," Walter Holbrook went on. " 'Well,' he said after he had again carefully closed my door, shook my hand, and sat down, 'well, do I get the fifty percent?'

"I told him that our consulting geologist had run an assay of his samples locally and that the stuff indeed showed some small uranium content, all right; that I'd communicated this fact to the Wilmington office and that it had somewhat reluctantly agreed to enter into a preliminary contract to pay him ten percent of the net, providing that the extent of the deposit, in our sole judgment, warranted mining it. 'We're only doing it because the country needs the uranium,' I added."

"What was his reaction to that?" I said, deciding to

put up a last fight for my partridge hunt.

"As I told you, this Robbins was a cool one. 'Mr. Holbrook,' he said, 'I assure you it's a tremendous comfort to know I'm dealing with such blazing patriots.' He smiled and even chuckled a little over his joke. Then he took a letter from his pocket and tossed it over to me. 'Read that and weep,' he said. It was addressed to him at a New York hotel—dated within the week—from a reputable New York assay laboratory reporting that the mineral samples he had recently left with them contained pitchblende assaying seventy-eight percent U_3O_8. That's uranium oxide, Mr. Traver. You see, pitchblende is the richest known ore of uranium. 'There's your "some small uranium content," ' Robbins said, smiling cynically at me. 'Perhaps you consulted a soothsayer about my samples rather than your assayer.' "

An excited D.A. interrupted at this point. "Seventy-eight per cent," I murmured. I tried vaguely to recall my high-school chemistry. The effort was not fruitful. "Is that good?"

"*Good!*" Walter Holbrook said, rolling his eyes up in his head. "Good Lord, son—it rivals the richest-known uranium ores in the world—the Katanga region in the Belgian Congo and the fabulous El Dorado in Canada. Uncle Joe Stalin'd give his—his favorite curved pipe to lay his peace-loving hands on stuff half as hot."

It was my turn to do some eye rolling. "You—you mean, Mr. Holbrook, we've got deposits of rich uranium ore like that—right here in this county?" The partridge were forgotten. Instead, my mind buzzed and sang with the sweet whine of Geiger counters.

"I don't know whether or not it's in this county.

That's the trouble. You see, we own scattered tracts of land all over this blessed state—not to mention Minnesota and Wisconsin—assuming that the damned stuff ever came from our land."

"Then you didn't learn where it came from? You and Robbins didn't make any deal?" I asked.

"Hell, no," Walter Holbrook answered. "My smiling friend, Robbins, calmly picked up his assay letter and walked to the door. He turned and spoke. 'Sorry we can't make a deal on my terms. Get in touch with me when you change your mind—providing I haven't changed mine. It's been nice knowing you. And in the meantime I hope you'll continue to so splendidly keep the secret I told you in strict confidence.'

" 'Thanks,' I said, and I hope just as sarcastically.

"Then Robbins paused, his hand on the door knob, and slyly added: 'I know that you're not apt to forget my terms, Holbrook, because I'm fully aware that you've recorded on wire our conversations of two weeks ago and again today. Or was it on tape? Tape generally has higher fidelity. And all of us appreciate a high degree of fidelity, don't we, Mr. Holbrook?' Then he *winked* at me. 'But you really shouldn't lean so far over your hidden microphone. It gives the thing away, you know, and also causes annoying distortion and voice blast. Good day, sir.' Then he and his mocking smile disappeared."

"Was he right, Mr. Holbrook?" I asked, smiling a little myself. "I mean about the hidden recorder?"

Walter Holbrook flushed, grimaced, and took the bit in his teeth. It appeared hard for him to be divulging such, should I say, intimate company strategy to a mere backwoods district attorney. "Yes, damn it," he answered, swallowing hard. "We have to deal with all sorts of people, you know, and sometimes on damned important deals—transactions, I mean. A verbatim recording often avoids misunderstandings later on, you know."

"Of course," I said, reflecting on how pleasant it was that the expanding marvels of science had kept so nicely abreast of the expanding distrust of men, one for the other.

"But mainly I keep a recorder for night dictation," he added, rather lamely and belatedly, I thought. "At any rate, our attorneys and I have played this damned recording over so often that I know it by heart. And then," he continued more brightly, "it should help a lot in court when we press the criminal prosecution against Robbins. Don't you think so?"

I heaved a sigh and decided that it was time for the D.A. to do a little talking. "Mr. Holbrook," I began. I explained to him that in my opinion he had so far failed to even remotely make out any criminal case against Robbins or anyone else; that all he had shown was that Robbins had claimed to have discovered some valuable minerals on the company's land; that he had tried to make a *transaction* regarding it, and having failed, had simply gone about his affairs.

"However eccentric or mysterious Robbins' conduct may have been," I went on, "he does not appear to have committed any crime. No one can compel him to show or prove where he found the uranium. And his conduct does not strike me as being particularly unnatural or suspicious. Try putting yourself in his place and him in yours. Would you honestly have shown *him* where you found the stuff before you—pardon me—had made a deal?"

Walter Holbrook grinned, almost boyishly, I thought. "No," he slowly admitted, tamping a new cigarette. "No, I guess not." The high-powered, staccato-talking executive was breaking down a little, relaxing a trifle. He might not, I thought, really be such a bad companion on a fishing trip.

"Perhaps," I gently suggested, "there are some things you haven't yet told me—things that might be relevant to this most interesting story." I felt in my bones that there were. Walter Holbrook and his battery of suave Eastern lawyers were too smart to have let me in on this much without there being more. "Isn't there something else?" I repeated. I was not wrong.

"Yes," Walter Holbrook said. "I hadn't quite finished. Was just taking a little breather. Been doing a lot of talking today." He sighed. "Damn that man Robbins! Wish I'd never laid eyes on him."

"I'm sorry if I interrupted you," I said. "Now suppose you proceed in your own words and tell me *all* the story, right to the end. I'll fire any necessary questions as you go along."

This, then, is the rest of the story that Walter Holbrook told me—and not, I may add, without considerable personal embarrassment—concerning the strange case of Kurt Robbins, prospector.

The moment Robbins had left Holbrook's office, following his first visit when he had left the uranium samples, apparently quite a scamper had taken place. Walter Holbrook had hastily summoned the company's chief consulting geologist and told him the startling story, played over for him the tape recording—indeed it *was* tape—and showed him the samples. The geologist had been impressed. They had then air-mailed several of the samples to the same "Robbins" laboratory in New York, and the geologist had assayed the rest locally. Results: Contents 77 and 79 percent U_3O_8, respectively.

They had then rounded up virtually every geologist they could beg, borrow, or steal—not to mention a flock of hurriedly mustered young student geologists from a neighboring mining college—and armed them with Geiger counters, and even a few new Canadian scintillometers, and sent them swarming out over the company's far-flung landholdings in search of Robbins' uranium. All this ostensibly, Walter Holbrook carefully explained, the result of a suddenly conceived program on the part of the company to patriotically determine if it had uranium on its lands.

"Did you find any?" I asked Walter Holbrook.

"Hell, no," he answered glumly. "A few low-grade whispers but nothing like *his* stuff. And we've still got 'em out prowling all over the damned state. Costing us thousands of dollars." He shrugged. "But what are we going to do? The stuff runs nearly eighty percent. We've simply got to find it—providing it's there."

"This is all very interesting, Mr. Holbrook, but I'm still afraid there's no provable crime," I said, refilling my pipe. "There must be something more you've neglected to mention." My complainant seemed oddly reluctant to tell me something important about his case. "Let's have it, Mr. Holbrook," I said quietly.

Walter Holbrook suddenly grasped hard at his side of the top of my desk, with both hands, fingers up, and sat staring at me. His knuckles whitened under the pressure. "Yes," he said slowly, "unfortunately there is more to tell. A hell of a lot more." He was flushing deeply. "I'll tell you. You see, when I learned that there appeared to be such a rich uranium deposit on our company's lands, I felt obliged to confide this important knowledge to my superiors in Wilmington. Sense of company duty, you know. In fact, I had to, to let them pass on his proposed 'deal.' And who was this Robbins to be saddling me with his unsought confidences?"

"Yes," I said, beginning to see daylight. "And what else? There must be something else."

"Well, we felt that such valuable new mineral discoveries on our lands would in the normal course naturally increase the value of our company's stock when the news broke." He hesitated and then took the plunge. "We also felt that—er—we might just as well profit, so to speak, from our inside knowledge by, in the meantime, sort of naturally enlarging our own personal holdings of company stock." Ah, the real story was finally coming out. Walter Holbrook's face had assumed the radiant hue of a red-brick schoolhouse.

"Naturally," I agreed, embarrassed at witnessing his embarrassment, suddenly studying the elaborate whirls and flourishes on my law-school diploma hanging on the far wall. "Then what happened?"

"So we—well, we went into the market and tried to buy up all the company stock we could lay our hands on. The word got out, as these things do, that *something* was cooking—they knew not what—and the more stock we bought up, the higher the price went." He paused and sighed. "It was then that we learned that a certain individual had beaten us to the punch. Singlehanded, he'd damned near cornered all the readily available stock on the market."

"And the name of this certain individual?" I asked, knowing.

"Kurt Robbins, of course," he replied harshly. "Always Robbins, Robbins, Robbins." He fumbled and lit a cigarette, ignoring his amber holder.

"Then what?" I said, wondering how this battle of the foxes would turn out.

"Though the news of the supposed uranium strike on our lands didn't break publicly—it hasn't to this day, as a matter of fact—naturally, with all the inevitable rumors of our heavy prospecting for uranium and the unusual demand and market activity over our stock, the price kept going up and up. And we—meaning me, our chief consulting geologist, a few cronies, yes, even my poor wife, and our associates in Wilmington—kept right on buying it. And paying, I may add, right through the nose. Knowing that Robbins was loaded only spurred us on. We were sure, then, that he had found the uranium on our land." He stopped and sighed deeply. "Then it happened."

"Yes?" I said.

"Kurt Robbins suddenly unloaded all of his holdings of our stock—at top prices. It started the very next day after he last left my office. Naturally, the damned stock went down immediately. As a matter of fact, even today it's a few points lower than when Robbins first saw me. He must have made a fortune. And our losses are way up in the thousands. I haven't even tried to count 'em." Walter Holbrook, the harried executive, was perspiring freely now. "And naturally, I'm in a devil of a hole with my superiors back in Wilmington—not to even *mention* my wife. I really don't know which way to turn. That's why I've come to you. Our Wilmington attorneys felt I should lay all the facts before you."

Walter Holbrook sighed, lit a new cigarette from his last one, and gloomily crushed out the butt in the growing mound in my ash tray. "What can be done?" he said.

I lit my pipe, sparring for time. I was already pretty well convinced what it was I had to tell him, but I wanted to make sure. I also thought I might at least let the poor man down easy. He'd had a pretty rough day of it. So I told him I wanted time to clarify my thinking about the situation and possibly to look up some law. I arranged to meet him at my office the next morning. For, uranium or no uranium, I was surely going partridge hunting the next afternoon. Perhaps, I thought, I'd even take along a battery of Geiger counters, too.

A rumpled, red-eyed, and unshaven Walter Holbrook was at my office the next morning promptly at nine. As we shook hands, I thought I detected the faint smell of whisky; but as I'd consumed a few "onions" myself the night before, perhaps I was mistaken.

"What's the verdict?" he asked, slumping into his chair across from me. His fingers were stained from smoking cigarettes. "Insomnia—couldn't sleep." He laughed briefly and without mirth. "My wife also abetted the insomnia," he wryly added.

Of all the victims of possible fraud a public prosecutor is ever obliged to listen to, none is at once more distasteful or more pathetic than one who is the victim of his own greed and cupidity. So, in as kindly a manner as I could manage, I explained to Mr. Holbrook that as matters then stood, he had not in my opinion produced any proof that Kurt Robbins had defrauded him, his company, or anyone, or that he had been guilty of committing any other criminal offense.

"Assuming that Robbins did find valuable uranium deposits on your land," I went on, "—which is something he need not prove and which you people can scarcely ever be able to finally disprove—wasn't it entirely natural and businesslike that he should act to protect his discovery by buying up your company's stock? All he needed to be able to do that was money. Wouldn't you have done the same thing? In fact, he could point to his heavy stock purchases as rather persuasive evidence that he *did* discover uranium on your land. Also, when you flatly turned down his proposition, wasn't it equally natural—or at least legal— for him to take his profit and run?"

"Perhaps," Walter Holbrook grudgingly admitted, shifting uneasily in his chair.

The relentless D.A. closed in. "After all, it was *you* men who tried to short-circuit Robbins by finding his uranium without him," I pressed on. "To call a spade a spade, weren't you trying to freeze him out of his discovery? Weren't you men trying to profit, and exclusively, from important information he had confided to you? Let's face it. These are all questions any competent defense attorney would throw at you, and throw at you hard, if Robbins were ever prosecuted."

"Oh, Lord," Walter Holbrook said, mopping his brow.

"If I may say so, Mr. Holbrook, your main complaint

seems to be that he outsmarted you at your own game."
I paused to let this sink in. "As a matter of fact, Robbins
seems rather to have banked shrewdly on your doing just
what you did. Quite a plan, quite a plan. . . . If this is a
fraud, it is one of the most subtle and airtight ones I have
ever seen or heard of. And I've run into a few."

"But look at the *money* we've lost!" Walter Holbrook said, hunching his shoulders and spreading out
both hands, palms up, in a most unexecutivelike gesture.

I quickly slammed the door on that. "Your losses
strike me as being largely paper losses. I assume that
you people still have your stock. Surely you have
enough faith in the future of your own company to
hang on and weather the storm. Or would you men
prefer to publicly testify in effect that you lack this
faith? Your stock might really nosedive if you did such
a thing." I paused. "But perhaps I'd better not be suggesting things that are more properly matters of company policy—your own resourceful staff of lawyers is
fully capable of that." (I could not resist this little professional shaft.) "After all, you came here with a criminal complaint to lay before me as D.A., so I'll try to
stick to analyzing that."

Walter Holbrook slumped lower in his chair. It was
rough, giving it to him that way, but it had to be done.
I felt like a gruff old country doctor removing a mustard
plaster from the chest of a quaking child. It was easier
in the long run if you just ripped it off.

"Generally speaking, Mr. Holbrook, an indictable
criminal fraud requires the combined presence of three
elements: an actual fraud or misrepresentation of an ex-
isting fact or situation; a reliance on this fraud by the

victim to his injury; and an enrichment of the suspected villain as a natural result of his fraud." I guess I am something of a pedagogue at heart. I was enjoying my little lecture on the subject of fraud. But Walter Holbrook was not sharing it.

"You mean," he said huskily, "I don't make out a criminal case because we can't prove the first and third elements, regardless of our losses?"

"You should have been a lawyer, Mr. Holbrook," I said, grading him an A. "You've put your finger on the two basic weaknesses of your case. Especially the first."

"Humph," he grunted. "I wasn't such a hot lawyer with that snake Robbins. I flunked that test."

"Perhaps you met a better lawyer," I ventured.

"Perhaps!" he flared. "You're damned right I did!"

"The only possible way I can see to begin to hold Robbins for fraud is to show that his uranium samples came from somewhere else," I continued. "But that is something which, under our American law, the People would first have to prove—not something that Robbins would first have to disprove. It might even help some, as a starter, if you could show he'd ever worked at or visited one of the big Canadian or African uranium mines; or, better yet, that his hot uranium samples came from one of them."

Walter Holbrook nodded glumly. "Our attorneys warned me about this proof business. But they made me come here, anyway. No, we can't prove where the lousy stuff came from. Like peroxide blondes, pitchblende is pitchblende, wherever you find it. As I've already suggested, all of it looks like a damned poor grade of coal. And we've already worked the African and Canadian angles. Even sent his leering, smiling picture around. Nobody ever saw him before. The guy must've crept out at night from under a damp plank." He brightened a little and sat up. "But couldn't our Atomic Energy Commission or Congress or *someone* force him to tell them where he got his damned uranium? God, our country needs the stuff, man!"

"Not under any present law or procedure in this country of which I am aware," I said. "And in any event, that would be a matter for the federal authorities, not me." I paused, feeling a wave of pity for the man. "And may I say this, Mr. Holbrook," I went on, "before you carry your complaint any further, might you not pause and reflect how you and your Wilmington associates would appear to the public, the business world, your competitors—not to even mention your own small stockholders—if you men were to take the witness stand and testify to such a story as you have told me?" I paused. "I think you'll agree that certain aspects of it would scarcely tend to glorify the loftiest aspirations of our free-enterprise system."

I had plunged the needle pretty far. He nodded his head glumly. "I wish I had a stiff drink," he said.

"But I've got an idea," I went on. "You might bury your pride and try meeting Robbins' own terms—that's if you know where he is. *Give* him his fifty percent. If he now refuses to accept, you might possibly have the opening wedge of a fraud case—though I doubt it. And if he should accept, then—when he showed you the uranium deposit and the big word got headlined around the country, as these things do—this should pull your stock out of its slump, and you, Robbins, and everyone should live happily ever after. Perhaps even your wife might rally. Remember, the stock went up before on a mere market hunch that something was cooking."

Walter Holbrook shook his head dolefully. "Hell, we've tried that. Guess I forgot to tell you—we've had detectives trailing Robbins ever since his last visit. He now calls 'em by their first names and invites them to drink with him. And I'm beginning to suspect they're accepting. And guess where the great Robbins is holed up? Over in Paris, shacked up with some foreign movie actress, the lucky devil, wading up to his hips in vintage champagnes—and all on our dough! Two days ago we cabled our acceptance of his original terms."

"Did he answer?"

"Answer!" Walter Holbrook shouted, suddenly pounding my desk with his fist. "He cabled back collect. This was his answer: 'Dear Holbrook: We're in bed. Wish you were here. This place is expensive, so my terms have jumped to seventy-five percent. Next time higher. Confidentially yours, Robbins.' " Walter Holbrook paused. "It —it's diabolical. The man is stark, raving mad."

"Like a fox," I said. "But I'm afraid that as things stand there's nothing my office can do about it. I'm sorry."

Walter Holbrook slumped back in his chair, a beaten man. "I'm in hot water from here clean to Wilmington." He wagged his head. "You're sure you've got nothing more to suggest?"

I was sorry to see any man in such a jam. "Well," I smiled, "possibly two things. Both are long shots."

"Name 'em," Walter Holbrook muttered.

"Keep looking for Robbins' uranium till you find it."

"And if I don't?"

"Then—heaven help you—turn author and write a bang-up mystery movie scenario for Hollywood."

"Movie scenario!" he said, bridling. "About what?"

"About your strange adventures with Prospector Robbins. You've already got most of the dialogue on your tape recorder. And I've already got a title for you: *The Great Uranium Hoax.*" I reached into my phone stand and quickly dredged up a bottle and a glass. "But before you embark upon the hideous travail of authorship, I suggest that you try a slug of this cooking whisky—for years the favorite of many peasants of extinction. You asked for it."

Walter Holbrook reddened and glared hard at me for several moments. Then he broke into a broad grin. With a shaking hand he poured himself a stiff drink. He raised his glass aloft and smiled at me gamely.

"Skoal, pal," he said. "I don't like your diagnosis, but I like your medicine. Here's uranium in your eye."

"Drink hearty, chum," I replied, vowing that someday we two really *would* go fishing.

The Wicked Cousin

When Simon Templar arrived in Los Angeles, there was a leaden ceiling of cloud over the sky and a cool wind blowing. A few drops of unenthusiastic rain moistened the pavements and speckled the shoulders of his coat. The porter who was loading his bags into a taxi assured him that it was most unusual weather, and he felt instantly at home.

Later on, comfortably stretched out on a divan in the sitting room of his suite at the hotel in Hollywood upon which he had chosen to confer the somewhat debatable honor of his tenancy, with a highball at his elbow and a freshly lighted cigarette smoldering contentedly between his lips, he turned the pages of the address book on his knee and considered what his next steps should be to improve that first feeling of a welcome return.

He was not there on business. To be quite accurate, none of the stages of the last few months of carefree wandering which had just completed their vague object of leading him across America from coast to coast had been undertaken with a view to business. If business had materialized on more than one occasion, it was because there was something about Simon Templar which attracted adventure by the same kind of mysterious but inescapable cosmic law which compels a magnet to attract steel or a politician to attract attention; and if much of that business was not looked upon favorably by the Law—or would not have been favorably looked upon if the Law had known all that there was to know about it —this was because Simon Templar's business had an unfortunate habit of falling into categories which gave many people good reason to wonder what right he had to the nickname of the Saint by which he was far more widely known than he was by his baptismal titles. It is true that these buccaneering raids of his which had earned him the subtitle of "The Robin Hood of Modern Crime" were invariably undertaken against the property, and occasionally the persons, of citizens who by no stretch of the imagination could have been called desirable; but the Law took no official cognizance of such small details. The Law, in the Saint's opinion, was a stodgy and elephantine institution which was chiefly justified in its existence by the pleasantly musical explosive noises which it made when he broke it.

Certainly he was not thinking of business. In Hollywood he had many genuine friends, few of whom gave much consideration to the sensational legends that were associated with his name in less unsophisticated circles, and his only immediate problem was to which one of them he should first break the dazzling news of his arrival. He paused at one name after another, recalling its personality: movie executives, directors, writers, actors and actresses, both great and small, and a certain number of ordinary human beings. He wanted—what did he want? A touch of excitement, preferably feminine, beauty, a little of the glamour and gay unreality with which the very name of Hollywood is inseparably linked in imagination if not in fact. He wanted some of these things very much. His last stop had been made in the state of Utah.

There was a girl called Jacqueline Laine whom Simon remembered suddenly, as one does sometimes remember people, with a sense of startling familiarity and a kind of guilty amazement that he should have allowed her to slip out of his mind for so long. Once she was remembered, he had no more hesitation. No one else could have been so obviously the one person in the world whom he had to call up at that moment.

He picked up the telephone.

"Hello, Jacqueline," he said when she answered. "Do you know who this is?"

"I know," she said. "It's Franklin D. Roosevelt."

"You have a marvelous memory. Do you still eat?"

"Whenever I'm thirsty. Do you?"

"I nibble a crumb now and then. Come out with me tonight and see if we can still take it."

"Simon, I'd love to; but I'm in the most frantic muddle—"

"So is the rest of the world, darling. But it's two years since I've seen you, and that's about seven hundred and thirty days too long. Don't you realize that I've come halfway around the world, surviving all manner of perils and slaying large numbers of ferocious dragons, just to get here in time to take you out to dinner tonight?"

"I know, but—Oh, well. It would be thrilling to see you. Come around about seven, and I'll try to get a bit straightened out before then."

"I'll be there," said the Saint.

He spent some of the intervening time in making

himself the owner of a car, and shortly after half past six he turned it westward into the stream of studio traffic homing toward Beverly Hills. Somewhere along Sunset Boulevard, he turned off to the right and began to climb one of the winding roads that led up into the hills. The street lights were just beginning to trace their twinkling geometrical network over the vast panorama of cities spread out beneath him, as the car soared smoothly higher into the luminous blue-grey twilight.

He found his way with the certainty of vivid remembrance; and he was fully ten minutes early when he pulled the car into a bay by the roadside before the gate of Jacqueline Laine's house. He climbed out and started toward the gate, lighting a cigarette as he went, and as he approached it, he perceived that somebody else was approaching the same gate from the opposite side. Changing his course a little to the left so that the departing guest would have room to pass him, the Saint observed that he was a small and elderly gent arrayed in clothes so shapeless and ill fitting that they gave his figure a comical air of having been loosely and inaccurately strung together from a selection of stuffed bags of cloth. He wore a discolored Panama hat of weird and wonderful architecture, and carried an incongruous green umbrella furled, but still flapping in a bedraggled and forlorn sort of way, under his left arm; his face was rubicund and bulbous like his body, looking as if it had been carelessly slapped together out of a few odd lumps of pink plasticine.

As Simon moved to the left, the elderly gent duplicated the maneuver. Simon turned his feet and swerved politely to the right. The elderly gent did exactly the same, as if he were Simon's own reflection in a distorting mirror. Simon stopped altogether and decided to economize energy by letting the elderly gent make the next move in the ballet on his own.

Whereupon he discovered that the game of undignified dodging in which he had just prepared to surrender his part was caused by some dimly discernible ambition of the elderly gent's to hold converse with him. Standing in front of him and blinking shortsightedly upward from his lower altitude to the Saint's six foot two, with his mouth hanging vacantly open like an inverted U and three long yellow teeth hanging down like stalactites from the top, the elderly gent tapped him on the chest and said, very earnestly and distinctly: "Hig fwmgn glugl phnihklu hgrm skhlglgl?"

"I beg your pardon?" said the Saint vaguely.

"Hig fwmgn," repeated the elderly gent, "glugl phnihklu hgrm skhlglgl?"

Simon considered the point.

"If you ask me," he replied at length, "I should say sixteen."

The elderly gent's knobbly face seemed to take on a brighter shade of pink. He clutched the lapels of the Saint's coat, shaking him slightly in a positive passion of anguish.

"Flogh ghoglu sk," he pleaded, "klngnt hu ughlgstghnd?"

Simon shook his head.

"No," he said judiciously, "you're thinking of weevils."

The little man bounced about like a rubber doll. His eyes squinted with a kind of frantic despair.

"Ogmighogho," he almost screamed, "klngt hu ughglstghnd? Ik ghln ngmnpp sktlghko! Klugt hu hgr? *Ik wgnt hlg phnihklu hgrm skhlglgl!*"

The Saint sighed. He was by nature a kindly man to those whom the gods had afflicted, but time was passing and he was thinking of Jacqueline Laine.

"I'm afraid not, dear old bird," he murmured regretfully. "There used to be one, but it died. Sorry, I'm sure."

He patted the elderly gent apologetically upon the shoulder, steered his way around him, and passed on out of earshot of the frenzied sputtering noises that continued to honk despairingly through the dusk behind him. Two minutes later he was with Jacqueline.

Jacqueline Laine was twenty-three; she was tall and slender; she had grey eyes that twinkled and a demoralizing mouth. Both of these temptations were in play as she came toward him; but he was still slightly shaken by his recent encounter.

"Have you got any more village idiots hidden around?" he asked warily, as he took her hands; and she was puzzled.

"We used to have several, but they've all got into Congress. Did you want one to take home?"

"My God, no," said the Saint fervently. "The one I met at the gate was bad enough. Is he your latest boy friend?"

Her brow cleared.

"Oh, you mean the old boy with the cleft palate? Isn't he marvelous? I think he's got a screw loose or something. He's been hanging around all day—he keeps ringing the bell and bleating at me. I'd just sent him away for the third time. Did he try to talk to you?"

"He did sort of wag his adenoids at me," Simon admitted, "but I don't think we actually got on to common ground. I felt quite jealous of him for a bit, until I realized that he couldn't possibly kiss you nearly as well as I can, with that set of teeth."

He proceeded to demonstrate this.

"I'm still in a hopeless muddle," she said presently. "But I'll be ready in five minutes. You can be fixing a cocktail while I finish myself off."

In the living room there was an open trunk in one corner and a half-filled packing case in the middle of the floor. There were scattered heaps of paper around it, and a few partially wrapped and unidentifiable objects on the table. The room had that curiously naked and inhospitable look which a room has when it has been stripped of all those intimately personal odds and ends of junk which make it a home, and only the bare furniture is left.

The Saint raised his eyebrows.

"Hello," he said. "Are you moving?"

"Sort of." She shrugged. "Moving out, anyway."

"Where to?"

"I don't know."

He realized then that there should have been someone else there, in that room.

"Isn't your grandmother here any more?"

"She died four weeks ago."

"I'm sorry."

"She was a good soul. But she was terribly old. Do you know she was just ninety-seven?" She held his hand for a moment. "I'll tell you all about it when I come down. Do you remember where to find the bottles?"

"Templars and elephants never forget."

He blended bourbon, applejack, vermouth, and bitters, skilfully and with the zeal of an artist, while he
waited for her, remembering the old lady whom he had
seen so often in that room. Also, he remembered the
affectionate service that Jacqueline had always lavished
on her, cheerfully limiting her own enjoyment of life to
meet the demands of an unconscious tyrant who would
allow no one else to look after her, and wondered if there
was any realistic reason to regret the ending of such a
long life. She had, he knew, looked after Jacqueline herself in her time, and had brought her up as her own child
since she was left an orphan at the age of three; but life
must always belong to the young. . . . He thought that for
Jacqueline it must be a supreme escape, but he knew that
she would never say so.

She came down punctually in the five minutes which
she had promised. She had changed her dress and put a
comb through her hair, and with that seemed to have
achieved more than any other woman could have shown
for an hour's fiddling in front of a mirror.

"You should have been in pictures," said the Saint,
and he meant it.

"Maybe I shall," she said. "I'll have to do something
to earn a living now."

"Is it as bad as that?"

She nodded.

"But I can't complain. I never had to work for anything before. Why shouldn't I start? Other people have
to."

"Is that why you're moving out?"

"The house isn't mine."

"But didn't the old girl leave you anything?"

"She left me some letters."

The Saint almost spilled his drink. He sat down heavily on the edge of the table.

"She left you some *letters?* After you'd practically been a slave to her ever since you came out of finishing school? What did she do with the rest of her property—leave it to a home for stray cats?"

"No, she left it to Harry."

"Who?"

"Her grandson."

"I didn't know you had any brothers."

"I haven't. Harry Westler is my cousin. He's—well, as a matter of fact he's a sort of black sheep. He's a gambler, and he was in prison once for forging a check. Nobody else in the family would have anything to do with him, and if you believe what they used to say about him, they were probably quite right; but Granny always had a soft spot for him. She never believed he could do anything wrong—he was just a mischievous boy to her. Well, you know how old she was. . . ."

"And she left everything to him?"

"Practically everything. I'll show you."

She went to a drawer of the writing table and brought him a typewritten sheet. He saw that it was a copy of a will, and turned to the details of the bequests.

To my dear granddaughter Jacqueline Laine, who has taken care of me so thoughtfully and unselfishly for four years, One Hundred Dollars and my letters from Sidney Farlance, knowing that she will find them of more value than anything else I could leave her.

To my cook, Eliza Jefferson, and my chauffeur,
Albert Gordon, One Hundred Dollars each, for their
loyal service.

The remainder of my estate, after these deductions, including my house and other personal belong-
ings, to my dear grandson Harry Westler, hoping it
will help him to make the success of life of which I
have always believed him capable.

Simon folded the sheet and dropped it on the table
from his fingertips as if it were infected.

"Suffering Judas," he said helplessly. "After all you
did for her—to pension you off on the same scale as the
cook and the chauffeur! And what about Harry—doesn't
he propose to do anything about it?"

"Why should he? The will's perfectly clear."

"Why shouldn't he? Just because the old crow went
off her rocker in the last days of senile decay is no reason
why he shouldn't do something to put it right. There must
have been enough for both of you."

"Not so much. They found that Granny had been
living on her capital for years. There was only about
twenty thousand dollars left—and the house."

"What of it? He could spare half."

Jacqueline smiled—a rather tired little smile.

"You haven't met Harry. He's—difficult . . . He's
been here, of course. The agents already have his instruc-
tions to sell the house and the furniture. He gave me a
week to get out, and the week is up the day after tomorrow. . . . I couldn't possibly ask him for anything."

Simon lighted a cigarette as if it tasted of bad eggs
and scowled malevolently about the room.

"The skunk! And so you get chucked out into the

wide world with nothing but a hundred dollars."

"And the letters," she added ruefully.

"What the hell are these letters?"

"They're love letters," she said; and the Saint looked as if he would explode.

"Love letters?" he repeated in an awful voice.

"Yes. Granny had a great romance when she was a girl. Her parents wouldn't let her get any further with it because the boy hadn't any money and his family wasn't good enough. He went abroad with one of these heroic young ideas of making a fortune in South America and coming back in a gold-plated carriage to claim her. He died of fever somewhere in Brazil very soon after, but he wrote her three letters—two from British Guiana and one from Colombia. Oh, I know them by heart—I used to have to read them aloud to Granny almost every night, after her eyes got too bad for her to be able to read them herself. They're just the ordinary simple sort of thing that you'd expect in the circumstances, but to Granny they were the most precious thing she had. I suppose she had some funny old idea in her head that they'd be just as precious to me."

"She must have been screwy," said the Saint.

Jacqueline came up and put a hand over his mouth.

"She was very good to me when I was a kid," she said.

"I know, but—" Simon flung up his arms hopelessly. And then, almost reluctantly, he began to laugh. "But it does mean that I've just come back in time. And we'll have so much fun tonight that you won't even think about it for a minute."

Probably he made good his boast, for Simon Templar

brought to the solemn business of enjoying himself the same gay zest and inspired impetuosity which he brought to his battles with the technicalities of the law. But if he made her forget, he himself remembered; and when he followed her into the living room of the house again much later, for a good-night drink, the desolate scene of interrupted packing, and the copy of the will still lying on the table where he had put it down, brought the thoughts with which he had been subconsciously playing throughout the evening back into the forefront of his mind.

"Are you going to let Harry get away with it?" he asked her, with a sudden characteristic directness.

The girl shrugged.

"What else can I do?"

"I have an idea," said the Saint; and his blue eyes danced with an unholy delight which she had never seen in them before.

Mr. Westler was not a man whose contacts with the law had conspired to make him particularly happy about any of its workings; and therefore when he saw that the card which was brought to him in his hotel bore in its bottom left-hand corner the name of a firm with the words "Attorneys-at-Law" underneath it, he suffered an immediate hollow twinge in the base of his stomach for which he could scarcely be blamed. A moment's reflection, however, reminded him that another card with a similar inscription had recently been the forerunner of an extremely welcome windfall, and with this reassuring thought he told the bellboy to bring the visitor into his presence.

Mr. Tombs, of Tombs, Tombs, and Tombs, as the card introduced him, was a tall lean man with neatly brushed white hair, bushy white eyebrows, a pair of gold-rimmed and drooping pince-nez on the end of a broad black ribbon and an engagingly avuncular manner which rapidly completed the task of restoring Harry Westler's momentarily shaken confidence. He came to the point with professional efficiency combined with professional pomposity.

"I have come to see you in connection with the estate of the—ah—late Mrs. Laine. I understand that you are her heir."

"That's right," said Mr. Westler.

He was a dark, flashily dressed man with small greedy eyes and a face rather reminiscent of that of a sick horse.

"Splendid." The lawyer placed his fingertips on his knees and leaned forward, peering benevolently over the rims of his glasses. "Now I for my part am representing the Sesame Mining Development Corporation."

He said this more or less as if he were announcing himself as the personal herald of Jehovah, but Mr. Westler's mind ran in practical channels.

"Did my grandmother have shares in the company?" he asked quickly.

"Ah—ah—no. That is—ah—no. Not exactly. But I understand that she was in possession of a letter or document which my clients regard as extremely valuable."

"A letter?"

"Exactly. But perhaps I had better give you an outline of the situation. Your grandmother was in her youth greatly—ah—enamored of a certain Sidney Farlance. Perhaps at some time or other you have heard her speak of him."

"Yes."

"For various reasons her parents refused to give their consent to the alliance; but the young people for their part refused to take no for an answer, and Farlance went abroad with the intention of making his fortune in foreign parts and returning in due course to claim his bride. In this ambition he was unhappily frustrated by his —ah—premature decease in Brazil. But it appears that during his travels in British Guiana he did become the owner of a mining concession in a certain very inaccessible area of territory. British Guiana, as you are doubtless aware," continued Mr. Tombs in his dry pedagogic voice, "is traditionally reputed to be the source of the legend of El Dorado, the Gilded King, who was said to cover himself with pure gold and to wash it from him in the waters of a sacred lake called Manoa—"

"Never mind all that baloney," said Harry Westler, who was not interested in history or mythology. "Tell me about this concession."

Mr. Tombs pressed his lips with a pained expression, but he went on.

"At the time it did not appear that gold could be profitably obtained from this district and the claim was abandoned and forgotten. Modern engineering methods, however, have recently revealed deposits of almost fabulous value in the district, and my clients have obtained a concession to work it over a very large area of ground. Subsequent investigations into their title, meanwhile, have brought out the existence of this small—ah—prior concession granted to Sidney Farlance, which is situated almost in the center of my client's territory and in a position which—ah—exploratory drillings have shown to be one of the richest areas in the district."

Mr. Westler digested the information, and in place of the first sinking vacuum which had afflicted his stomach when he saw the word Law on his visitor's card, a sudden and ecstatic awe localized itself in the same place and began to cramp his lungs as if he had accidentally swallowed a rubber balloon with his breakfast and it was being rapidly inflated by some supernatural agency.

"You mean my grandmother owned this concession?"

"That is what—ah—my clients are endeavouring to discover. Farlance himself, of course, left no heirs, and we have been unable to trace any surviving members of his family. In the course of our inquiries, however, we did learn of his—ah—romantic interest in your grandmother, and we have every reason to believe that in the circumstances he would naturally have made her the beneficiary of any such asset, however problematical its value may have seemed at the time."

"And you want to buy it out—is that it?"

"Ah—yes. That is—ah—provided that our deductions are correct and the title can be established. I may say that my clients would be prepared to pay very liberally—"

"They'd have to," said Mr. Westler briskly. "How much are they good for?"

The lawyer raised his hands deprecatingly.

"You need have no alarm, my dear Mr. Westler. The actual figure would, of course, be a matter for negotiation, but it would doubtless run into a number of millions. But first of all, you understand, we must trace the actual concession papers which will be sufficient to establish your right to negotiate. Now it seems that in view of the relationship between Farlance and your grandmother, she would probably have treasured his letters as women do even though she later married someone else, particularly if there was a document of that sort among them. People don't usually throw things like that away. In that case you will doubtless have inherited these letters along with her other personal property. Possibly you have not yet had an occasion to peruse them, but if you would do so as soon as possible—"

One of Harry Westler's few Napoleonic qualities was a remarkable capacity for quick and constructive thinking.

"Certainly I have the letters," he said, "but I haven't gone through them yet. My lawyer has them at present, and he's in San Francisco today. He'll be back tomorrow morning, and I'll get hold of them at once. Come and see me again tomorrow afternoon, and I expect I'll have some news for you."

"Tomorrow afternoon, Mr. Westler? Certainly. I think that will be convenient. Ah—certainly." The lawyer stood up, took off his pince-nez, polished them, and revolved them like a windmill on the end of their ribbon. "This has indeed been a most happy meeting, my dear sir. And may I say that I hope that tomorrow afternoon it will be even happier?"

"You can go on saying that right up till the time we start talking prices," said Harry.

The door had scarcely closed behind Mr. Tombs when

he was on the telephone to his cousin. He suppressed a sigh of relief when he heard her voice and announced as casually as he could his intention of coming around to see her.

"I think we ought to have another talk—I was terribly upset by the shock of Granny's death when I saw you the other day and I'm afraid I wasn't quite myself, but I'll make all the apologies you like when I get there," he said in an unfamiliarly gentle voice which cost him a great effort to achieve, and was grabbing his hat before the telephone was properly back on its bracket.

He made a call at the bank on his way, and sat in the taxi which carried him up into the hills as if its cushions had been upholstered with hot spikes. The exact words of that portion of the will which referred to the letters drummed through his memory with a staggering significance: *"My letters from Sidney Farlance, knowing that she will find them of more value than anything else I could leave her."* The visit of Mr. Tombs had made him understand them perfectly. His grandmother had known what was in them; but did Jacqueline know? His heart almost stopped beating with anxiety.

As he leaped out of the taxi and dashed toward the house, he cannoned into a small and weirdly apparelled elderly gent who was apparently emerging from the gate at the same time. Mr. Westler checked himself involuntarily, and the elderly gent, sent flying by the impact, bounced off a gatepost and tottered back at him. He clutched Harry by the sleeve and peered up at him pathetically.

"Glhwf hngwglgl," he said pleadingly, "kngnduk glu bwtlhjp mnyihgli?"

"Oh, go climb a tree," snarled Mr. Westler impatiently.

He pushed the little man roughly aside and went on.

Jacqueline opened the door to him, and Mr. Westler steeled himself to kiss her on the forehead with cousinly affection.

"I was an awful swine the other day, Jackie. I don't know what could have been the matter with me. I've always been terribly selfish," he said with an effort, "and at the time I didn't really see how badly Granny had treated you. She didn't leave you anything except those letters, did she?"

"She left me a hundred dollars," said Jacqueline calmly.

"A hundred dollars!" said Harry indignantly. "After you'd given up everything else to take care of her. And she left me more than twenty thousand dollars and the house and everything else in it. It's—disgusting! But I don't have to take advantage of it, do I? I've been thinking a lot about it lately—"

Jacqueline lighted a cigarette and regarded him stonily.

"Thanks," she said briefly. "But I haven't asked you for any charity."

"It isn't charity," protested Mr. Westler virtuously. "It's just a matter of doing the decent thing. The lawyers have done their share—handed everything over to me and seen that the will was carried out. Now we can start again. We could pool everything again and divide it the way we think it ought to be divided."

"As far as I'm concerned, that's been done already."

"But I'm not happy about it. I've got all the money,

and you know what I'm like. I'll probably gamble it all away in a few months."

"That's your affair."

"Oh, don't be like that, Jackie. I've apologized, haven't I? Besides, what Granny left you is worth a lot more than money. I mean those letters of hers. I'd willingly give up five thousand dollars of my share if I could have had those. They're the one thing of the old lady's which really means a great deal to me."

"You're becoming very sentimental all of a sudden, aren't you?" asked the girl curiously.

"Maybe I am. I suppose you can't really believe that a rotter like me could feel that way about anything, but Granny was the only person in the world who ever really believed any good of me and liked me in spite of everything. If I gave you five thousand dollars for those letters, it wouldn't be charity—I'd be paying less than I think they're worth. Let's put it that way if you'd rather, Jackie. An ordinary business deal. If I had them," said Mr. Westler with something like a sob in his voice, "they'd always be a reminder to me of the old lady and how good she was. They might help me to go straight. . . ."

His emotion was so touching that even Jacqueline's cynical incredulity lost some of its assurance. Harry Westler was playing his part with every technical trick that he knew, and he had a mastery of these emotional devices which victims far more hard-boiled than Jacqueline had experienced to their cost.

"I'm thoroughly ashamed of myself and I want to put things right in any way I can. Don't make me feel any worse than I do already. Look here, I'll give you ten thousand dollars for the letters, and I won't regret a penny of it. You won't regret it either, will you, if they help me to keep out of trouble in future?"

Jacqueline smiled in spite of herself. It was not in her nature to bear malice, and it was very hard for her to resist an appeal that was made in those terms. Also, with the practical side of her mind, she was honest enough to realize that her grandmother's letters had no sentimental value for her whatever, and that ten thousand dollars was a sum of money which she could not afford to refuse unless her pride was compelled to forbid it; her night out with the Saint had helped her to forget her problems for the moment, but she had awakened that morning with a very sober realization of the position in which she was going to find herself within the next forty-eight hours.

"If you put it like that I can't very well refuse, can I?" she said, and Harry jumped up and clasped her fervently by the hand.

"You'll really do it, Jackie? You don't know how much I appreciate it."

She disengaged herself quietly.

"It doesn't do me any harm," she told him truthfully. "Would you like to have the letters now?"

"If they're anywhere handy. I brought some money along with me, so we can fix it all up right away."

She went upstairs and fetched the letters from the dressing table in her grandmother's room. Mr. Westler took them and tore off the faded ribbon with which they were tied together with slightly trembling fingers which she attributed to an unexpected depth of emotion. One by one he took them out of their envelopes and read rapidly through them. The last sheet of the third letter was a different kind of paper from the rest. The paper was brown and discolored and cracked in the folds, and the ink had the rust-brown hue of great age; but he saw the heavy official seal in one corner and strained his eyes to decipher the stiff old-fashioned script.

We, Philip Edmond Wodehouse, Commander of the Most Noble Order of the Bath, Governor in the name of His Britannic Majesty of the Colony of British Guiana, by virtue of the powers conferred upon us by His Majesty's Privy Council, do hereby proclaim and declare to all whom it may concern that we have this day granted to Sidney Farlance, a subject of His Majesty the King, and to his heirs and assigns being determined by the possession of this authority, the sole right to prospect and mine for minerals of any kind whatsoever in the territory indicated and described in the sketch map at the foot of this authority, for the term of nine hundred and ninety-nine years from the date of these presents.

Given under our hand and seal this third day of January, Eighteen Hundred and Fifty-Six.

At the bottom of the sheet below the map and description was scrawled in a different hand: *"This is all for you. S.F."*

Harry Westler stuffed the letters into his pocket and took out his wallet. His heart was beating in a delirious rhythm of ecstasy and sending the blood roaring through his ears like the crashing crescendo of a symphony. The gates of Paradise seemed to have opened up and deluged him with all their reservoirs of bliss. The whole world was his sweetheart. If the elderly gent whose strange nasal garglings he had dismissed so discourteously a short time ago had cannoned into him again at that moment, it is almost certain that Mr. Westler would not have told him to go and climb a tree. He would probably have kissed him on both cheeks and given him a nickel.

For the first time in his life, Harry Westler counted out ten thousand-dollar bills as cheerfully as he would have counted them in.

"There you are, Jackie. And I'm not kidding—it takes a load off my mind. If you think of anything else I can do for you, just let me know."

"I think you've done more than anyone could have asked," she said generously. "Won't you stay and have a drink?"

Mr. Westler declined the offer firmly. He had no moral prejudice against drinking, and in fact he wanted a drink very badly, but more particularly he wanted to have it in a place where he would not have to place any more restraint on the shouting rhapsodies that were seething through his system like bubbles through champagne.

Some two hours later, when Simon Templar drifted into the house, he found Jacqueline still looking slightly dazed. She flung her arms around his neck and kissed him.

"Simon!" she gasped. "You must be a mascot or something. You'll never guess what's happened."

"I'll tell you exactly what's happened," said the Saint calmly. "Cousin Harry has been here, told you that he'd rather have dear old Granny's love letters than all the money in the world, and paid you a hell of a good price for them. At least I hope he paid you a hell of a good price."

Jacqueline gaped at him weakly.

"He paid me ten thousand dollars. But how on earth did you know? Why did he do it?"

"He did it because a lawyer called on him this morning and told him that Sidney Farlance had collared an absolutely priceless mining concession when he was in British Guiana, and that there was probably something about it in the letters which would be worth millions to whoever had them to prove his claim."

She looked at him aghast.

"A mining concession? I don't remember anything about it—"

"You wouldn't," said the Saint kindly. "It wasn't there until I slipped it in when I got you to show me the letters at breakfast time this morning. I sat up for the other half of the night faking the best imitation I could of what I thought a concession ought to look like, and apparently it was good enough for Harry. Of course I was the lawyer who told him all about it, and I think I fed him the oil pretty smoothly, so perhaps there was some excuse for him. I take it that he was quite excited about it—I see he didn't even bother to take the envelopes."

Jacqueline opened her mouth again, but what she was going to say with it remained a permanently unsolved question, for at that moment the unnecessarily vigorous ringing of a bell stopped her short. The Saint cocked his ears speculatively at the sound, and a rather pleased and seraphic smile worked itself into his face.

"I expect this is Harry coming back," he said. "He wasn't supposed to see me again until tomorrow but I suppose he couldn't wait. He's probably tried to ring me up at the address I had printed on my card and discovered that there ain't no such lawyers as I was supposed to represent. It will be rather interesting to hear what he has to say."

For once, however, Simon's guess was wrong. Instead of the indignant equine features of Harry Westler, he confronted the pink imploring features of the small and shapeless elderly gent with whom he had danced prettily around the gateposts the day before. The little man's face lighted up, and he bounced over the doorstep and seized the Saint joyfully by both lapels of his coat.

"Mnyng hlfwgl!" he crowed triumphantly. "Ahkgmp glglgl hndiuphwmp!"

Simon recoiled slightly.

"Yes. I know," he said soothingly. "But it's five o'clock on Fridays. Two dollars every other yard."

"Ogh hmbals!" said the little man.

He let go of the Saint's coat, ducked under his arms, and scuttled on into the living room.

"Oi!" said the Saint feebly.

"May I explain, sir?"

Another voice spoke from the doorway, and Simon perceived that the little man had not come alone. Someone else had taken his place on the threshold—a thin and mournful-looking individual whom the Saint somewhat pardonably took to be the little man's keeper.

"Are you looking after that?" he inquired resignedly. "And why don't you keep it on a lead?"

The mournful-looking individual shook his head.

"That is Mr. Horatio Ive, sir—he is a very rich man, but he suffers from an unfortunate impediment in his speech. Very few people can understand him. I go about with him as his interpreter, but I have been in bed for the last three days with a chill—"

A shrill war whoop from the other room interrupted the explanation.

"We'd better go and see how he's getting on," said the Saint.

"Mr. Ive is very impulsive, sir," went on the sad-looking interpreter. "He was most anxious to see somebody here, and even though I was unable to accompany him, he has called here several times alone. I understand that he found it impossible to make himself understood. He practically dragged me out of bed to come with him now."

"What's he so excited about?" asked the Saint as they walked towards the living room.

"He's interested in some letters, sir, belonging to the late Mrs. Laine. She happened to show them to him when they met once several years ago, and he wanted to buy them. She refused to sell them for sentimental reasons, but as soon as he read of her death he decided to approach her heirs."

"Are you talking about her love letters from a bird called Sidney Farlance?" Simon asked hollowly.

"Yes, sir. The gentleman who worked in British Guiana. Mr. Ive is prepared to pay something like fifty thousand dollars—Is anything the matter, sir?"

Simon Templar swallowed.

"Oh, nothing," he said faintly. "Nothing at all."

They entered the living room to interrupt a scene of considerable excitement. Backing toward the wall, with a blank expression of alarm widening her eyes, Jacqueline Laine was staring dumbly at the small elderly gent, who was capering about in front of her like a frenzied redskin, spluttering yard after yard of his incomprehensible adenoidal honks interspersed with wild piercing squeaks apparently expressive of intolerable joy. In each hand he held an envelope aloft like a banner.

As his interpreter came in, he turned and rushed toward him, loosing off a fresh stream of noises like those of a hysterical duck.

"Mr. Ive is saying, sir," explained the interpreter, raising his voice harmoniously above the din, "that each of those envelopes bears a perfect example of the British Guiana one-cent magenta stamp of 1856, of which only one specimen was previously believed to exist. Mr. Ive is an ardent philatelist, sir, and these envelopes—"

Simon Templar blinked hazily at the small crudely printed stamp in the corner of the envelope which the little man was waving under his nose.

"You mean," he said cautiously, "that Mr. Ive is really only interested in the envelopes?"

"Yes, sir."

"Not the letters themselves?"

"Not the letters."

"And he's been flapping around the house all this time trying to tell somebody about it?"

"Yes, sir."

Simon Templar drew a deep breath. The foundations of the world were spinning giddily around his ears but his natural resilience was unconquerable. He took out a handkerchief and mopped his brow.

"In that case," he said contentedly, "I'm sure we can do business. What do you say, Jacqueline?"

Jacqueline clutched his arm and nodded breathlessly.

"Hlgagtsk sweghlemlgl," beamed Mr. Ive.

WALTER S. TEVIS

The Hustler

They took Sam out of the office, through the long passageway, and up to the big metal doors. The doors opened, slowly, and they stepped out.

The sunlight was exquisite; warm on Sam's face. The air was clear and still. A few birds were circling in the sky. There was a gravel path, a road, and then, grass. Sam drew a deep breath. He could see as far as the horizon.

A guard drove up in a gray station wagon. He opened the door, and Sam got in, whistling softly to himself. They drove off, down the gravel path. Sam did not turn around to look at the prison walls; he kept his eyes on the grass that stretched ahead of them, and on the road through the grass.

When the guard stopped to let him off in Richmond, he said, "A word of advice, Willis."

"Advice?" Sam smiled at the guard.

"That's right. You got a habit of getting in trouble, Willis. That's why they didn't parole you, made you serve full time, because of that habit."

"That's what the man told me," Sam said. "So?"

"So stay out of poolrooms. You're smart. You can earn a living."

Sam started climbing out of the station wagon. "Sure," he said. He got out, slammed the door, and the guard drove away.

It was still early, and the town was nearly empty. Sam walked around, up and down different streets, for about an hour, looking at houses and stores, smiling at the people he saw, whistling or humming little tunes to himself.

In his right hand he was carrying his little round tubular leather case, carrying it by the brass handle on the side. It was about 30 inches long, the case, and about as big around as a man's forearm.

At ten o'clock he went to the bank and drew out the six hundred dollars he had deposited there under the name of George Graves. Only it was six hundred eighty; it had gathered that much interest.

Then he went to a clothing store and bought a sporty tan coat, a pair of brown slacks, brown suede shoes, and a bright green sport shirt. In the store's dressing room he put the new outfit on, leaving the prison-issued suit and shoes on the floor. Then he bought two extra sets of underwear and socks, paid, and left.

About a block up the street there was a clean-looking beauty parlor. He walked in and told the lady who seemed to be in charge, "I'm an actor. I have to play a part in Chicago tonight that requires red hair." He smiled at her. "Can you fix me up?"

The lady was all efficiency. "Certainly," she said. "If you'll just step back to a booth, we'll pick out a shade."

A half hour later he was a redhead. In two hours he was on board a plane for Chicago, with a little less than six hundred dollars in his pocket and one piece of luggage. He still had the underwear and socks in a paper sack.

In Chicago he took a fourteen-dollar-a-night room in the best hotel he could find. The room was big, and pleasant. It looked and smelled clean.

He sat down on the side of the bed and opened his little leather case at the top. The two-piece billiard cue inside was intact. He took it out and screwed the brass joint together, pleased that it still fit perfectly. Then he checked the butt for tightness. The weight was still firm and solid. The tip was good, its shape had held up; and the cue's balance and stroke seemed easy, familiar; almost as though he still played with it every day.

He checked himself in the mirror. They had done a perfect job on his hair; and its brightness against the green and brown of his new clothes gave him the sporty, racetrack sort of look he had always avoided before. His once ruddy complexion was very pale. Not a pool player in town should be able to recognize him: he could hardly recognize himself.

If all went well, he would be out of Chicago for good in a few days; and no one would know for a long time that Big Sam Willis had even played there. Six years on a manslaughter charge could have its advantages.

In the morning he had to walk around town for a while before he found a poolroom of the kind he wanted. It was a few blocks off the Loop, small; and from the outside it seemed to be fairly clean and quiet.

Inside, there was a short-order and beer counter up front. In back there were four tables; Sam could see them through the door in the partition that separated the lunchroom from the poolroom proper. There was no one in the place except for the tall, blond boy behind the counter.

Sam asked the boy if he could practice.

"Sure." The boy's voice was friendly. "But it'll cost you a dollar an hour."

"Fair enough." He gave the boy a five dollar bill. "Let me know when this is used up."

The boy raised his eyebrows and took the money.

In the back room Sam selected the best 20-ounce cue he could find in the wall rack, one with an ivory point and a tight butt, chalked the tip, and broke the rack of balls on what seemed to be the best of the four tables.

He tried to break safe, a straight pool break, where you drive the two bottom corner balls to the cushions and back into the stack where they came from, making the cue ball go two rails and return to the top of the table, killing itself on the cushion. The break didn't work, however; the rack of balls spread wide, five of them came out into the table, and the cue ball stopped in the middle. It would have left an opponent wide open for a big run. Sam shuddered.

He pocketed the fifteen balls, missing only once—a long shot that had to be cut thin into a far corner—and he felt better, making balls. He had little confidence on the hard ones; he was awkward. But he still knew the game; he knew how to break up little clusters of balls on one shot so that he could pocket them on the next. He knew how to play position with very little English on the cue, by shooting "natural" shots, and letting the speed of the cue ball do the work. He could still figure the spread, plan out his shots in advance from the positions of the balls on the table, and he knew what to shoot at first.

He kept shooting for about three hours. Several times other players came in and played for a while, but none of them paid any attention to him, and none of them stayed long.

The place was empty again and Sam was practicing cutting balls down the rail, working on his cue ball and on his speed, when he looked up and saw the boy who ran the place coming back. He was carrying a plate with a hamburger in one hand and two bottles of beer in the other.

"Hungry?" He set the sandwich down on the arm of a chair. "Or thirsty, maybe?"

Sam looked at his watch. It was one thirty. "Come to think of it," he said, "I am." He went to the chair, picked up the hamburger, and sat down.

"Have a beer," the boy said affably. Sam took it and drank from the bottle. It tasted delicious.

"What do I owe you?" he said, and took a bite out of the hamburger.

"The burger's thirty cents," the boy said. "The beer's on the house."

"Thanks," Sam said, chewing. "How do I rate?"

"You're a good customer," the boy said. "Easy on the equipment, cash in advance, and I don't even have to rack the balls for you."

"Thanks." Sam was silent for a minute, eating.

The boy was drinking the other beer. Abruptly he set the bottle down. "You on the hustle?" he said.

"Do I look like a hustler?"

"You practice like one."

Sam sipped his beer quietly for a minute, looking over the top of the bottle, once, at the boy. Then he said,

"I might be looking around." He set the empty bottle down on the wooden chair arm. "I'll be back tomorrow; we can talk about it then. There might be something in it for you, if you help me out."

"Sure, mister," the boy said. "You pretty good?"

"I think so," Sam said. Then when the boy got up to leave, he added, "Don't try to finger me for anybody. It won't do you any good."

"I won't." The boy went back up front.

Sam practiced, working mainly on his stroke and his position, for three more hours. When he finished, his arm was sore and his feet were tired; but he felt better. His stroke was beginning to work for him; he was getting smooth, making balls regularly, playing good position. Once, when he was running balls continuously, racking 14 and 1, he ran 47 without missing.

The next morning, after a long night's rest, he was even better. He ran more than 90 balls one time, missing, finally, on a difficult rail shot.

The boy came back at one o'clock, bringing a ham sandwich this time and two beers. "Here you go," he said. "Time to make a break."

Sam thanked him, laid his cue stick on the table, and sat down.

"My name's Barney," the boy said.

"George Graves." Sam held out his hand, and the boy shook it. "Just"—he smiled inwardly at the thought—"call me Red."

"You *are* good," Barney said. "I watched you a couple of times."

"I know." Sam took a drink from the beer bottle. "I'm looking for a straight pool game."

"I figured that, Mister Graves. You won't find one here, though. Up at Bennington's they play straight pool."

Sam had heard of Bennington's. They said it was a hustlers' room, a big money place.

"You know who plays pool there, Barney?" he said.

"Sure. Bill Peyton, he plays there. And Shufala Kid, Louisville Fats, Johnny Vargas, Henry Keller, a little guy they call 'The Policeman'. . . ."

Henry Keller was the only familiar name; Sam had played him once, in Atlantic City, maybe fourteen years ago. But that had been even before the big days of Sam's reputation, before he had got so good that he had to trick hustlers into playing him. That was a long time ago. And then there was the red hair; he ought to be able to get by.

"Which one's got money," he asked, "and plays straight pool?"

"Well"—Barney looked doubtful—"I think Louisville Fats carries a big roll. He's one of the old Prohibition boys; they say he keeps an army of hoods working for him. He plays straights. But he's good. And he doesn't like being hustled."

It looked good; but dangerous. Hustlers didn't take it very well to find out a man was using a phony name so he could get a game. Sam remembered the time someone had told Bernie James whom he had been playing, and Bernie had got pretty rough about it. But this time it was different; he had been out of circulation six years, and he had never played in Chicago before.

"This Fats. Does he bet big?"

"Yes, he bets big. Big as you want." Barney smiled. "But I tell you he's mighty good."

"Rack the balls," Sam said, and smiled back. "I'll show you something."

Barney racked. Sam broke them wide open and started running. He went through the rack, then another, another, and another. Barney was counting the balls, racking them for him each time. When he got to 80, Sam said, "Now I'll bank a few." He banked seven, knocking them off the rails, across, and into the pockets. When he missed the eighth, he said, "What do you think?"

"You'll do," Barney said. He laughed. "Fats is good: but you might take him."

"I'll take him," Sam said. "You lead me to him. Tomorrow night you get somebody to work for you. We're going up to Bennington's."

"Fair enough, Mister Graves," Barney said. He was grinning. "We'll have a beer on that."

At Bennington's you took an elevator to the floor you wanted: billiards on the first, pocket pool on the second, snooker and private games on the third. It was an old-fashioned setup: high ceilings, big, shaded incandescent lights, overstuffed leather chairs.

Sam spent the morning on the second floor, trying to get the feel of the tables. They were different from Barney's, with softer cushions and tighter cloths, and it was a little hard to get used to them; but after about two hours he felt as though he had them pretty well, and he left. No one had paid any attention to him.

After lunch he inspected his hair in the restaurant's bathroom mirror; it was still as red as ever and hadn't yet begun to grow out. He felt good. Just a little nervous, but good.

Barney was waiting for him at the little poolroom. They took a cab up to Bennington's.

Louisville Fats must have weighed three hundred pounds. His face seemed to be bloated around the eyes like the face of an Eskimo, so that he was always squinting. His arms, hanging from the short sleeves of his white silk shirt, were pink and doughlike. Sam noticed his hands; they were soft looking, white and delicate. He wore three rings, one with a diamond. He had on dark-green wide suspenders.

When Barney introduced him, Fats said, "How are you, George?" but didn't offer his hand. Sam noticed that his eyes, almost buried beneath the face, seemed to shift from side to side, so that he seemed not really to be looking at anything.

"I'm fine," Sam said. Then, after a pause, "I've heard a lot about you."

"I got a reputation?" Fats's voice was flat, disinterested. "Then I must be pretty good maybe?"

"I suppose so," Sam said, trying to watch the eyes.

"You a good pool player, George?" The eyes flickered, scanning Sam's face.

"Fair. I like playing. Straight pool."

"Oh." Fats grinned, abruptly, coldly. "That's my game, too, George." He slapped Barney on the back. The boy pulled away, slightly, from him. "You pick good, Barney. He plays my game. You can finger for me, sometime, if you want."

"Sure," Barney said. He looked nervous.

"One thing." Fats was still grinning. "You play for money, George? I mean, you gamble?"

"When the bet's right."

"What you think is a right bet, George?"

"Fifty dollars."

Fats grinned even more broadly; but his eyes still kept shifting. "Now that's close, George," he said. "You play for a hundred, and we play a few."

"Fair enough," Sam said, as calmly as he could. "Let's go upstairs. It's quieter."

"Fine. I'll take my boy if you don't mind. He can rack the balls."

Fats looked at Barney. "You level with that rack, Barney? I mean, you rack the balls tight for Fats?"

"Sure," Barney said, "I wouldn't try to cross you up."

"You know better than that, Barney. OK."

They walked up the back stairs to the third floor. There was a small, bare-walled room, well lighted, with chairs lined up against the walls. The chairs were high ones, the type used for watching pool games. There was no one else in the room.

They uncovered the table, and Barney racked the balls. Sam lost the toss and broke, making it safe, but not too safe. He undershot, purposely, and left the cue ball almost a foot away from the end rail.

They played around, shooting safe, for a while. Then Fats pulled a hard one off the edge of the rack, ran 35, and played him safe. Sam jockeyed with him, figuring to lose for a while, only wanting the money to hold out until he had the table down pat, until he had the other man's game figured, until he was ready to raise the bet.

He lost three in a row before he won one. He wasn't playing his best game; but that meant little, since Fats was probably pulling his punches, too, trying to take him for as much as possible. After he won his first game, he let himself go a little and made a few tricky ones. Once he knifed a ball thin into the side pocket and went two cushions for a breakup; but Fats didn't even seem to notice.

Neither of them tried to run more than 40 at a turn. It would have looked like a game between only fair players, except that neither of them missed very often. In a tight spot they didn't try anything fancy, just shot a safe and let the other man figure it out. Sam played safe on some shots that he was sure he could make; he didn't want to show his hand. Not yet. They kept playing, and, after a while, Sam started winning more often.

After about three hours he was five games ahead, and shooting better all the time. Then, when he won still another game, Sam said, "You're losing money, Fats. Maybe we should quit." He looked at Barney and winked. Barney gave him a puzzled, worried look.

"Quit? You think we should quit?" Fats took a big silk handkerchief from his side pocket and wiped his face. "How much money you won, George?" he said.

"That last makes six hundred." He felt, suddenly, a little tense. It was coming. The big push.

"Suppose we play for six hundred, George." He put the handkerchief back in his pocket. "Then we see who quits."

"Fine." He felt really nervous now, but he knew he would get over it. Nervousness didn't count. At six hundred a game he would be in clover and in San Francisco in two days. If he didn't lose.

Barney racked the balls, and Sam broke. He took the break slowly, putting to use his practice of three days, and his experience of twenty-seven years. The balls broke perfectly, reracking the original triangle, and the cue ball skidded to a stop right on the end cushion.

"You shoot pretty good," Fats said, looking at the safe table that Sam had left him. But he played safe, barely tipping the cue ball off one of the balls down at the foot of the table and returning back to the end rail.

Sam tried to return the safe by repeating the same thing; but the cue ball caught the object ball too thick, and he brought out a shot, a long one, for Fats. Fats stepped up, shot the ball in, played position, and ran out the rest of the rack. Then he ran out another rack, and Sam sat down to watch; there was nothing he could do now. Fats ran 78 points and then, seeing a difficult shot, played him safe.

He had been afraid that something like that might happen. He tried to fight his way out of the game, but couldn't seem to get into the clear long enough for a good run. Fats beat him badly—125 to 30—and he had to give back the six hundred dollars from his pocket. It hurt.

What hurt even worse was that he knew he had less than six hundred left of his own money.

"Now we see who quits." Fats stuffed the money in his hip pocket. "You want to play for another six hundred?"

"I'm still holding my stick," Sam said. He tried not to think about that "army of hoods" that Barney had told him about.

He stepped up to the table and broke. His hand shook a little; but the break was a perfect one.

In the middle of the game Fats missed an easy shot, leaving Sam a dead set-up. Sam ran 53 and out. He won.

It was as easy as that. He was six hundred ahead again, and feeling better.

Then something unlucky happened. Downstairs they must have closed up because six men came up during the next game and sat around the table. Five of them Sam had never seen, but one of them was Henry Keller. Henry was drunk now, evidently, and he didn't seem to be paying much attention to what was going on; but Sam didn't like it. He didn't like Keller, and he didn't like having a man who knew who he was around him. It was too much like that other time. That time in Richmond when Bernie James had come after him with a bottle. That fight had cost him six years. He didn't like it. It was getting time to wind things up here, time to be cutting out. If he could win two more games quick, he would have enough to set him up hustling on the West Coast. And on the West Coast there weren't any Henry Kellers who knew that Big Sam Willis was once the best straight-pool shot in the game.

After Sam had won the game by a close score, Fats looked at his fingernails and said, "George, you're a hustler. You shoot better straights than anybody in Chicago shoots. Except me."

This was the time, the time to make it quick and neat, the time to push as hard as he could. He caught his breath, held steady, and said, "You've got it wrong, Fats. I'm better than you are. I'll play you for all of it. The whole twelve hundred."

It was very quiet in the room. Then Fats said, "George, I like that kind of talk." He started chalking his cue. "We play twelve hundred."

Barney racked the balls, and Fats broke them. They

both played safe, very safe, back and forth, keeping the cue ball on the rail, not leaving a shot for the other man. It was nerve-racking. Over and over.

Then he missed. Missed the edge of the rack, coming at it from an outside angle. His cue ball bounced off the rail and into the rack of balls, spreading them wide, leaving Fats at least five shots. Sam didn't sit down. He just stood and watched Fats come up and start his run. He ran the balls, broke on the fifteenth, and ran another rack: 28 points. And he was just getting started. He had his rack break set up perfectly for the next shot.

Then, as Fats began chalking up, preparing to shoot, Henry Keller stood up from his seat and pointed his finger at Sam.

He was drunk; but he spoke clearly, and loudly. "You're Big Sam Willis," he said. "You're the World's Champion." He sat back in his chair, heavily. "You got red hair, but you're Big Sam." He sat silent, half slumped in the big chair, for a moment, his eyes glassy, and red at the corners. Then he closed his eyes and said, "There's nobody beats Big Sam, Fats. Nobody *never.*"

The room was quiet for what seemed to be a very long while. Sam noticed how thick the tobacco smoke had become in the air; motionless, it was like a heavy brown mist, and over the table it was like a cloud. The faces of the men in the chairs were impassive; all of them, except Henry, watching him.

Fats turned to him. For once his eyes were not shifting from side to side. He looked Sam in the face and said, in a voice that was flat and almost a whisper, "You Big Sam Willis, George?"

"That's right, Fats."

"You must be pretty smart, Sam," Fats said, "to play a trick like that. To make a sucker out of me."

"Maybe." His chest and stomach felt very tight. It was like when Bernie James had caught him at the same game, except without the red hair. Bernie hadn't said anything, though; he had just picked up a bottle.

But, then, Bernie James was dead now. Sam wondered, momentarily, if Fats had ever heard about that.

Suddenly Fats split the silence, laughing. The sound of his laughing filled the room; he threw his head back and laughed; and the men in the chairs looked at him, astonished, hearing the laughter. "Big Sam," he said, "you're a hustler. You put on a great act; and fool me good. A great act." He slapped Sam on the back. "I think the joke's on me."

It was hard to believe. But Fats could afford the money, and Sam knew that Fats knew who would be the best if it came to muscle. And there was no certainty whose side the other men were on.

Fats shot, ran a few more balls, and then missed.

When Sam stepped up to shoot, he said, "Go ahead, Big Sam, and shoot your best. You don't have to act now. I'm quitting you anyway after this one."

The funny thing was that Sam had been shooting his best for the past five or six games—or thought he had—but when he stepped up to the table this time, he was different. Maybe it was Fats or Keller, something made him feel as he hadn't felt for a long time. It was like being the old Big Sam, back before he had quit playing the tournaments and exhibitions, the Big Sam who could run 125 when he was hot and the money was up. His stroke was smooth, steady, accurate, like a balanced, precision instrument moving on well-oiled bearings. He shot easily, calmly, clicking the shots off in his mind and then pocketing them on the table, watching everything on the green, forgetting himself, forgetting even the money, just dropping the balls into the pockets, one after another.

He did it. He ran the game: 125 points, 125 shots without missing. When he finished, Fats took twelve hundred from his still-big roll and counted it out, slowly, to him. He said, "You're the best I've ever seen, Big Sam." Then he covered the table with the oilcloth cover.

After Sam had dropped Barney off, he had the cab take him by his hotel and let him off at a little all-night lunchroom. He ordered bacon and eggs, over light, and talked with the waitress while she fried them. The place seemed strange, gay almost; his nerves felt electric, and there was a pleasant fuzziness in his head, a dim, insistent ringing sound coming from far off. He tried to think for a moment; tried to think whether he should go to the airport now without even going back to the hotel, now that he had made out so well, had made out better, even, than he had planned to be able to do in a week. But there was the waitress and then the food; and when he put a quarter in the jukebox, he couldn't hear the ringing in his ears anymore. This was no time for plane trips; it was a time for talk and music, time for the sense of triumph, the sense of being alive and having money again, and then time for sleep. He was in a chromium and plastic booth in the lunchroom, and he leaned back against the padded plastic backrest and felt an abrupt, deep, gratifying sense of fatigue, loosening his muscles and killing, finally, the tension that had ridden him like a fury for the past three days. There would be plane flights enough tomorrow. Now, he needed rest. It was a long way to San Francisco.

The bed at his hotel was impeccably made; the pale-blue spread seemed drum-tight, but soft and round at the edges and corners. He didn't even take off his shoes.

When he awoke, he awoke suddenly. The skin at the back of his neck was itching, sticky with sweat from where the collar of his shirt had been pressed, tight, against it. His mouth was dry, and his feet felt swollen, stuffed, in his shoes. The room was as quiet as death. Outside the window a car's tires groaned gently, rounding a corner, then were still.

He pulled the chain on the lamp by the bed, and the light came on. Squinting, he stood up, and realized that his legs were aching. The room seemed too big, too bright. He stumbled into the bathroom and threw handfuls of cold water on his face and neck. Then he dried off with a towel and looked in the mirror. Startled, he let go the towel momentarily; the red hair had caught him off guard; and with the eyes now swollen, the lips pale, it was not his face at all. He finished drying quickly, ran his comb through his hair, straightened out his shirt and slacks hurriedly. The startling strangeness of his own face had crystallized the dim, half-conscious feeling that had awakened him, the feeling that something was wrong. The hotel room, himself, Chicago; they were all wrong. He should not be here, not now; he should be on the West Coast, in San Francisco.

He looked at his watch. Four o'clock. He had slept three hours. He did not feel tired, not now, although his bones ached and there was sand under his eyelids. He could sleep, if he had to, on the plane. But the important thing, now, was getting on the plane, clearing out, moving West. He had slept with his cue, in its case, on the bed. He took it and left the room.

The lobby, too, seemed too bright and too empty. But when he had paid his bill and gone out to the street, the relative darkness seemed worse. He began to walk down the street hastily, looking for a cab stand. His own footsteps echoed around him as he walked. There seemed to be no cabs anywhere on the street. He began walking faster. The back of his neck was sweating again. It was a very hot night; the air felt heavy against his skin. There were no cabs.

And then, when he heard the slow, dense hum of a heavy car moving down the street in his direction, heard it from several blocks away and turned his head to see it and to see that there was no cab light on it, he knew—abruptly and lucidly, as some men at some certain times know these things—what was happening.

He began to run; but he did not know where to run. He turned a corner while he was still two blocks ahead of the car and when he could feel its lights, palpably, on the back of his neck, and tried to hide in the doorway, flattening himself out against the door. Then, when he saw the lights of the car as it began its turn around the corner, he realized that the doorway was too shallow, that the lights would pick him out. Something in him wanted to scream. He pushed himself from his place, stumbled down the street, visualizing in his mind a place, some sort of a place between buildings where he could hide completely and where the car could never follow him. But the buildings were all together, with no space at all between them; and when he saw that this was so, he also saw at the same instant that the carlights were flooding him. And then he heard the car stop. There was nothing more to do. He turned around and looked at the car, blinking.

Two men had got out of the back seat; there were two more in front. He could see none of their faces; but was relieved that he could not, could not see the one face that would be bloated like an Eskimo's and with eyes like slits.

The men were holding the door open for him.

"Well," he said. "Hello, boys," and climbed into the back seat. His little leather case was still in his right hand. He gripped it tightly. It was all he had.

LEO HAMALIAN is a professor of English at The City College of New York. He has taught at the California Institute of the Arts, the University of Damascus, and the University of Tehran.

Mr. Hamalian has served as educational editor of *Harper's* and is currently editor of *Ararat,* an arts and letters quarterly. He has written a great number of articles and essays and, in addition to his books on writing and criticism, is known for his anthologies. Recently he collaborated with his wife Linda on SOLO: *Women on Woman Alone.* He co-edited NEW WRITING FROM THE MIDDLE EAST, and a collection of essays, BURN AFTER READING, will appear in 1979. ROGUES is his first anthology for young readers.

Mr. Hamalian lives with his wife in New York City.